IN HIS
RIGHT MIND

IN HIS RIGHT MIND

Philip R. Sullivan

Foremost Press
Cedarburg, Wisconsin

Also by Philip R. Sullivan

The World According To Homo Sapiens
The Same Lonely Songs
Coming Home Again
A Peaceful, Easy Feeling
The Wolf Tree

Copyright © 2017 Philip R. Sullivan. All rights reserved. Reproduction of any part of this publication in any way requires written permission from the author.

Published by Foremost Press
www.foremostpress.com

ISBN-10: 1-939870-33-X
ISBN-13: 978-1-939870-33-9

This is a work of fiction. Any similarity of characters or events to real persons or actual events is coincidental.

*To anyone who has been
threatened or harassed
along the path of life*

PREFACE

The events depicted in this story happened more than thirty years ago; yet as I review my notes and the transcripts of the time, I am struck by how rapid has been the pace of technological change during this interval. For instance, the dependence by physicians of that time on communication via land phones and answering services already seems utterly archaic, and "solo practice" among physicians is now well on the way to becoming an anachronism in most of our metropolitan areas.

Nevertheless, one vital aspect of our society remains unchanged during this interval, and it forms a strong reason for publishing this account. As any woman who's been threatened by a partner will be the first to attest: no adequate societal protection exists against the viciousness of a determined predator who has another person doggedly in his sights, but who has not yet performed a hostile act that can be clearly attributed to him. The instance presented here differs from the common case just mentioned in only one respect. The person in search of protection was a physician, a psychiatrist named Kevin Kiley, who had drawn implacable ire on the basis of a disability report that had been unfavorable to the litigant's interests.

2017   Philip R. Sullivan

PART I

CHAPTER 1

"Hello . . . Yes, this is Doctor Kiley. . . . No, I'm sorry I don't recall you, Mr. Polito. . . . Air Traffic Controller? Oh, yes, I remember now. I saw you at the request of the Department of Labor for a disability evaluation. . . . No, I'm not allowed to discuss my report with you. . . . No, I'm sorry. . . . I'm sorry you feel that way, but I'm obliged to give an opinion as I see it. . . . I certainly don't think that I've destroyed your life as you say. In any case, you can always seek another opinion. . . . Mr. Polito, there's nothing to be gained by talking intemperately like that. . . . Yes, I know you're upset, but . . . I'm sorry. I'm going to have to hang up now."

Kevin Kiley put the receiver down with a deliberate motion and settled back in his chair as if to shake off the effects of the other man's wrath. Performing a disability evaluation is so different from seeing someone as your patient, thought Kevin. People become doctors in order to help other people—to lessen their pain, to restore their health. Doctors and patients don't always agree, but at least they have that common goal. Examining disability litigants is a completely different ballgame. They're not coming because they want a doctor's help. They're coming because they want compensation, and, if you don't agree, naturally you're the enemy.

Kevin ran his hand through his early graying hair and considered whether he should refuse to do further evaluations of this sort. That would not be right, he thought. It's good to compensate a person who gets injured on the job. It's fair. And there will always be disputed cases. Someone then has to make a judgment, and if those responsible in society for the application of medical expertise don't do it, who can?

He shook his head and sighed inaudibly. The day had seemed long now, but as he glanced over his desk at the digital clock on the mahogany bookcase, he noted it was only six thirty. That's the usual time he finished office hours after completing his phone calls. The late summer sun cast a bright hue, captured by the large bay windows arcing around the northwest end of his consulting room. Looking out at the Charles River basin, he noted the sailboats gliding in the easy breeze of day's end. He never grew tired of that view. Just, sometimes, he grew tired.

After glancing distractedly at the day sheet in the outer office, he locked the cabinet and headed down the three flights of stairs to the parking area in back. Now nearing fifty, the forward balance of his athletic shoulders was starting to form a slight stoop. Concerned about his appearance, he'd sometimes tell himself to straighten up. That's what he told himself now as he unlocked his Subaru in the bricked area adjoining the deserted back alley. But this time, he was speaking figuratively, reminding himself not to take professional troubles home.

CHAPTER 2

On the following Monday at the end of the day, Kevin's secretary was putting on her coat to leave. Nodding toward the daily list on her desk, she mentioned that Mr. Polito had phoned again. "He wanted me to apologize to you for his having gotten so hot under the collar last time, but he said he needed some information and advice."

Kevin frowned—almost a wince. "Have a good evening, Frances," he said. "I'll see you tomorrow." Then picking up the phone list, he returned to his own office. Seated in the swivel chair behind his large mahogany desk, he pencil-dialed the first number. Almost forty minutes later, he came to the last name, one that he'd skipped. Usually he returned any urgent calls first, then the other calls in order. But he had been undecided about this one. What good could come from another conversation? Probably nothing but additional frustration and hostility. Leaning back in the chair, he was not really conscious of weighing his thoughts. As the late-afternoon sun through the window outlined the settling effects of midlife on the still handsome oval of his face, he seemed instead to be scanning the distance for some object that had not yet come into view. Then he found himself dialing the number, as if an agency within him which was not really himself had made the decision.

"Mr. Polito, please. This is Doctor Kiley returning his call."

A woman's voice answered that she'd get him. Then a short period of silent waiting.

"Hello, *Kiley?*" A now familiar phone-voice spoke.

"Yes, this is Doctor Kiley." Already annoyed, Kevin had placed a bit too much emphasis on the word "Doctor," and in that subtle resonation between people, he knew that he'd not breasted his cards sufficiently. He'd given his unchosen adversary the satisfaction of getting his goat.

"Oh, *Doc-tor* Kiley, good of you to call back. Look, I need your help and your advice. Since you took away my disability, I've been awfully upset; I've been in a terrible state. When no check came again this week, my wife started to cry. 'How're we gonna pay the rent?' she says. I told her something would work out, and she told me that's all right for me to say but she's got to do the shopping, and these chains don't give credit like Mr. Genero's old grocery store. And she looks at the kids and eats her heart out. 'How're we gonna feed them?' she asks me. What would you say, Doc? What would you do? How would you advise me?"

"I think it would be a good idea for you to get some professional help at this time." Kevin found himself consciously attending to the proper modulation of his voice.

"Fine, Doc, *real fine*! But how's that going to put food on the table?" Angry sarcasm saturated every syllable.

Keeping control of his voice, Kevin responded, "I got the impression you were feeling so badly that you were unable to work . . . that you were in effect disabled. It would make sense to me for you to get help."

"Look, Doc, I'm okay. It was just the awful pressures of that job . . . the planes coming in. Too much to keep track of all the time. Not enough relief. No wonder I cracked up!"

"I agree that the job was probably unsuitable for you. But if you got appropriate help with your condition—and I would recommend that you make use of the AA program also—I think you might adjust better at different work."

"*Sure, sure!* What other sort of work am I going to do? I don't have a fancy education like you. You know from the questions you asked me yourself that I never even finished my second year at Northeastern. What do you want me to do? Get a job at the minimum wage washing dishes somewhere? How could I support my family with that, never mind pay my alimony? Tell me, would *you* do that?"

Kevin experienced a turbulent mixture of anger and compassion. He could see the realistic and, in a way, insoluble difficulties of Mr. Polito's situation. Yet he strongly resented his own position as scapegoat. He had not been asked how this man was going to take care of himself and support his family. Rather, he had been asked two limited questions that required specific medical expertise. First, did this man, who had in fact not been working for the past four years, remain disabled as an air traffic controller? Second, did Mr. Polito's job cause or permanently aggravate his condition?

Kevin had made a diagnosis of Bipolar Disorder and Alcoholism. It was his opinion that Mr. Polito could not function at this time in his former position. It was also his opinion—and this part had led to

Mr. Polito's problem—that the job had not caused either of these conditions. He believed, on the contrary, that a man with these concurrent illnesses, both in poor control, could not function adequately in such a responsible job.

Outwardly, he said, "Mr. Polito, I can see that you're presently in a difficult position. I can also see that there's nothing I can do to help. I assume what you would really want is for me to change my opinion, but I can't do that. I suggest, in terms of an appeal, that you consult a lawyer. I would also advise you to see a doctor, and if you are right now in acute financial hardship, the welfare office. Otherwise, there's nothing I can do. I'm sorry."

"You're *sorry?* There's nothing you can do? Look, Doc, I don't think you understand. I'm a desperate man. You don't really think I'm going to let you get away with this, do you?"

Kevin felt an ominous tone now in the other man's voice, but ignored it. "There's nothing to be gained by further discussion," he answered. "I'm going to hang up now."

"Wait a minute! You're going to have to pay for . . ." Click. And the fading words ended abruptly in midsentence as Kevin placed the receiver gently down. Clouds from a late summer storm blocked out the rays of sunset, and the somber evening sky matched an uneasy foreboding in Kevin's chest as he headed home.

CHAPTER 3

Doctor Kiley chose not to answer any of the subsequent calls and instructed Frances to tell Mr. Polito that he should address further inquiries directly to the Department of Labor. Still, the persistence of those phone messages over the next few weeks troubled him. Sometimes they were listed on his secretary's pad and occasionally delivered by his answering service during the evening.

One day, in reviewing the call list, Frances noted a new patient's name. "James Burgess. He got your name from the hospital. The first opening was a week from Tuesday. When he told me that it was sort of urgent, I said you might be able to see him at the hospital tomorrow morning. He thought he could wait till next week if he could just ask you something over the phone. I told him I'd give you the message."

"Thanks," said Kevin. "Have a good evening."

"See you tomorrow," said Frances with a broad smile. It had been a smooth day. As he went down the phone list, he took the Burgess call in order. "Hello, may I please speak with Mr. Burgess."

The man's voice on the other end replied, "Speaking."

"This is Doctor Kiley."

"I *know*," said the other voice. "You know who this is?"

The now irrevocably familiar voice bounced off Kevin's ear, though he did not let on. "Who is it?" he said, a businesslike tone entering his own voice.

"Sorry about the phony name, but you and I have something we need to talk over, and you've been acting like an ostrich. You know, head in the sand?"

"We have nothing further to talk about." Hostility had now involuntarily entered Kevin's voice.

"Not so fast! Being a shrink, you should be the first to understand that a serious problem doesn't go away by ignoring it. You know, that could make a bad situation dangerous. *Very* dangerous."

The ominous tone came across to Kevin even more than the words. He felt his anger buttressed now by a definite component of fear. Yet his own voice sounded strangely calm to himself. "What are you getting at, Mr. Polito?"

"*Getting at?* You destroy my life and my dignity. You endanger my family. And then you have the nerve to ask what I'm getting at? Oh, no! You're in big trouble. No way am I going to let you get away with that!"

"Mr. Polito, you are now threatening me."

"Who, *me*?" And the tone abruptly changed from anger to sweet reasonableness. "Would I threaten you? Why, we both know that would be a crime. You might even bring charges against me that I would have to deny. Let's just say, I'm asking you to reconsider your report . . . you know, find the error in it."

Kevin was so shaken, he slammed the receiver down. It's not just the words, he thought once more. It's the tone of voice—and his persistence, the fact that he won't let go.

* * *

Driving home on the expressway, Kevin experienced one of those times when he didn't even attempt to leave his work concerns at the office. How did this whole business come about? he asked himself. And he mentally reviewed the notes on Mr. Polito, whose record he had reread shortly after the first phone call. Joseph Polito was a forty-six-year-old man who had been on disability close to four years at the time of his recent reevaluation.

When Kevin had digested a rather formidable sheath of medical reports supplied by the Department of Labor, he found considerable evidence to support the diagnoses that had originally been made in 1977. At the time, Mr. Polito had become loud, overactive, and disruptive on the job. He started arguments about safety procedures, and his coworkers were sometimes at a loss to follow the gist of his complaints. When he started talking about a conspiracy where "they"— not his colleagues but some ill-defined group of evil men—were trying to sabotage air safety, his supervisor knew something had to be done. Joe's behavior for several months before had stood in marked contrast. He seemed sad and preoccupied, not his usual outgoing self, and he looked haggard. When his coworkers tried to help, he'd brush them off with statements like "It's nothing. I'm just not sleeping too good lately."

The hospital report from 1977 had reconstructed the symptoms of these preceding months as a depressive state, followed abruptly by an overactive manic episode requiring hospitalization. The last day at work had been a real horror show, his condition progressing from wound-up to racing. The last straw occurred when Charlie at the next desk was scratching his head absently while concentrating his attention on the big screen. Joe had misinterpreted that innocent motion as a special message. Outraged that Charlie was now commanding him—presumably with subtle signals—to violate air safety codes, he raised his voice in angry objection. When Charlie said he must be crazy, Joe started punching him. The other controllers finally got Joe to the floor, somehow managing to keep the planes from cracking into each other during the scuffle, and the police brought him to the emergency ward where psychiatric hospitalization had been arranged.

Undoubtedly, Joe's program of self-medication had made matters worse. He had upped his booze consumption to the point where sometimes he couldn't even remember the drive home, or what time he got to bed, or how he got there. One morning he'd gone out to the driveway and noted the crumpled right fender of his car with "not the faintest idea" of what had happened.

Before 1977, there was no overt history of psychiatric illness. Hindsight certainly suggested that his morose spells of many years duration were minor depressive episodes. Additionally, there had been times of cantankerous behavior, and his first wife had finally obtained a restraining order to keep him out of the house.

But is he *dangerous*? Kevin wondered. The problem was that psychiatrists work with stone-age tools on that question. The best they can often do is to look at the past track record—about as effective as picking a pari-mutuel winner after studying the race sheet. But now he studied Joe's race sheet, looking mostly for reassurance. On the plus side, Joe had never to his knowledge hurt anyone seriously and had never attacked anyone with a dangerous weapon. On the minus side, Joe was known to have grossly misinterpreted reality in a paranoid way and had on more than one occasion been involved in physical assaults.

Not the most reassuring picture in the world, Kevin considered, as he turned his Subaru off the road onto his long dirt drive. He pulled his car up alongside the lonely country ranch house and noted the porch light shining warmly in the afterglow of evening. "Yes, sirree," Kevin said facetiously to himself, "all the comforts of home." A growing feeling of peace was not disturbed by the raucous honking of his farmyard geese as he approached.

CHAPTER 4

"But I left explicit instructions for you never to do that!" Kevin's professional cool gave way completely over the phone to an anger of exasperation.

"Well, I'm *very sorry*, Doctor, but I never saw any instructions like that. Besides, the caller said he was another doctor, and he needed to reach you directly. I was just trying to help." The answering-service worker sounded put upon that her efforts had evoked an intemperate display from a professional who should be more dignified.

Kevin now felt additionally upset—at himself—for losing his cool so thoroughly. What was done was done, and berating the service person wouldn't undo it. Tomorrow, he'd change his home phone to another unlisted number and withhold that one from the service. In the future, they could contact him through a beeper, and he'd call back for messages.

Regaining his composure, Kevin terminated the conversation by thanking the worker for her effort to be helpful. Inside, he was still shaking a bit, like the lower pitch of a coin just before it stops rattling after being dropped on the floor. It was the invasion of his home that had separated him from his equanimity—if not the physical invasion, the telephone invasion at least. Bad enough when you're sitting down to dinner and a modern day update of the door-to-door salesman intrudes as boorishly over the phone as any foot-stuck-in-the-doorway salesman of yore. This was far worse because it was targeted, effectively timed, and ominous.

About a week had passed since the "Burgess" call. Kevin was beginning to think, or at least hope, that the whole business was going to blow over. Then this call came, eleven-forty-seven at night, shortly after dropping off to sleep. An almost disembodied hand had groped in dark discoordination for the receiver. "Hello," he'd said tentatively, fighting against his sleep drive to gain full consciousness.

"Hello, is this Doctor Kiley?" It was a man's voice.

"Yes, it is." Kevin's voice was still hooked up to automatic pilot, flying out of a pea soup fog.

"Did I wake you up?"

Now Kevin's faculties started coming back fast. "Who is this?" he asked of the now familiar voice.

"Just like a shrink, answer a question with a question!"

"Who is this?" Kevin repeated.

"That's for me to know and you to find out!"

Anger surged within Kevin, but he resisted his arm's automatic drive to bang the receiver down. Keep your cool, he told himself. Get him to commit himself. And outwardly he spoke again without pause. "Look, I don't find a late night call like this humorous. If you have business with me, state it."

"Oh . . . you know what my business with you is." And the voice had taken on an almost dreamlike, detached quality.

Outwardly Kevin responded, "No, I'm afraid I don't know what your business with me is, or even who you are."

"Playing dumb, huh? Well, I suppose that may be because you really *are* dumb. You think you're so smart and so educated and so high and mighty, and you can run people's lives for them—and ruin their lives. You *are* dumb. And you're *evil*. You should be done away with. The world will be better for it! The world and the grasslands!"

The phone voice had revved up to an angry level now, but Kevin managed to keep an even tone. "What's this about grasslands?" he asked.

"Grass lands, ass lands, ash cans, what's the difference? You know anyway, you stupid asshole!"

Kevin decided to use the direct approach. "You're Mr. Polito, aren't you?"

"Mr. Polito, Mr. Poleeto, MR. POLEE-EETO—NO, YOU FUCKIN' ASSHOLE" and the voice rose to a screaming crescendo.

Kevin was processing the data now as he went along. Apparently irrelevant concepts like "grasslands," clang associations like "grass-land-assland," unmodulated vulgarity indicating loss of emotional control, all consistent with the sort of psychotic decompensation Joe Polito might be expected to have. Kevin felt calmer again as he was assuming his more comfortable clinical role. In conversational tone, he said, "Well, if you're not Mr. Polito, who are you?"

"Who am I? Who am I? *Who-oo-oo am I?* I'll tell you who I am. You can call me the Avenger. Yes, sir, you can call me the *Avenging*

Angel." And the voice laughed with a sense of pleased self-discovery—and kept laughing, and kept laughing, into a cold sadistic trough.

Kevin felt the hair standing up on the back of his neck. And strangely enough, thoughts about the wonders of the nervous system distracted him: that his brain had processed the threat automatically and had sent messages through thousands of tiny nerve fibers to contract thousands of minuscule muscles attached to the puny hairs on his skin. In unity with the lower animals who puff their fur out to increase their apparent size and formidability in response to a potential predator, he was doing likewise—uselessly of course, since his atrophic pelt would hardly enlarge through such a maneuver, even if his telephone adversary could have seen it. Just like a human though, he thought ironically, reacting to the present with responses appropriate only to the past.

The distracting thoughts seemed to calm him, and as the bristling subsided, he asked, "Who or what are you avenging?"

"You know that, don't you?" the voice said, returning to an ethereal calm.

"How did you get my number?"

"Your answering service was very cooperative, once they knew it was another doctor who wanted to reach you." And it was the Avenger who hung up then in a fading flurry of laughter.

Two minutes later, the phone rang, and Kevin lifted it up calculatedly. Nothing! Heavy breathing. Kevin hung up. Another few minutes elapsed and the phone rang again. He picked it up. Nothing. He put it down again, but this time he got out of bed, releasing the clear plastic connector from the wall plug. This represented the first instance where Kevin's dealings with the Avenger interfered with professional care. Had hospital or patient needed to reach Doctor Kiley for the rest of that night, they would have been unable to do so. He thought about it carefully and decided upon this course of action as the lesser evil. If he were to be continually interrupted by those silently menacing phone calls, he believed he would be in absolutely no condition to help any of his patients the following day.

Rest! Try to get some rest tonight. But his self-exhortation accomplished little. It was then that he'd gotten out of bed irritably, flicked on the lights, replugged the phone for a time, and engaged in futile remonstrance with the woman at the answering service. After that foolishness, he'd switched the lights back off and returned to bed. Following a few almost jumping turns from left side to right, he lay on his back, hands folded on his chest, with the tucked-in blanket trying to bend the toes down uncomfortably on his size eleven feet. The thought struck him then with gallows humor that he was in perfect position for the funeral home.

Eventually, he sank—or was it rose—into sleep. Moving, shifting, sometimes twisting, until all motion stopped. Then a moaning began, followed by paroxysmal gasping, the struggle to wake, and a breaking through to the consciousness of our ordinary waking state. Kevin heard the tail end of himself crying out in fear.

Fully awake now, Kevin regarded the transparency of the dream that had just troubled him: A herd of impala leaping with fawnlike grace across an African veldt had scattered suddenly in the face of a jaguar's powerful pursuit. Having centered on one animal, the spotted feline pursued its quarry with singleness of purpose, ignoring all the others as they scattered back and forth every which way. Twisting and turning, trying to hide in the herd, doubling back in an effort to throw off its lethal follower, the impala, with undefending prongs, grew in swelling terror and tiring acceptance of the inevitable. And Kevin, at the very same time in the dream, was both external observer and the pursued animal itself, unable to elude the jaguar or distract its attention to a confusion of other quarry.

As he shook off his fright with gathering wakefulness, Kevin marveled at the imagery of his own slumbering brain, whose effortless symbolism had represented his situation so precisely. He felt like the member of a preyed-on species who, for some luckless reason of being here at a particular time in a particular place, becomes helplessly targeted in the relentless crosshairs of a monomaniacal predator.

Comforted nonetheless by a reverential appreciation for the workings of his own brain, Kevin managed to fall asleep once more. Tossing and turning, he logged a few hours before the early gray of morning shed its light on the off-white bedroom walls, the stained-wood framings, and the foot-wide floorboards of knotty pine.

CHAPTER 5

Morning will come from the east with a smile
Infusing new strength for another day's trial.

Looking in the mirror as he finished shaving, Kevin found himself half-humming, half-singing those lines from the country song, "Blue Cowboy." And he vividly experienced the truth encapsulated in that rhymed couplet.

What had expanded Kevin's interest from Mozart to country involved not only the simplicity of the music but the symbol of the cowboy: solitary and strong, independent yet principled, not just another clone running with the crowd. This cowboy wasn't the transient version from the Old West, though some of those hard laborers no doubt qualified. This cowboy could exist anywhere, though pictured gloriously out on the range astride a horse. But being a cowboy meant not just adding something like a broad-brimmed hat atop one's head; rather, it had to do with developing one's inner strength and the courage of one's own convictions.

Alone now with his thoughts and alone in his house, Kevin tried to decide what to do. During the hours just past, he'd beaten back an endless number of fears and worries. He knew from long experience that things usually seem worse in the still of the night. But now he recalled a selected group of the ideas that had come to him unbidden in that darkness. Make a formal complaint to the police, since threatening another person already constitutes a crime; get advice from a lawyer; initiate a direct confrontation with Joe Polito. Go over the facts with him. Face him, head on.

As he walked out onto his screened porch, the early morning coolness ascended with his first breath, and an immediate rush of vigor circulated through his body. He'd never snorted cocaine, but he knew he would never want to swap this experience. Often, he thought, the best things in life really *are* free. Three steps down from the screened porch, a deck came forward to join the two-car garage. As he walked through an opening in the adjoining trellis, he noted that the beautiful blooms of his clematis vines had finally faded.

Nothing lasts forever, he thought. But funny how this reality must be brought home again, and again, because we don't really want to believe it. Viewed from without, the kaleidoscopic changes of our universe give rise to our sense of its magnificence. Yet viewed from within, continuing change leads eventually to the sadness and dissolution of death.

His musings were interrupted by the familiar greeting of his white geese as he slipped over the wood-rail fence to the back meadow. Walking along the pasture that sloped downward in gracefully repetitive undulations, he saw his African sheep gathering at his approach. Beautiful animals, they looked nothing like Mary's little lamb. Doelike in their quickness, and just as shy, they foraged equally on meadow grass and adjoining wood thickets, thinning the latter to a pleasant arboretum of larger remaining trees.

Spreading some horse checkers on the ground, Kevin watched the sheep eating their food-supplement with the avidness of small children running for candy. Then as he strode back to his car in the front drive, his decision about how to handle the "Avenger" situation came suddenly and spontaneously to mind. He decided the best action at this point was continued inaction. Most unstable people don't tend to stick to things too long. Unless there's some active response to keep their attention, they generally get distracted by something else. To notify the police on the other hand would accomplish little. Mr. Polito would clearly deny everything, and a police inquiry might only inflame the situation further.

As he made the long drive into the hospital—Kevin judged the hour's commute a worthwhile trade-off for his place in the country—he had the additional thought that contacting Mr. Polito's own psychiatrist might help. He knew of Doctor Sanderson only from that doctor's medical reports on Mr. Polito. Kevin had not been impressed. The first report detailed some of the day-to-day stresses of the air traffic controller's job and concluded that the pathological stresses of that position had in fact caused Mr. Polito's illness.

Kevin saw an inverse catch-22 in that report. As Doctor Sanderson had grimmed out the diabolical rigors of the job, no sane man would have taken it in the first place. Then a few months later when Mr. Polito wanted to withdraw his disability application, Doctor Sanderson sent in another report stating that his patient's condition had stabilized, and that he was now fit to return to duty at his former job.

Granted that the majority of bipolar states, especially if uncomplicated by additional problems like alcoholism, respond effectively to treatment and allow as normal a life as that of, say, a person with diabetes or arthritis. But after all, if you're going to say that a pathological environment has made your patient sick, don't come back a few months later with a recommendation that he be sent back into the jaws of the lion.

Kevin could only conclude that Doctor Sanderson was not exactly lying, but slanting the facts as much as possible, like an attorney defending his client: make the strongest possible case you can with the facts available to represent your client's interests. I suppose, thought Kevin, if a patient's own doctor isn't in his corner, who would be? And he'd noticed the same tendency in himself, though he hoped never to this blatant an extreme. But that inclination on the part of a patient's doctor certainly did contribute to the need for independent evaluations around issues of medical litigation.

* * *

After breakfast at the Long Valley Hospital, a small private sanatorium where Kevin usually started his workday, he went to the phone and contacted his tormentor's psychiatrist. "Hello, Doctor Sanderson, this is Doctor Kiley. I saw a patient of yours a while back for disability evaluation. Joe Polito. He's been angry because, in my opinion, his psychiatric condition wasn't caused by his work. He's been harassing me the past few weeks and now is definitely threatening me."

"Doctor Kiley," came the reply, "I won't comment on the wisdom of your report. That's between you and the agency that paid you for your opinion. But you obviously know I can't violate professional confidence without a written release from the patient." Doctor Sanderson's tone of voice stayed level throughout, imbued with a devastatingly put-down cool.

Kevin fought to control a flush of anger. First, the dig about being paid for his opinion. He would have expected that from a lawyer in front of a jury, and he would have been careful to make the distinction that he was being paid for his professional time, not for a bought opinion. But he didn't expect that sort of gamesmanship from a fellow doctor.

As for the matter of a written release, Doctor Sanderson was, of course, technically correct. That regulation served a good purpose by protecting the patient's confidentiality. But even the best rules suffer from not being able to take all the specifics of a situation into account. Therefore, in real life, rules bend. Doctors do sometimes communicate with each other rapidly and informally. If, for instance, an emergency room doctor called, a patient's regular doctor would be hardly likely to wait for a formal release before sharing pertinent information.

After an overly long pause during which Kevin tried to regain composure, he spoke—anger unfortunately showing through in his voice. "I'm glad to hear about your professional concern for confidentiality, but there happens to be another issue at stake here also. *My life!* And, as you darn well know from whatever the name of that decision was in California; you have the duty to inform me and the police of your patient's targeted dangerousness."

Like a fighter in the ring, Kevin observed that most often a person gets tanked when he loses his cool. But occasionally an instinctive flurry of punches hits the mark and puts an opponent back on the defensive. That's what had happened here. He knew the remark, which had come to him spontaneously, wasn't particularly well thought out. The situations were different. In the earlier California case, a patient had shared with his psychiatrist the intent to kill. For all Kevin knew, Joe Polito might never have told Doctor Sanderson of his threats.

"I don't know anything about it." The cold control in the other doctor's voice had given way to the pressured speech of anxiety. "I haven't even seen him for more than a month. He wouldn't take his lithium. He's not my patient anymore. I have nothing to say!"

Kevin pressed his advantage: "You can't just *resign* from a case. From a legal perspective, that would constitute abandonment! Don't you think that under the circumstances he is of immediate danger to others if not himself, and therefore should be committed for observation and treatment in the controlled environment of a psychiatric hospital?"

Doctor Sanderson fought back. "When I last saw him, he was mentally competent and able to make his own decisions. Of course, it was unwise of him to stop his medicine and stop his treatment. But you can't put a patient behind bars for that. How many patients continue to smoke, continue to drink too much, don't follow their diet, or don't continue with their blood pressure medicines? All these things are dangerous to their health and can hurt their family and community, but we can't put all those patients in the hospital. We wouldn't have anyone left outside!"

"*Come on*, Doctor Sanderson, let's not compare someone smoking with someone threatening to kill another person. You've got a responsibility here!"

"Well, I don't recall his threatening you, and when he was my patient, he wasn't an acute danger—and he was legally free to stop seeing me. I'm not *responsible*, I'll stand by that!" Doctor Sanderson's anxiety, still evident in his run-on speech, was abating into a hardening posture as he continued to fashion a defense for his position that obviously seemed more tenable to him now.

"Okay, you yellow bastard, cover your own ass! But thanks anyway for the clinical information you gave me without a release!" In his anger and frustration, Kevin had lost all professionalism. Not only had he stooped to open vulgarity, he had also not been able to resist the dig about Doctor Sanderson's pharisaical adherence to the letter of the law—and the immediate crumbling of that supercilious position at the first threat to his professional position.

Following the phone conversation, Kevin leaned back in the desk chair, his anger gradually subsiding in contemplation. That habit gave him greater distance from an event, but also a weird sense of unreality, as if what was going on wasn't really happening at all—as if it were simply some fictional drama he was watching from the outside.

Reflecting on the conversation with Doctor Sanderson from this perspective, he could understand it, and not even feel angry at the other man. Self-preservation runs deep. It is heroism that represents occasional deviation from the norm. And pompous professionalism, like all "insolence of office," serves the need for self-preservation.

A person in Doctor Sanderson's situation had to confront risks to his professional status from all sides. If he gave out confidential information without permission, he could be sued for malpractice. If he did not give out such information in a case like this, he could lay himself open to suit from a victim of his patient's actions (or posthumously, Kevin thought grimly, from relatives of the victim). Then too, when dealing with an unbalanced individual who could be dangerous, going out of your way to lasso him might cause a change of course in the individual's pursuit of a victim.

Yes, Kevin reflected, it was quite understandable for Doctor Sanderson to try to keep as far away from this one as he could, following that old adage: "Better you than me." Still, he had provided some useful information. When last seen professionally more than a month earlier, Mr. Polito was not obviously out of control. At the same time, he was not cooperating with treatment. Probably he had not made homicidal threats, though Doctor Sanderson's behavior suggested that he didn't consider Mr. Polito to be a tame and toothless tabby either.

Kevin glanced down at his watch and almost shot from his chair. He'd have to really move in order to be on time for his first office appointment.

CHAPTER 6

Squash: a vegetable grown in backyard gardens, or what happens when you dump six kids in the back of your car, but also the name of a racquet sport that Kevin played every Tuesday and Friday nights after work. The appearance of a squash court would be easy to imagine for handball players and the growing legion of racquetball enthusiasts. Picture a large, high-ceiling room, white in color throughout except for a couple of red lines on the front wall and a large, red T with curlicues striped across the rear part of the floor. There are no windows to let in the outside world, and even the solitary doorway recedes into the rear wall like the hidden entrance to a secret passageway, ostensibly to allow the speeding ball to careen off that wall too with bounce untrued by jutting door frames or hinges.

Kevin saw the whole arrangement, however, in more metaphorical terms as a world set apart, as far detached from the universe of ordinary reality as a spaceship chamber in 2001 when that year still seemed far away. On entering this pristine cave, his usual cares most often subsided in a frenzy of dashing forward, back, and sideways, pursuing a small rubber ball that he leveraged along its way with far greater velocity because of the elongated racket handle than he could ever have accomplished with his unaided hand.

Every game has its rules, and what's good for one game may be bad for another. Hit a little white golf ball straight down the center of the fairway, and you're in good shape. Hit the little black squash ball down the center of the court and you're usually in deep trouble—too many different things the opponent can do with it. So Kevin and his regular Friday night adversary, Bernie Schafter, spent most of their time trying to crack the ball up and down along the side wall. All their countermoves, all their crafty plans to outwit one another, built on that basic strategy.

But tonight Kevin hit too many bad shots—or was it that Bernie had hit too many good ones? On the last point of the match, Kevin hit the ball too far out from the wall. Bernie banked his return off the sidewall up front and Kevin had to dash toward the other front corner to retrieve the ball. Hopelessly out of position then, he watched

Bernie hit a crisp shot by him that bounced twice on the floor before he could get there.

"Come on. I'll let you buy me a drink," Bernie spoke with a winner's pleasure. "You know," he added, "I don't think I've ever seen you play better," and they both laughed at this old back-handed self-compliment as they headed downstairs to the locker room. After showering, they walked into the lounge and collapsed comfortably into a couple of leather chairs.

"How'd your week go?" Kevin asked.

"Pretty well," answered Bernie, stretching his muscular legs onto the adjoining chair and adjusting his steel-rimmed glasses. "How about you?"

"A pretty good week," said Kevin, his present state of relaxation adding a degree of retrospective distortion to the ever-present tendency of keeping troubles to oneself.

But Bernie persisted. "Kev, what about that nut who's been threatening you?"

"*That* part's not too good. He's so darn persistent. It's gotten to be like trying to anticipate the next move in a match."

"What's the latest?"

"Well, after I changed my unlisted number and kept it from the answering service, I did all right for several days. Then the new beeper I'd gotten started going off at all hours, so there was no way of getting a night's sleep. Got more middle of the night calls in two days than I ordinarily do in a year."

Kevin continued, his voice firming into seriousness. "So it was *my* move next. There's no way you can leave it to the answering service to screen bogus calls, so I had to tell them not to beep me between eleven and six. If the caller says he's from the hospital, the service girl is to call back the ward and verify that fact before beeping. If patients express an emergency that can't wait till morning, they just have to be referred to the emergency ward to a resident who doesn't even know them. Not very satisfactory for a doctor trying to render personalized service, but right now it seems the lesser of the evils. Better than my not being able to pay attention to *any* of my patients the next day because I'm just too tired. Anyway, I'm fortunate that the type of emergency involved doesn't come up very frequently."

"A real drag," agreed Bernie. "By the way, I was right about that phone business. You can't legally introduce recorded evidence of a phone threat unless the other party agrees to be recorded. You can imagine his response to that. But I think you could have him into the office and record him without his knowledge, and then introduce that into court. I think *that* would be legal."

"Nice you're so certain of the law, Bernie." In his anxiety, Kevin's effort at facetiousness crossed over the line to sarcasm.

"Come on, Kev, don't get impatient. You know I'm in corporate law, so this criminal stuff isn't exactly down my alley. And remember last winter when I was taking that trip to Mexico. I asked you about *Tourista,* and you rambled on about the risk-benefit ratio of preventative antibiotics, but you couldn't answer my specific question either!"

Kevin had to laugh at himself. "Sorry, Bernie, this darn thing has been getting to me." After a pause, he continued, "But you know, lawyers really should do what doctors do—organize formal specialties. People know I'm a psychiatrist and Salty Whittier over there's a gynecologist. It's easy for patients to realize you've got to tip the table different ways for our examinations. But with lawyers, things are left so vague that it promotes misunderstanding. It's easy for an outsider who's not in on all the complexities to believe naively that *any* lawyer can do it all—a bit like that charming old fantasy about the family doctor with his little black bag.

"Besides," added Kevin, brightening a little, "Think of all the opportunity to increase the number of your organizations: specialty boards, diplomates, officers, issues about recertification, bundles of paperwork, and all that sort of thing!"

Bernie laughed. "Not a bad idea, but what would you think about asking him into your office to try to get him to commit himself verbally on your own home ground?"

Not only psychiatrists, but lawyers too have to keep bringing people back to the point, thought Kevin. "Maybe that would be the best thing. Maybe that will be my next move if he won't let go. I've even thought of relisting my number and putting a tracer on the calls. I know telephone harassment is a legal offense in itself. But that bastard's probably clever enough to use pay phones anyway."

"What the hell are you two looking so serious about?" Salty Whittier, a wiry, middle-age physician with abundant hair everywhere on his body except for his head, was in the midst of moving over from the next table. He evidently wanted someone to talk to while he finished his martini, and perhaps he was taking exception to this deviation from the usual locker room banter—locker rooms are for fun, for relaxing, for unwinding, not for continuing the seriousness of the day.

"Let me tell you guys this story," said Salty. "It's about a kid who comes home late. You heard it?"

"How the hell should we know?" said Bernie. "A kid comes home late. That could be anything. So go on."

"Well, this kid . . . he's sixteen, and he just got his license. So his mother's waiting up for him. His curfew's eleven, but he doesn't get home till quarter of one. She's pacing down by the front door, and she's all worried. Finally he comes in and she says, 'Son, we've been worried half to death about you.' And he says, 'Relax, Mom. There's nothing to worry about. I just got laid.' Well, the mother nearly has a fit, and she screams upstairs to her husband who's asleep: 'Get down here right now and talk to your son. He's an animal!' So the father comes downstairs as the mother leaves the room hysterically. He asks his son what's happened. 'Nothing, Dad,' the son says. 'I just got laid tonight for the first time.' With ill-concealed approval, the father shakes his head knowingly, then says in a conspiratorial tone, 'Congratulations, son. But, for Christ sake, there are some things you just don't talk about in front of women. Now get up to bed.'

"So the following night, the kid goes out again. His mother's still a little shell-shocked and insists that her husband wait up this time. Same curfew, eleven o'clock. The father's waiting and starts pacing around impatiently as it gets to midnight, then one, then two o'clock. Finally his son comes home. By this time, the father's pretty pissed off from waiting up. So as his kid comes in the door, he says sharply, 'Where the hell have you been? I suppose you've been out getting laid again!' 'Hell, no,' answers his son. 'My ass is still too sore from last night!'"

The three of them broke up at this spoofing of their macho tendencies—though Kevin might well have reflected additionally that it helps to be sure of your facts before you react.

CHAPTER 7

"When I go to sleep, I never count sheep, I count all the charms about Linda." Kevin sang in a happily relaxed tone, trying simultaneously to remember from his childhood the name of the fellow who had made the hit.

"Don't give me that line," interrupted Linda playfully as she lay beside him, her crescent eyes laughing in the nakedness of her own afterglow. "I've heard about you, living alone out there with those sheep."

"Who told you?" Kevin mocked dismayed surprise, and they both laughed, almost with the giggle of children. They often kidded about that. Just like children, he thought. Find mirth in something, and they want to repeat it over and over.

Kevin's thoughts drifted without conscious choice to his days as a young father. Jessica would sit dwarfed in his leather reading chair, scrunched in one of its overstuffed corners, knees under her chin, nothing seeming to show but a blissful smile, long sandy hair, and large, wide-open hazel eyes. It all seemed unreal now, little different than the insubstantial daydreams of youth. Yet the fledglinged child and still unfailed marriage had been in those earlier times as actual as his waking dream of the present moment.

"What are you thinking?" Linda was stretched out on her side now, her head resting on her right hand, elbow crooked for support, and the fingers of her left hand playing deftly with the hair on his chest. At times like this, their silences were mostly easy, and conversations often repeated might break off at any point. Still, Linda was sensitive to even the minute stiffenings of his body, the trouble lines on his face, or that peculiar upward gaze which transfixed him occasionally—out toward another world, back in time, onward to something else. It had a disquieting effect on her.

A couple of weeks had passed since the strategy talk with Bernie, and Kevin proceeded to relate the intervening events. ". . . so the following Monday, I called Mr. Polito at home. No answer in the morning, but that afternoon one of his kids picked up the phone. Told me his father was asleep but seemed impressed that I was a doctor and said he'd get him. What the heck, I figured that he woke me up enough.

"Anyway, I told him I was very concerned about the things that had been happening, and that I'd like to meet with him. He asked what good that would do now, and I said it might help to clear the air. Naturally I didn't add 'And I want to tape some of those threats you've been making.' Well, he said he could understand that my conscience was bothering me, and under the circumstances he thought it certainly should. But it was too late now. Finally, after needling me a while longer, he reluctantly agreed to come to my office. Then he never showed.

"I also checked with my answering service. They'd still been receiving an occasional bogus call. He must have figured out that he was successfully harassing me this way, because if his calls weren't getting through, other calls weren't either. So I explained the situation to Ma Bell. They installed another line for me and put a tracer on my regular phone. Then I gave my number to the answering service with instructions to give it out directly to callers at night. The idea was, when he phoned, I had to keep him on the line and then alert the phone company through the other line. I felt like some sort of novice juggler, or one of those executives who gets satirized with all the phones. But it worked, though I had to listen to a lot of that angrily irrational howling in the process."

Linda's eyes lit up. "Oh good! You finally caught him with something you could prove."

"I wish you were right. The guy may be crazy, but like a fox. Pay phones all over town! That's what I figured would happen. Still it does puzzle me that he seems so out of control when he's raving over the wires; then he's so craftily in control the way he goes about it. Well, I remember when I saw him that I thought he'd have the equipment to make a good air traffic controller, except for his psychiatric problems. He seemed to have good intelligence and quick wits. But you know, I can't for the life of me recall clearly what he even looks like. I recall he was dark complexioned and had a receding hairline. He was just starting to show a little gray, and he had prominent eyes. I had even reviewed his medical record to make sure a thyroid test had been done. But those bulging eyes did give him a sort of wild look, especially when he spoke with intensity. He was a little shorter than I am, maybe just touching six feet, but he was a lot heavier." Still lying on his back, Kevin pounded his flat abdomen a couple of times with the palm of his right hand, noting that contrast with a trace of irrelevant pride.

Picking up on that and trying to lighten the conversation, Linda stroked his abdomen and said with playfully exaggerated admiration, "I *know*. Your tummy is so strong and so flat . . . and so handsome."

He smiled in a halfway response to her gear shifting effort toward another mood. But at the same time, he found himself reflecting that the impersonalness of urban life causes some of our most important transactions to occur with people who otherwise remain faceless, and he wondered if Mr. Polito had a better picture of him.

Sitting up in bed, Kevin looked across the room at a now-familiar hanging, the large outline of a melancholy leopard, printed on a burlap backing. He had always admired the solitary strength of this animal in its sleek black variety, but it had never looked like this sad-sack caricature. Why did Linda, whose temperament seemed as pleasant as her long-legged ballerina's figure was beautiful, give this sorrowfully faced and heavy-hearted creature a place of such prominence in her boudoir? He realized that he had never asked. There's a lesson here somewhere, he thought. Did Florence Nightingale fantasies not only dictate her choice of career but also her avocations from Animal Shelter advocate to a friend who was still licking his inner wounds?

"How about some Mallomars and milk?" Linda's cheerfulness continued, finally infecting him.

"Great! Hey, that reminds me of a story I heard at the club tonight. I thought you'd appreciate it. Seems this guy wasn't feeling well, so he went to his doctor. After a thorough examination, the doctor approached him gravely." As Linda started walking out to the kitchen—sweeping her long, brown hair back over her shoulders as she went—Kevin continued with a decibel adjustment in his voice. " 'I have some very bad news,' he says. 'You're suffering from a rare and fatal illness. Unfortunately, there's no cure for it. You have only three months left to live. I'm sorry.'

"Well, the guy's really shook up, and he starts imploring the doctor. 'Look, there's got to be something you can do for me! With all the wonderful breakthroughs in modern medicine, there must be some new operation or wonder drug or something.' The doctor shakes his head sadly, then pauses. 'What are you thinking of?' the guy asks anxiously. The doctor answers, 'Well, there is an old folk cure that's been reported to have helped this condition. Nothing scientifically proven, you understand.' 'I'll take it, I'll do it, I'll do anything,' the guy says, as if he's just been given a reprieve by the governor. 'It's mother's milk,' replies the doctor. And the guy collapses back in his chair again. 'There might as well not be any treatment,' he says sadly. 'How could I ever get that?' 'No problem there,' answers the doctor. 'All I have to do is write you out a prescription for a wet nurse.'

"So the doctor makes the arrangement for him. At first he's a bit embarrassed, but after a while he's going right at it. Meantime, the wet nurse starts getting a little excited. She looks down at him and asks seductively, 'Is there anything else I can do for you?' He looks up into her eyes and answers, 'Yeh, can I have a cookie?' "

At this point, Linda was walking back into the bedroom with the Mallomars and milk. Her sudden laugh jiggled the mug, and some milk sloshed out over her hand, the carpet, and the edge of the bed. "Couldn't you have held that punchline till I put this stuff down?" she admonished facetiously.

"Couldn't do it!" he said. "Timing is everything in life." And it's true, there's a time to ventilate one's troubles and a time to suppress their useless rumination. But which time was it now, he wondered, as his thoughts returned to Joe Polito before crunching the first Mallomar—for once, he had hardly noticed Linda's beautiful long-legged figure.

"What sort of condition does this fellow have?" she asked.

Kevin paused, because ordinarily he spoke to no one about patients he had seen. But the personal threat he felt in this case had opened him up a little with Bernie and Linda, though he still hadn't mentioned Joe Polito by name. He had kept that confidence. Out of prudence though, he had documented the threats in his record and had mentioned the matter specifically to his secretary, albeit facetiously. "Frances, if the police should drop by some day to ask: 'Did the doctor have any enemies, anyone who'd want to hurt him?' Be sure to put this Polito fellow on the top of the list!" Now, however, he felt an almost irrepressible urge to talk about it, so he answered Linda's question. "He's got a bipolar state with some highs, but not the pleasant euphoric type. More the hyperirritable kind that lapse over into paranoid delusions when he's severely agitated."

"Well, if he gets so ill, why *isn't* he disabled?" Linda inquired neutrally.

"He *is* disabled," answered Kevin, "especially given the added complication of his alcoholism—at least for a very responsible job like air traffic controller. But that's not the issue here. The question I was asked concerned whether his job *caused* the condition, or permanently aggravated it."

"I've read that the controller's job is very stressful," said Linda cautiously, "so how can you be sure it wasn't the cause?"

"*Every* job has stress!" Kevin replied emphatically. "But that stress is usually healthier than the opposite, the stress of lack of stress. It's like stress on bones. Take a person off his feet for a while, remove the stress of moving and lifting and pulling and so forth, and his bones weaken. The calcium starts to come out, and he's more prone to fracture. The stress of exercise is essential for physical health. Not the extreme stress that will break bones in a bad accident, but a reasonable amount of stress. It's the same thing with work stress and psychic health. Take away that reasonable amount of stress, and full health becomes impossible. It's the doing something meaningful and coping with associated problems that produces the healthy stimulation.

"You know, since most of us have to work for a living, we often oversimplify things, thinking that money's the only reason we work. But work is *therapy*, occupational therapy, even though it's too basic a health need to ordinarily refer to it by that name. It'd be like calling food *medicine*. But since work always involves stress, you could *always* make a case for work causing a stress-related illness.

"If you followed that line of reasoning, establishing a psychiatric diagnosis would be tantamount to accepting a work-caused condition. Well, if the citizens of the country want to be extremely generous, they can choose that option . . . and the increased taxes that'd go with it. But I don't think that's their intent in the present law. And if the law should be rewritten or, much the same thing, grossly reinterpreted, there'd be other problems. Reward any activity, and it will occur more commonly. Give a man three quarters of his pay without any of the expenses involved in going to work, and what do you expect to happen? Jogging may be good for your health, but it's still a drag to get out and do it. Working is good for your health, but the same thing goes. And with many modern jobs, the chief meaningfulness is found in the act of supporting self and family. Take away that financial meaningfulness because there's an easier way, and many folks are sapped of the main sense of purpose they've been able to experience with their work."

"I know what you're saying," Linda said earnestly. "But isn't the air traffic controller's job something special?"

"Not entirely," Kevin answered. "There's been some sort of mystique cultivated about that job, as if it's prone to all kinds of extraordinary and unique hazards. Maybe it has to do with the whole aura of man being airborne. I'm not knocking the position. It's very important work, requiring intelligence, attentiveness, and good judgment. But for Heaven's sake, to hear some people talk, there's more stress involved than in flying the planes themselves.

"Look, all sorts of jobs require direct responsibility for the lives of others—jobs as different as bus driving and cardiac surgery. Take your nursing job, Linda. When you give out meds, one misread might contribute to a patient's death. One extra squirt of potassium in the IV bottle, one contamination of the hyperalimentation tubing. You name it. The stress of your job is *life and death*. But if you should develop a nervous breakdown, will workman's compensation say that your job did it?

"Marriage can be one hell of a stress. Why not say that this guy's marriages caused his illness? He's had three of them. But they never get mentioned, and for one reason. There's no issue of compensation! Too bad he hadn't married a rich woman. At least then he could have tried for alimony." And a smile came to Kevin's face as his tone changed to humorous.

"What *did* cause his illness then, and why did it take such a downhill course?"

"Who knows?" answered Kevin, sitting straight up in bed now. "I mean, who really knows why anyone gets ill. Why does a patient come onto your floor with a heart attack? Does he eat a high cholesterol diet? Does he smoke? Does he have a time-and-performance-oriented personality? Does he have a history of family susceptibility? Answer yes to all these questions and it puts him in a group more likely to have a heart attack. But there'll be a thousand other guys without any symptoms walking the streets that same day with that same profile, and another heart attack patient in the very next hospital room without any of those factors. So if we can't even say for sure what causes a heart attack, something as demonically simple as the death of a piece of heart muscle due to a clogging of the blood vessel that's supposed to feed it, how in the world are we to know what causes the subtle imbalance of bipolar disorder in the subtlest of all organs, the brain? Undoubtedly a number of interacting factors are involved, some of them inherited, some of them experienced.

"Take this air controller guy. His father took off when he was a little kid . . . later died in a hushed up way, so the patient doesn't know to this day what happened. It left his mother distressed and the family bereft, one heck of a depressing circumstance in which to grow up. So did that experience cause his illness? Not by itself, that's for sure. Too many people have had the misfortune of losing a parent during childhood without suffering this disorder later.

"And before focusing exclusively on the impact of early environment here, consider another possibility. Perhaps the father had a similar illness, and this contributed to his own instability in leaving home. And his hushed up death, that might have been due to suicide, not a rare complication of bipolar disorder. So maybe the patient inherited the tendency. Most likely, the condition resulted from a combination of his father's genetic contribution, the problems produced by his absence, and a bunch of other things.

"At any rate, the bottom line here as to cause has to be: unknown. But there's no reason for me to believe his job contributed a necessary link in its development. It might even have provided a somewhat stabilizing and self-esteem-building influence, helping to stave off a more rapid deterioration in his condition. One thing's for sure though. He hasn't had an easy life from the word go. I could empathize with him more, however, if he didn't behave like such a bastard."

Linda smiled and cuddled closer, her dark hair flowing gracefully over her shoulders. Sometime between finishing his cookies and this part of the conversation, Kevin had slipped down again along the pillow, lying on his back as he talked. She's so nice, so tactful, thought Kevin, and he drifted off pleasantly—for his nightly encounters in the land of troubled dreams.

CHAPTER 8

Kevin left his office each night now with some trepidation. The end of daylight saving had accentuated nature's own shortening of the days, and the early darkness illuminated his mood of apprehensiveness. A pair of small floodlights lit up the brick parking area down back. This more or less point source of illumination, coming from an angle about twenty feet up on the building, brightened an immediate space, but produced long shadows of eeriness and faded abruptly into the surrounding darkness. If a person looked back toward the building, the light's intensity at its source would attract his eyes like a blinding magnet.

Walking out to his Subaru, Kevin noticed the right front tire first, rim to the ground. He cussed to himself, thinking he had picked up a nail, and headed immediately around to the station wagon's rear door—before he remembered that the spare tire hung out in the "engine room" of this car. He smiled at the thought of that term, "engine room," used in the owner's manual to describe a smallish space under the hood. The phrase had always connoted to him some extensive area down below, with pipes and valves everywhere, and sweaty men in T-shirts, usually trying frantically to keep the ship from going awash in some World War II movie. For Heaven's sake, he thought, with all the cars they're selling, at least the manufacturers could have afforded an American technical writer to edit the darn manual.

His thoughts came back to the business at hand as he unlocked the front door to release the hood latch. There is absolutely no good time to get a flat tire, but there are worse times, and this was one of them. After a long day, the flat fettered him just when he was headed home. Then he noticed something else: not the tire itself, but the fact that the car showed not the slightest tilt. He stepped back a couple of paces and looked more carefully. Sure enough, the left front tire was as flat as the right. He walked around the back of his wagon to confirm what at this point he already knew. Both rear tires were also flat.

No obvious slashes, probably ice-picked, he thought. The young repair truck driver, sporting a full beard that somehow looked incongruous atop his grease-stained overalls, had confirmed his suspicion: clean punctures in all four tires. Kevin informed the police, who could do little beyond adding it to their crime statistics. Nothing further happened that week—unless one were to count the daily repetition of apprehensive anticipation, subtle occurrences that leave no more of a scar than repeated drops on the forehead during a Chinese Water Torture.

* * *

The following Tuesday, Kevin descended the back stairway at day's end and went out the rear door. He had seen nothing from his office window, and the car showed no obvious damage as he approached it. Raising his collar against the chill of this late November evening, he inserted the key in his car door. As he started to lift the door latch, he heard the sound from behind: half-cackle, half-laugh. He fairly jumped, as he turned to see the long, shining tubes of a double-barreled shotgun glinting harshly in his direction. A large, dark-jacketed, stocking-masked figure moved forward into the edge of light and said, "I've been waiting for you."

"Will you put that gun down!" Kevin heard his own voice, as if coming from somewhere else—with a firmness that stood in absolute contradiction to the shaking weakness that had suddenly grasped arms, legs, and bladder.

"Still giving orders, huh, Doc?" And the humor of that absurdity under the circumstances evidently evoked the peals of insanely snorting half-laughter that followed. "No more shit from you, Doc. No more fuckin' shit from you." A blinding flash, followed immediately by a second echoing discharge. Kevin collapsed onto the ground, searing pain in his face and a tight sensation in his chest, followed by total unconsciousness.

CHAPTER 9

Something. Nothing. Something glimmering. Nothingness again. Something receding into annihilation, a pulsing of something, finally a flicker of actual consciousness, giving way again to undifferentiated awareness. Nothingness again, then back and forth through the "something" to that flicker of focused consciousness. Self-consciousness. Kevin—Kevin Kiley—Doctor Kevin Kiley—waking. Waking up. But not waking up as from sleep. No, not that oftentimes pleasant drift from slumber to alertness, the continuity of self an unquestioned certainty. This was like returning from the void of nothingness, an absolute interruption of the self. This was like returning from death. It was a foretaste of death.

As the pulses of self-consciousness grew stronger, Kevin experienced the frailty of his own inner being, a being whose existence till now had seemed independent of its bodily container. But the persistence of consciousness had proven more fragile even than his body! He grasped the entirety of those reflections in one clear moment, though it took the several weeks following to think it out fully in words. Thoughts accompanied by somber intimations of mortality.

But as full consciousness finally returned with a sudden rush, so did the key to his sense of continuing self. Memory. He suddenly remembered the frightening events, and he felt his body against the ground. Turning fully on his side, then his back, he felt the cold bricks on his underside. Hard, uncomfortable. He remembered that he'd been shot at close range, with both barrels of a shotgun. His mind told him that his head should have been blown off, that he should have been blown away. Yet, as his hands automatically explored his head and body, he seemed to be intact. No holes. Then he felt a sore spot, wet to the touch, high on his left cheekbone. And another one up on his temple. And the back of his head hurt. Sore to touch, but no wetness.

He checked his fingers after sending them on their reconnaissance trip. No blood. And he felt relieved that he could see, though now he became clearly aware of the spotlight shining at him blindingly from its perch on the building. And his body. He remembered from a moment ago that it had moved. He checked it again, mobilizing arms and legs and fingers and toes, then curving and straightening his trunk.

With clear-headed rapidity now came the tentative explanation that his assailant had removed the pellets and had shot at him with the equivalent of blanks. The sore spots on his cheek were probably powder burns, and the back of his head was hurting from the fall. I must have fainted, he thought, forcing himself to use that word though he didn't like it. The connotation was of weakness. He'd been *faint-hearted*.

And only then, though he considered that he had been clear-headed before, did he notice that he'd wet himself. Worse still, he had defecated involuntarily. Sitting up cross-legged, he smelled his own body with feelings of revulsion—feelings that reinforced the revulsion he experienced at his own cowardice. He raged inwardly at Joe Polito for puncturing, worse than his body, his heroic sense of self.

He'd have to return to the building for emergency repairs. But looking around, he couldn't find his keys. He checked his pockets. No luck. He stood up, but could see no more from that vantage point. He tried the back door, but it was locked. He knew it would be. He leaned on the doorbell hopelessly, remembering that the part-time building superintendent was seldom there Thursday nights.

A sense of shame grew stronger within him, though his mind well recognized its irrationality. Moving over to a darkened corner of the yard, he took off his car coat without feeling the cold. Then he took off his shoes and socks, not wanting to soil them in the subsequent act of removing trousers and underpants. Wiping himself off the best he could with the upper corner of his soiled underwear, he cast it aside and dressed again in his trousers, now turned cold as well as wet and odoriferous. With shoes, socks and coat back on, he walked the several townhouses width to the side alley. Apparently not a soul had heard the shots or noticed any commotion. In the city at night, people know to shut things out, a selective inattention that happens automatically with enough experience.

Back along Beacon Street several numbers, he entered the front hall of his own building without noticing on this occasion the handsome ogival doorway that he'd found so esthetically appealing on first seeing his office many years ago. He rang all the bells, hoping that someone was working late. Of all nine tenants, he was the sole psychiatrist remaining. Psychologists, marriage counselors, social workers, a seeming host of mental health professionals. But the other psychiatrists had retreated (or advanced) to the medical office buildings and a closer embrace with the rest of medicine.

Ben Walters's "Hello" sounded over the intercom. Kevin had never been happier to hear a sex therapist's voice. "Ben, this is Kevin Kiley. I've just been attacked. Could you let me in and call the police?"

"Christ!" answered Ben and the buzzer immediately formed an exclamation point. After checking to see that he was all right, Ben walked back upstairs to attend to his clients, troubled as that couple was by the quickest release since Joe Namath left football. Concentrating on a different use for those private organs, Ben said nothing about Kevin's wet pants or associated odor. Maybe it's not so noticeable, thought Kevin. Then the corrective of reality: more likely he's just being tactful.

The police were sympathetic, but only to a point. Ages no more than twenty-five or thirty, they'd already seen too much to react strongly to this sort of thing. But Kevin continued to talk and explain, talk and explain, nonstop. After a while, he became aware of his own nervous pressure of speech and tried to stop. Then the officer with the Clark Gable moustache went out to view the scene of the crime, while the baby-faced one told Kevin they'd drive him over to the City Hospital Emergency Ward to get checked out medically. That was the last thing Kevin wanted at this point. However, he felt too drained to do anything but go along.

The moustached officer returned with the keys. Turned out that Kevin had left them in the car door! When the baby-face officer mentioned driving over to the hospital, his companion said they should call the police ambulance. A flick of his eyes sideways toward Kevin's pants, followed by a moment's intense eye contact with his fellow officer, accompanied by an involuntary twitch of his moustache, spoke volumes. Kevin could not have felt more humiliated if he'd said: "I'm not going to ride in the same car with that shit."

How many times have I seen that eerie flicker from a police ambulance revolving in the darkness of some city street like the last drunken beacon of mankind, thought Kevin, as he walked out the doorway with the baby-face officer a little while later. But its siren always tolled for someone else, not me. Always someone playing out one of life's little dramas, most of them as prosaic as this.

The revolutions of light gave brilliant glimpses of the surroundings, but not long enough to grasp their reality. The ride to the hospital, the emergency ward staff, patients and family members waiting in chairs or in huddled groups standing in corridors, x-rays, physical exam, the taxi back to his car, the long ride home, all revolved around him with intense pulses of clarity that seemed to come and go with the same eerie flashings of unreality.

Once home, he showered, and in the water's warm envelopment, he felt the sins of the world being washed away. If cleanliness is not really next to Godliness, there are times when it at least seems so. Turning on his electric blanket, he dropped naked into bed. And some lines from "Blue Cowboy" entered his mind:

Blue Cowboy, let me sing you to sleep
Lullabies and nursery rhymes that won't make you weep.

In total exhaustion, he drifted immediately off. Physically, however, he had used much less energy than on a squash night.

CHAPTER 10

Kevin called Bernie the next morning for the name of an appropriate lawyer, and his friend immediately recommended a fellow named Mike Grady. "He's one of the best criminal lawyers around," said Bernie, "sharp as a tack, and he's tough. I'll check and see if he can see you right away, maybe after office hours today."

So Kevin had canceled his last appointment (really should have canceled out the whole bloody day, he thought) and walked along Beacon Street, slanting gradually up its incline over the front of Beacon Hill, with the Common on his right. Then he wound his way down along the old cow-path streets to Post Office Square. So many of the lawyers huddled their offices in the uncleanable old buildings of that area, the best ones showing a decadent elegance of marble entrances and foyers.

Kevin hated lawyers, hated his present position, and at this moment hated most of all having to wait. Shortly, however, Mike Grady's apparently boundless energy was upon him. "Doctor Kiley? Sorry to keep you waiting. Come on in." Shaking hands enthusiastically, he shepherded Kevin into his large office. "Bernie Schafter told me a bit about the situation. Sounds like you have a real headache there. Tell me about it."

Despite his negativity toward lawyers, Kevin felt an immediate rapport. Just a few correct cues from the square-jawed, broad-shouldered stranger had been sufficient to win the client over. In response to Mike's subsequent questioning, Kevin poured out all he could remember about what had happened and what had led up to it.

Mike listened intently, interrupting only when Kevin's account wandered too far afield. Then he summed the situation up succinctly. "Our problem is this. You've just told me in effect that you can't identify your assailant, nor the fellow who threatened you over the telephone, even assuming that they're the same person."

"But I *know* who it was," Kevin insisted, "this Polito fellow. *No question about it.*" And Kevin's voice rose with alarming suddenness, both in pitch and volume, apparently trying to convince by intensity after his earlier words had failed to do so on their own.

"I'm not trying to discourage you," Mike replied matter of factly, "but let's look at the evidence. You're sure it was this Polito fellow because he had threatened you, and because you thought you recognized his voice raised in anger. I'm convinced that won't wash unless we can get something more, or that we can trip him up. But if you feel you can identify him, that ought to be enough to get an informal hearing before the clerk at the district court. If he can get some more information, or if this Polito fellow doesn't show up, a warrant can be issued for a probable cause hearing. The only risk there is in getting the guy even more vindictive than he is now.

"Considering the present state of affairs, we don't seem to have much to lose though. On the plus side, at the very least, we would be pinpointing him as *the* person to suspect in the case of any future harassment. That in itself would make him think two or three times before getting onto your case again."

"That's the thing to do then." Kevin spoke with a resolve born out of his desperate need to do something. "How do we proceed from here?"

"I'll handle that," said Mike. "Tomorrow morning, I'll contact the detective division to see who's handling the case and what progress they've made. Likely not too much, given the circumstances . . . the fact that no one was seriously injured, and that you're not a public figure. Then I'll call the Clerk of Court and see what we can arrange."

"Thanks," said Kevin. He still hated lawyers in general. But right now he liked *his* lawyer. He felt grateful to Mike. Something positive would be done.

CHAPTER 11

Kevin sat on a bench in the courthouse lobby—actually a long corridor that ran at right angles to the vestibule. As nine o'clock neared, the benches became progressively filled, and people started milling about in small groups, like waiting at a subway station for an infrequent train. He tried to occupy his time constructively by reading one of his medical journals, but couldn't concentrate. He read a full page of words that seemed to have become detached from their meanings, and he felt a retrospective camaraderie with all those patients whom he had seen through the years, struggling to keep their jobs or stay in school while subject to this kind of disorganizing anxiety.

Putting the journal down, he started an inner review of the testimony he'd gone over with the prosecutor (that is, with the assistant district attorney who had graduated from law school in June of the preceding year). What he would say came back to him readily, and he felt too restless to bother focusing on it again now.

Just then, a white-shirted court officer, handcuffs attached around his belt, opened the main courtroom door immediately across from the vestibule, and a slowly gathering flow of people headed in. Kevin entered with them and sat down in the back row—as he had done years earlier in the classroom, the better to observe his surroundings. The wood-paneled hall within, unlike the outside waiting area, was bright and in good repair. Though relatively large, the room had only about ten rows of benches, all placed in its rear half, with side aisles like church for easier access.

Very much like a church, thought Kevin, and the analogy struck him explicitly for the first time—except that the "altar" railing was placed too far toward the room's center, evidently to allow space for the desks and chairs used by lawyers, prosecutors, defendants, and ancillary personnel. And when His Honor entered the room, everybody stood up, just the way it happened when the priest walked out onto the elevated altar. And as a priest's robes hide the human form so that people may see only the instrument of God, the judge's robes hide his body, allowing the audience to see but the pure instrument of Justice.

A sample of courtroom procedures began, and Kevin found himself alternately attending to his own inner musings, then focusing on the external events that were evolving. Right now, a traffic case.

An earnest young man, standing at a microphone facing the judge, was explaining that he did not know why the car behind him had suddenly speeded up, turning its revolving police light on, until the officer told him that he had not given way sufficiently at the Yield sign.

"I had to slam on my brakes or I'd have rammed into you," the policeman had remonstrated.

"That was obviously false," the young man said, pressing the center of his horn-rim glasses against the bridge of his nose. "He was far enough back that he had to speed up to me from behind. In fact, when I saw his flashing light, I pulled aside so that he could pass easily when he reached me. I assumed he must have just gotten an emergency call."

Having listened to the conflicting testimony, the judge leaned forward and spoke earnestly, eye to eye. "Mr. Morsely, the issue here is whether or not you operated your motor vehicle unsafely and to the danger of other citizens during the incident in question. You look like a sincere young man who has come to court because you believe you have not. But you're asking me to set aside the observations of an officer, whose duty is to police the highways for your own safety, as well as for all of us. I'll admit there can be close calls in this type of situation, as in the refereeing of a basketball game, and that your perspective at the time can represent a mitigating circumstance. Therefore, I am reducing your fine from twenty-five to fifteen dollars."

A real Solomon, thought Kevin. Cut the body in half! The young man, still standing at the microphone, head now bowed a little but moving in a negative direction that expressed perhaps equal mixtures of frustration, disagreement, and hopelessness about his cause, spoke again doggedly with a quiet tremble in his voice. "Your Honor, I'm an electrician. For me to take off this time to get to court today has cost more than twenty-five dollars. That cop over there who bullied me gets paid to come here. It looks to me like I can't win either way, and he can't lose. 'Cause even if I won my case, I'm already fined by losing this morning's money, while he's made himself thirty-five bucks just for showing up. But I didn't want to let him get away with giving a bum ticket. I don't know his problem. Maybe he just had a fight with his wife that day, but . . ."

"*Mr. Morsely*," the judge interrupted now quite sternly. "The court has listened closely to your side and has been most patient with all the time you took to describe this incident. That will be all." And the firmness of each equally intoned word of his last sentence was reinforced by a not-so-gentle grip on the defendant's right elbow by a court officer whose facial expression showed clearly the indignation he felt at this impertinence. The young man turned and left meekly, head still bowed, expression almost dazed, as if he'd been dealing with an issue of great importance.

How does a "court" go about listening? Kevin wondered ironically. And why did this young fellow bother to come to court to dispute a crummy little traffic violation, especially when he had it sized up that the lesser of two evils was really just to pay the bloody fine and have done with it? It's this idea of justice, he thought: *"It isn't fair!"*

But where does the whole issue of fairness come from, given the fact, on every page and every day, that life is anything but fair. We are born in good or bad times, in opulent or penurious circumstances, to loving parents or child beaters, with minds facile or slow, looks sparkling like Adonis or grungy like Grendel, with muscles that tend to ripple or wilt, and with reflexes like Doctor J. or Mr. Hyde. We suffer the luck of our defense mechanisms against illness, the vagaries of the marketplace, the often unpredictable eventuality of the fantasy that we marry, the consequences of mechanical breakdown and operator error, susceptibility to our own passions that can sometimes sweep us to chaos like an irresistible undertow, together with a rebellious Nature's "acts of god." Should we weather all these elements with good fortune, we then face inevitable decrepitude and dissolution. Yet we persist in processing the data of our experience through this filter of fairness. In fact, we cannot help but process our experiences in this way.

More still, imposed below the limits of our conscious minds! For it had suddenly occurred to Kevin that a relationship existed between this category of fairness and the so many miles of irrational guilt he had observed in his patients over the years. If they had experienced good luck in emerging unscathed while their comrades-in-arms were demolished or their fellow travelers were maimed, they felt guilty. It wasn't fair. But catch–22. If they had bad luck, then "God must have punished me."

The thought of Job entered his mind, and he tried to recall the details of that old bible story. If Job had just hit a run of bad luck, if the roulette wheel had just stopped landing on his number, the whole story with its ceaseless ruminations would have been pointless. But the whole business was processed through the prism of fairness, and that's, of course, what produced the enigma.

Where did this idea of *fairness* come from? His childhood catechism had announced that man was made in the Image of God: The Big Referee in the sky, All-Perfect and therefore All-Fair. But if you found it hard to believe in a humanoid God who went around toying with a guy named Job, what would you make of this story? You'd probably see God as the externally projected ideal within men's minds, able thus to turn "fairness" into "Fairness."

But that still wouldn't explain where man's instinct of fairness came from. And as soon as the word came to mind, Kevin smiled. No mystery that the word *instinct* should have come to him, given his extensive biological training. But it did thrust his mental exploration in a different direction, that of Darwin's Natural Selection. The sense of fairness in a social animal gives an advantage, because it enhances the likelihood of cooperative interaction sufficient for the group to survive. So this trait would have been positively selected over time because of its adaptiveness for the group and the group's imperious gene pool. . . .

"Doctor, will you please rise." And Kevin's thoughts were interrupted with some embarrassment as the court officer brought him back to external reality. The other participants were already standing to be sworn in together. His case was to begin.

* * *

The police officer provided his testimony regarding the scene of the crime, the hospital report had been introduced to attest to the minor injuries sustained, and Kevin had recounted in response to the prosecutor's questions the whole sequence of threats and harassments. During this entire time, Mr. Polito had sat on a separate bench over to the left side (the right side, now that Kevin was standing in the witness box just down from the judge's throne).

Beside Mr. Polito sat a small woman with graying brown hair and a tired expression. When the group of witnesses had been sworn in, she had stood up in her brown cloth coat and raised her right hand with the rest. The defendant had remained seated, since his lawyer would not allow him to be called. In fact, Kevin was almost surprised to see him since his presence was not strictly necessary at a probable cause hearing, and his lawyer might have asked the judge to waive his appearance, pleading emotional duress or whatever. I suppose, thought Kevin, that young defense lawyers working as public defenders have a lot to learn.

Dressed in a lined canvas car coat that he had unzipped after entering the courtroom, Mr. Polito's ruddy complexion against his plaid flannel shirt was consistent with the doctor's memory. Kevin reflected though that he never would have been able to pick him out of a police lineup with certainty. Well, perhaps those prominent eyes would have provided the necessary marker, he reassured himself. Looking ill at ease, with tension showing in the way he folded and unfolded his arms repeatedly, Mr. Polito did not come across like a dangerous man. He seemed discouraged and a little bit scared.

During all the prosecution testimony, the defense attorney had said virtually nothing. Not even any I-object-your-Honor. Obviously youthful despite his full brown beard and stooped shoulders, he would have done well with his frail frame to avoid any real fights. Kevin thought, I'll bet all his hostility, from years of kowtowing in the schoolyard, has been channeled into verbal altercations in the courtroom. Yet he had seen no sign of combativeness, just a methodical note-taking on yellow legal paper and the construction of what from a distance looked like some sort of flow chart on a separate paper attached to a dark brown clipboard.

* * *

Then it was the defense's turn. The lawyer stood up with the effort of an older man, guided himself around the flat-topped table where his papers lay, and almost lurched forward toward the star witness. A knowing smile now lit his face, much like a hyena about to worry its prey, Kevin thought.

"Doctor Kiley," his tone was crisp, "you're aware that this is a most serious charge you're making."

"Yes," Kevin answered laconically.

"That another man has assaulted you with a deadly weapon?"

"Yes."

"And that if convicted of such a crime, he would face a stringent prison sentence?"

"Yes."

"And that Mr. Polito, a family man, whom I understand has already been heavily weighed down with problems, would be harshly separated from his loved ones?"

"I object, your Honor!" And the young prosecutor, a clean-cut graduate of Boston College, the local Jesuit School, was on his feet.

"Sustained."

"So it is no small matter that we be certain of our facts." The defense counsel continued without skipping a beat, as if his last question had been answered like the others. "Do you see the defendant, Mr. Polito, sitting in this room with his wife?" And the lawyer seemed intent on dramatizing this fellow as a family man.

Kevin nodded.

"Will you please point to him now?" the lawyer asked, and Kevin promptly did so.

The lawyer nodded, then turned to the court stenographer and said, "Let the record show that Doctor Kiley did point to the good gentleman sitting beside Mrs. Polito." And with this aside, he turned back to Kevin. "If I remember correctly, you said that it was dark when you left your office on the night in question?"

"Yes."

"And that the man who accosted you stood just at the periphery of the floodlights?"

"Yes."

"And that when he took a step forward, his face seemed to be covered with a stocking mask?"

"Yes."

"Well, Doctor Kiley, let me see if I have this straight. You saw your assailant, briefly, in the dark, disguised by a mask, and you want us to believe you were able to make a positive identification of that furtive figure as none other than Mr. Joseph Polito?" He paused to let the impact settle in, then continued, "You must have truly extraordinary powers of visual observation, Doctor."

Kevin felt flustered, as the lawyer's segregation of visual cues for identification had made him look silly. "Well, it wasn't his looks. It was that voice." And his words were defensively pressured.

"Again, Doctor, then, let me see if I understand you correctly. You did not make an identification by sight but, rather, by the sound of his voice?"

"Well, it was the total gestalt."

"Total *gestalt*? What do you mean by that, Doctor? Perhaps you could enlighten us plain-speaking laymen?"

"The total impression I got from everything."

"From *everything*, Doctor? Do you mean from all your senses?"

Kevin paused. He felt frustrated, angry, and, worst of all, not able to think straight.

"We're waiting for you to clear this matter up for us." The lawyer seemed in no hurry at all.

"More the way he *sounded* than the way he looked." Kevin just blurted out words.

"Let me see if I understand?" The lawyer stroked his beard thoughtfully with his left hand, thumb and opposed fingers forming the legs of a loosely closing pair of tweezers. Then he stretched his right arm forward in a gesture of reaching out toward the witness. "You were unable to identify him by sight. You depended on the sound of his voice."

Kevin still hesitated. He did not want to be led, but he could see no alternative.

"Well, Doctor, unless medical science has just made some startling new discovery, I believe the old division into five senses still holds. Now, in your testimony, you mentioned seeing and hearing your assailant. You mentioned neither touching him, smelling him nor," and the lawyer paused with the faintest of smiles, "tasting him."

"Yes, it was his voice." Kevin decided to go with that.

"So the identification of your assailant is based on the sound of his voice."

"Principally."

The lawyer was not going to let go of his point. "What else besides his voice?"

"All right . . . his voice." Kevin decided not to add: "And I knew he was the one who was harassing me." In the cold light of court, that would sound too insubstantial, too paranoid.

"Now, Doctor, you mentioned that your assailant's voice had an unnatural quality: sharp, shrill, maniacal. Am I correct?"

"Yes."

"That is very striking, most noteworthy, don't you think?"

"Yes."

"I would like to hand you this report to read, Doctor." And, stooping across to the defense table in his awkward way, the lawyer had shuffled through some papers with apparent carelessness till he hit upon the one he produced for his witness. "Do you recognize this?"

Kevin saw that it was a copy of his original report to the Department of Labor, and it was so received by the court as evidence. The lawyer now continued to stand, the tweezers of his left hand stroking the brown beard in slow repetition, while a look of quiet puzzlement gradually crescendoed on his face. Kevin stood above him, paper in hand, imagining himself pounding the young bastard before him through the floorboards, like a hammer on a dull nail.

Finally, the lawyer spoke, with a questioning, almost diffident hesitation in his voice. "Doctor, I've read . . . and I've reread your report. I paid very special attention to the Mental Status examination included in it. But I've been able to find no mention of this extraordinary quality of Mr. Polito's voice. Perhaps you could bring it to my attention."

Kevin shoved the paper out at him impatiently. "Of course there's no mention of it. He didn't talk that way when he was in the office."

"Oh," and the lawyer again allowed pause enough for effect, then continued, "I don't understand. Since the voice was so different, so strange . . . so maniacal, how did you develop such extraordinary skill in making an absolute identification?"

Kevin was furious. As his whitened knuckles clutched the witness stand, a pause developed simply because he could not get untracked enough to think straight.

"I suppose, for example, Doctor, that having heard the prosecutor and myself talking today in ordinary fashion, you could unerringly, beyond the shadow of a reasonable doubt, identify us if you heard the sound of a few words we might yell out stridently and in some strangely altered tone?"

"It was the *telephone*!" And Kevin heard his own voice like a yell, yet with a husky tightness that seemed to him weird. "It was the same voice I recognized from the telephone. It was his threatening telephone voice."

"*Whose* telephone voice?" the lawyer shot back quickly, his own voice raised now to signify strong objection.

"Mr. Polito's."

"The voice told you it was Mr. Polito by name?"

"No, but he had called before."

"*Who* had called before?"

"Mr. Polito."

"How did you know it was Mr. Polito?"

"Because he told me."

The staccato cadence of questions subsided now as abruptly as it had begun. The lawyer paused and looked intently at his witness, his head slowly slanting to the left in quizzical lack of belief. Then, with quiet earnestness: "Doctor, you have previously testified that the vulgar, threatening voice you heard on the telephone did not identify itself as Mr. Polito. I believe it called itself the Avenger. Now, are you telling me that you're contradicting your earlier statements that were made under oath?"

"The Avenger calls came later in the sequence. But, earlier, when he was still identifying himself as Mr. Polito, he was making veiled threats anyway." The words tumbled out.

"Before you spread your witch-hunting net any further, Doctor Kiley, with additional allegations regarding so-called *veiled* threats, I suggest that we stick to the more serious charge you've already made. You have accused my client of a truly grievous offense, attack with a deadly weapon. You single him out, not because you saw him but because of his voice. And not because of *his* voice, but because of some similarity between your assailant's voice and some telephone voice you say you've heard. And now you throw one weak link at us after another, telling us that . . ."

"Objection, your Honor." As the prosecutor rose to his feet, Kevin marveled that the fellow was still alive.

"Sustained. This isn't the time for speeches, Counselor. Please confine yourself to questioning the witness."

"I'm sorry, your Honor," said the lawyer humbly. "I'll rephrase the question."

How could he rephrase a question when he had never gotten to the point of asking one? Kevin thought. The fellow had certainly lost nothing. Another person can never fully erase the emotional impact of what he's already heard, even if he wears a black robe every day.

"Doctor Kiley, you referred to a sequence of calls. That implies one following another in a connected series. What proof have you given us that there was indeed *any* connection between the calls that Mr. Polito understandably made to your office, and which your secretary received, with the vulgar and threatening calls you received some time later? What proof, that is, other than your own apparently unshakeable conviction?"

"I never got calls before like that until this happened, and there was a subtle quality, both in tone and attitude that was . . . similar." Kevin paused before the last word, trying to find the one that suited best.

"Well, then let me see if I have this straight again, Doctor. You identified your assailant positively, beyond any reasonable doubt, because, clear headed as you were at the time, you were able to identify with unerring accuracy the few words you heard as the same voice you had heard coming over the telephone wire. Furthermore, you were able to match up *that* disturbed telephone voice with complete fidelity to the voice of Mr. Polito when heard sometime earlier in the total course of three brief telephone conversations."

Kevin looked away in silent fury.

"Doctor, how many patients do you have?"

"That's hard to answer."

"You don't *know* how many patients you have?"

The lawyer was making him appear like a bumbling idiot again, thought Kevin. "I have some patients whom I see every week, some whom I see intermittently at intervals that may range from a month to a year, and others whom I just see from time to time when something comes up." His voice showed obvious pique.

"I see. Well, Doctor, could you estimate how many patients you have seen in your years of practice?"

"A rough estimate?"

"That will do."

"A couple of thousand, or more . . . and I've *never* been threatened before!"

"A couple of thousand or more. Over two thousand patients." He paused for effect. "I take it, Doctor, that as a board-certified specialist in psychiatry, these were all psychiatric patients?"

Kevin had to answer "Yes," though he could see the double entendre clearly enough. A person who sees a psychiatrist becomes by definition a "psychiatric patient," though that term so often becomes imbued with dire connotations, especially in the press.

"So, in your practice, you have seen well over two thousand psychiatric patients—more than two thousand emotionally disturbed people."

"Not *disturbed*," Kevin interrupted. "The majority have simply been depressed, or suffered anxiety, or have been troubled in some way."

"Well, aren't such patients said to be suffering from emotional disturbance?"

Kevin knew that, in one respect, "emotional disturbance" and "emotionally disturbed" were equivalent. Still, those two phrases had different connotations. An *emotionally disturbed person,* in the press, was always being reported as doing something troublesome or dangerous. Kevin hesitated, then started to answer, "Yes, but the words—"

This time it was the lawyer's turn to interrupt. "Please, Doctor, let's not quibble excessively about words. You admit that you have seen over two thousand patients, more than two thousand psychiatric patients; that is, more than a couple of thousand emotionally disturbed people, people with mental or emotional disturbance. Any one of them might be harassing you. More than one of them might be harassing you. And now with the barest of evidence, with the flimsiest shreds of questionable data, you single out one of these poor souls in what I can only describe as a New Salem witch hunt! I have no further questions of the witness, your Honor." And the lawyer turned away, shaking his head in disgust.

Kevin felt himself guided back to one of the spectator benches, like a blind man, in tow of the court officer. Though sitting now, he could scarcely feel the hard wood pressing against his back and bottom.

In an oneiric state, he saw the police officer take the stand again. And involuntarily, Kevin's eyes panned in on the moustache, waiting for it to twitch.

"Now, Officer, you've testified that you saw Doctor Kiley shortly after he reported the assault. Would you say that he was calm and fully collected at that time?" The tone of the lawyer's voice indicated that he knew what the answer would be.

"No, sir, I would not." The police officer spoke with the crisp tones of a good soldier.

"How would you describe his state?"

"I'd say he was in shock, sir."

"And what do you mean by *shock*, Officer?"

"Well, he was really unraveled. He was way out of it."

"Objection, your Honor." The prosecutor was still alive.

"I'll rephrase the question." The lawyer anticipated the nature of the objection and in any case had already made his emotional—and therefore motivational—point. "Officer, would you tell the court what you observed that led you to conclude that Doctor Kiley was not exactly calm and fully collected?"

"Yes, sir. For one thing, he kept talking and rambling on, hopping from one thing to another, so I couldn't always follow him."

"Anything else? Anything that might suggest some limitation in his powers of observation at that time?"

"Yes, sir. He had locked himself out of the building and couldn't find his keys."

"And you subsequently found them, Officer?"

"Yes, sir."

"Where were they?"

The moustache twitched for the first time as the policeman smoothed his hair down with a sudden motion upward of the right hand from his side.

"Right in the car door where he had left them."

Kevin couldn't believe it. A quiet but discernible titter had gone through the courtroom. The lawyer, though undoubtedly pleased, gave no trace of it in his appearance. He was not here to ridicule the prosecution witness, just to get at the facts in this very serious business.

"Did you notice anything else?"

"Yes, sir, the doctor was so upset that he had soiled himself—and he didn't even seem to realize it."

"Thank you, Officer, that will be all."

Then the defense lawyer made a decision. The other side was on the run. Try to wrap it up right here. Don't hold back the ace when another court appearance probably can be avoided. He called Mrs. Polito to the stand. Kevin knew right away, of course, what her testimony would be. The alibi.

She testified that her husband indeed had been home with her at the time of the crime. The best the prosecutor could do (lackluster novice compared to shining prodigy) was to point out that, as the defendant's wife, she had strong personal reason to be protective, and that earlier she had refused to give testimony to the DA's office. He had of course considered that tantamount to not wanting to testify against her husband.

"I have one final witness I wish to call, your Honor," the lawyer was saying matter of factly. "Mr. Polito." The defendant looked nervous as Mrs. Polito had just taken her seat beside him again. Kevin was incredulous, having been told by Mike that a defendant's lawyer almost never puts the accused on the stand in a probable cause procedure. "Don't give the prosecution any ammunition they don't already have!" Had this young lawyer's brilliance turned to pride that goeth before the fall? Would this prosecutor have the ability to take advantage of it, in any case? Kevin, completely demoralized by now, thought not.

"Mr. Polito, will you please take the stand?" The court clerk spoke the repetitive formula and the defendant moved forward.

"Will you please state your full name?"

"Robert L. Polito."

The clerk hesitated, then corrected him: "Joseph."

"This is Robert Polito, the defendant's brother," said the lawyer.

The impact was like a haymaker, telegraphed from way back, landing on an opponent already too numb to move. The perfunctory questions about where this witness had been on the night of the crime gave way to the lawyer's rising intonation as he said dramatically to the stenographer, "Let it be noted on the court record that this witness is the person who was carelessly and callously misidentified by Doctor Kiley, this very day, in this very room, as Mr. Joseph Polito, his supposed assailant!"

CHAPTER 12

Schmitt's. A funny name for a restaurant in ethnically Irish South Boston. Yet it had become one of Linda's favorite eating places; partly, she supposed, because of her pleasant association of dinners there with Kevin. Also, she was particularly fond of Finnan Haddie, that locally appreciated dish of smoked cod, successfully embroidered with a rich cream sauce, served behind a circular retaining wall of whipped potato.

The restaurant's decor was also intriguing—large booths of dark and olden wood, a brass-railed bar, and a large albeit faded green campaign sign, urging citizens to vote for Mayor James Michael Curley. This evening, however, there was little gaiety at her table (certainly far less than at an Irish wake). Kevin's mood following the court debacle had become darker than a chimney sweeper's brush.

"Why didn't Mike go to court with you?" Linda was asking.

"We'd discussed that. Mike said he would if I wanted him there. He also explained that at a probable cause hearing he could play no formal role, since I was the prosecution's witness. Therefore, it might not be too efficient a use of his time, which I figured translated into the fact that at his prices, it would amount to pretty expensive hand-holding. So I decided against it."

"What did he say about it afterward?" Having felt horrified herself when Kevin told her about the hearing, she assumed his lawyer shared that reaction.

Kevin leaned back in his seat and shook his head ruefully. "He laughed—actually paid homage to that clever little bastard of a defense lawyer—like watching someone get cut up and admiring the artistry of the sadist wielding his knife."

"Well, I certainly wouldn't go back to *him*!"

"Oh, Mike's all right. He did try to reassure me then. He said that we knew we had a weak case. Our goal really was to put Joe Polito on notice that he was to be the chief suspect in case of any *future* harassment, and that we had sort of achieved that goal. Only thing is, I don't really think so. You know, when I went out after the hearing, I did see Joe Polito—well, it had to be Joe this time—standing with his brother and wife. He looked at me straight on with this big grin and then nodded knowingly, like 'there's more cumin', buddy.' It was chilling."

"He's so sick. How does he keep his cool?"

"Good question. I don't know. I've seen very ill people get, say, a religious conversion, and suddenly their life becomes orderly and goal-directed beneath this protective umbrella. Unless a person's mental state is completely disorganized, there's nothing like a *cause* to galvanize a persevering and disciplined course of action. I have a funny feeling that I've become Joe Polito's *cause*, his purpose in life."

As he talked, Kevin looked up at some decorative shamrocks tucked in behind beer mugs on the wall. Perhaps this extraneous perception influenced his train of thought in a humorous manner. "Reminds me of the situation in Northern Ireland," he said. "Did you hear about the guy walking down the street in Belfast?"

"No."

"Well, as he's walking along, he suddenly feels this gun shoved into his ribs from behind, and a sinister voice asks, 'Be ye Catholic or Protestant?' The guy's frightened out of his wits, and he figures: If I say I'm Catholic, he's probably a Protestant terrorist, and he'll shoot me. If I say I'm Protestant, he's probably a Catholic terrorist, and he'll shoot me. So thinking fast, he replies, 'I'm neither; I'm a Jew.' To which the voice behind responds triumphantly: 'And I'm the luckiest Ay-rab in all of Belfast.' "

Linda broke up, more from relief at the lightening up of their conversation than in response to the joke itself. But the relief lasted only a moment before Kevin was into his heavy mood again. "We in fact seem confronted by two choices: illusions of reality fostered by society, or illusions rising from within."

Linda, having finished her dinner by now, looked over at Kevin's plate. Hardly touched, partly because he'd been talking so much, partly because he'd just been pushing food around his plate without apparent appetite. The skin of his face, especially around the corners of his eyes and mouth, seemed almost drooping like a planter of unwatered flowers, matching the depressing tone of his voice. Linda had the unaccustomed urge to shake him, at least out of his pessimistic doldrums. "Look, how do you know this guy is really all that sinister?" she asked. "How do you know he'd really do something bad? Maybe he's all bluff, and you're worrying too much. Anyway, how can you really be sure he's the one? Maybe his lawyer did have a point."

Linda knew in an instant that she'd said the wrong thing. Kevin's face firmed like a fitted sheet pulled suddenly taut over the bed's end, and he spoke one clipped word, "Maybe." Then without further conversation, he shoveled his food furiously from plate to mouth till it was gone. When the waitress came by, he said "No thanks" to coffee, explaining that he might have trouble sleeping. He shepherded Linda rather briskly to the parking lot around back. "How about a little traveling music?" he said with a forced effort at joviality, and flipped on the car radio as they drove off.

The strains of old-wave rock swelled from all four speakers a little louder than usual, and the words, "Ya know it don't come easy . . ." came blaring out repetitively between hammering guitar cords and riffs. Amen, thought Linda.

After a while, she said softly, "What will you do, Kevin?"

Both hands gripping the wheel, he answered laconically, "I don't know." Then after a pause: "I'll just have to see what happens." That night, Kevin did not stay at her apartment, saying only, "I'm too darn restless to sleep."

CHAPTER 13

The next several weeks went by uneventfully, unless one wanted to count Kevin's state of hyperalertness (and more than three thousand dollars invested fruitlessly in a private detective who tailed and investigated Joe Polito for ten days straight). Especially after dark, Kevin exercised for a while what some might have considered an excess of caution. But even in the face of nothing happening, he felt confirmed in his belief that Joe Polito had been the culprit. The lack of new occurrences was consistent after all with Mike's idea that taking the fellow to court would label him as the prime suspect and warn him off efforts at future harassment.

Turning off the expressway along the small country highway—it was six weeks to the day of his court appearance—he felt almost sleepy. Moving at a leisurely rate, he had little reaction to the headlights approaching rapidly from behind. Higher set from the road, that likely meant a pickup truck, he thought. Probably some guy hustling home late for dinner after staying one drink and one conversation too many at an after-work tavern.

Pulling across the double line along a stretch that seemed to wind blindly through a deserted area of woods, the half-ton pickup driver revved his engine in order to pass. Not exactly thrilled by the potential danger of this maneuver, Kevin edged his little Subaru over to the side of the road. What a jerk, he thought, but I'd better help the guy get by so he can take his craziness away with him.

Not until the truck had pulled alongside did Kevin become alarmed. The nondescript vehicle seemed suddenly large and near. Drawing its nose just three or four feet ahead of his car, the truck was already starting to pull back into Kevin's lane, and the dark faded enamel of its finish seemed mere inches from Kevin's eyes. A reflex increase of pressure on the gas pedal brought pings from the pistons but no sudden acceleration. In another flick, Kevin's foot switched pedals, and the Subaru was braking while he tried to find a few spare inches of road between his wheels and the soft shoulder.

"BAM!" The sideswiping sound was followed by a sensation that his car had been clutched and tossed by a massive grip of steel. The Subaru landed with a bounce that threw Kevin forward against the

cutting restraint of his seat belt, hands ripped off the steering wheel by its sudden jolt. Spineless like Raggedy Ann, his body, neck, and head joggled in different directions through a daze punctuated by an abrupt stop.

Moments or minutes later, he could not tell, he became aware that he was he, still alive, sitting tilted in his bucket seat. The right side of the steering wheel pressed against the middle of his chest, and the dashboard was clamping his knee. Wetness that he thought must be blood was moving down between his trousers and the calf of his leg. A young tree, almost six inches in diameter, had indented the right front bumper, and the fender on that side was crinkled into an obvious hump with receding satellite humps producing an appearance more like tin foil than sheet metal. Thank God, the soft shoulder slowed me some before the car hit that tree, he thought appraisingly. And he believed himself cool and clear-headed, just before he passed out again.

A car pulled up, stopping immediately behind the wreck. Then another car, and another still, plus a couple of other cars coming from the opposite direction. Kevin regained consciousness, saw the group of headlights peering through the dark, and heard the voices talking back and forth—voices that seemed distant, though they were right outside.

"Yeh, it's bad, all right."

"Hey, get the police."

"Yeh, good."

"No, we tried the door; he's really jammed in."

"Best not to move him anyway."

The sentences he heard didn't seem to follow each other, just a potpourri of alarmed assessments and disjointed advice.

Then one of the men, noticing Kevin's movement, came over to the car window again and asked, "You all right, buddy?"

In the background, one of the others asked someone righteously, "Was he drinking?"

Kevin had already given himself the toe-wiggling and hand-moving test to check against a dreaded spinal cord injury. Thank God, the car didn't catch fire with me pinned in it, he thought. He started to shiver, slowly at first, then uncontrollably. Is it the fear of what might have happened, he wondered—those fates worse than death descending in the form of quadriplegia or massive third degree burns? Or is it the cold, or am I in shock? And his hand told him the wet on his leg was definitely blood. No crepitation from a broken bone, no displacement or point tenderness. He decided it was most likely soft tissue injury from the grip-wrench effect.

Then he mused about the advantages and disadvantages of being a physician at a time like this. He was better able to assess and, therefore, to reassure himself than an ordinary citizen. He was more able to think of the complications and grim possibilities—like bleeding out before he could be freed. Knowledge sure is a two-edged sword, he thought. So often, as with the Serpent in the Garden, it seems to come down to the *knowledge of good and evil*.

The flashing blue light and whooping siren pulled up at that moment—squad car door left open to the cold, static, and police messages spewing out through the cold night air. "Doctor Kiley!" Recognition and concern entered the small town officer's voice. "You all right?"

"I'm okay, but I'm bleeding, and I'm really pinned in." Kevin spoke with a calm that he did not feel.

"Don't worry, we'll get you out." And the officer shined his bright hand lantern inside to assess the damages. The passenger compartment had been compressed by the accordion effect on the car's frame, and the driver was caught between steering wheel in front and bucket seat behind. Both front doors were jammed.

Moving back to the rear door, the officer managed to pry it open and then slide the back of the bucket seat into a semi-recumbent position. Slipping over on his left side, Kevin managed to worm his way out with the aid of the officer and assorted other helping hands. Once outside, Kevin surveyed the damages himself. His right knee was swollen and bruised, with a four-inch laceration just below. Someone brought over a T-shirt to use as a temporary tourniquet, but Kevin put it right over the cut, whose jagged edges he placed together. Then he pressed firmly to stop his own bleeding.

A memory suddenly intruded. Dedicated medical student at the Boston City Hospital Emergency Ward, he saw the chalky laborer carried in by his two frightened coworkers, dark blood now only weakly spurting from his tourniqued arm. The surgical intern quickly released the strapping and Kevin, surprised, waited for the deluge. Instead, the bleeding almost stopped. "These tourniquets are no damn good," the intern had explained. "People never get them tight enough to cut off the arterial circulation, so the blood keeps flowing into the arm. The tourniquet's just tight enough to keep the venous blood from getting back out, so it flows from the wound like traffic through a detour." Working continuously while he was talking, the intern soon had things under control, leaving an admiring Kevin to wipe the blood off the floor.

Just then, the approaching beacon of an ambulance brought Kevin forward more than twenty-five years to the present moment. He was glad he wouldn't have to sit up in the police car as they drove to the small town hospital. He felt too weak and faint. But as he lay on the movable cot, wound now temporarily bandaged with sterile gauze and knee splinted against painful motion, Kevin noted a transition in his own feelings. Numbness, apprehensiveness, and resignation had given way slowly to a cold wrath. No way, he thought, am I going to live in fear and trembling, waiting for the other shoe to drop. If he's covered his traces so the law can't help me out, I'll do it myself. I'm going to have to get him before he gets me.

CHAPTER 14

"Hello!" With a cheery intonation that turned two syllables into three, Linda entered the doorway from the porch, walked through the kitchen-dining area into the pine-walled living room and greeted Kevin with a smile. "How's the invalid?" she asked, facetiously accenting the second syllable.

Kevin was sitting back leisurely in one of his easy chairs, white-duck upholstery contributing to the room's informality. His splinted right leg lay stretched out on an ottoman toward the brick fireplace, and the many green plants around the room created an inner extension of his outdoor surroundings. "Nice to see you, babe," he said, and his face lit up.

"How's the leg?"

"Great! First time I've had a full week's vacation at home." He looked relaxed and was obviously trying to emphasize the positive side of the coin. "The housekeeper lasted three days till her car broke down, so they sent over someone new today."

"I wish you had let me take care of you, Kevin. I really would have been happy to take the week off."

"I appreciate that, but I couldn't have let you ask for unplanned time away."

The words didn't matter. Linda had intuited that he wanted to keep his distance to avoid greater emotional entanglement. Changing the subject, she asked cheerfully, "Well, what've you been doing with yourself today?"

"Nothing much. Wading through these references in preparation for that review article I'm going to write." Kevin nodded in the direction of a pile of photocopied manuscripts, each with its identifying form from the Countway Library. The explosion of medical knowledge during recent years had necessitated reviews to correlate the data and theory on any given subject—material that was scattered through many different journals over numbers of years.

"Nice to see you're keeping yourself constructively occupied." The lilt in her voice conveyed her tendency to kid him about his compulsive need to keep busy with one or another project.

He laughed good humoredly.

"Anything new?" She did not have to say in reference to what.

Kevin shook his head with a frown. "They found the truck... abandoned, with some blue paint from my Subaru newly scratched along its right side. Stolen, of course. They found it at the Columbia Point housing project. The owner had reported it stolen from outside a South End tavern."

"What about Mr. Polito?"

"What about him?" Kevin said with involuntary irritability. "He was at home—of course—resting in his room at the time. And his wife corroborated his story."

"What are you going to do?"

"I don't know. One thing's for sure. I can't go on living this way—always waiting for the other shoe to drop. This time, what he did could well have been lethal. He keeps upping the ante, and meantime I've got this anticipatory dread that's getting harder to keep under control. Unless he gets really sick again, sick enough that he becomes so disorganized he can't cover his traces, the police won't get him. I'm convinced of that. They can't afford to put him under constant surveillance for the sake of one private citizen, *anymore than I can myself.*

"I never thought, as a doctor, I'd want to see someone get sicker. But I sure do now. Though in the process, he'd probably kill me anyway. Then the police would react, and I'd be dead right."

Linda made no effort to conceal her worry. "Isn't there anything else that can be done?"

Kevin decided to launch his trial balloon. "I could kill *him* first."

The words didn't frighten Linda. How many times had she heard such statements from people when they felt really frustrated. She had even thought them herself. What scared her was his tone of voice. "Don't even talk that way," she said.

"I'm serious, Linda. I'm being bullied, and I'm close to being fully intimidated. I can't stand that in myself. And I don't plan to be a martyr to the slow and imperfect wheels of justice in our land of the free—where free has especially come to mean freedom for criminals and an absurd extreme in protecting their civil rights." Kevin was by this time sitting on the edge of his chair, the intensity in his voice matching the tautness of his body.

Trying to lighten the conversation, Linda exclaimed, "But then they'd send you to jail, and I'd have to visit you every Sunday like one of those prison groupies."

Kevin ignored the effort at humor. "I've thought of that," he said. "If I could make it look like legitimate self defense . . ." His voice trailed off as if giving way to inner thoughts about how to arrange that.

"But anyway, Kevin, he's sick. You have to remember that." Linda had returned to his level of dead seriousness.

"Sure, he's sick. And sickness has been used as an excuse for all sorts of behavior. How many psychotic patients have I seen over the past twenty years? Has to be a thousand. And until now, not one has done anything like this. I've decided there are just a certain number of bad asses around. Take a thousand anythings—Irish, Methodists, Legionnaires, bridge players, asthmatics, you name it—and you'll have a few bad eggs. But let the bad ones belong to the group called *mental patients*, and they're suddenly excused of culpability.

"If some guy's walking down the street and a buddy whispers in his ear that he should knock off the corner liquor store, he's to blame, even though he's been *influenced*. He still knows it's wrong. But if some hallucinatory voice gives the same advice, the guy's not to blame? Why? I've had hundreds of patients with voices telling them to do bad things. Yet these folks haven't done them. And still, so many of my colleagues will go to court and testify that the defendant was unable to *adhere to the right*. How do *they* know? All they really know is that he had the impulse to do something, and that in fact he didn't resist it."

Linda was reaching a quiet state of alarm. Was she upset because of fear for Kevin's welfare, or was she distressed that this man whom she loved could seriously consider such violence? Though she was learning something more about him, she felt she knew him less. The kindly helping doctor, the friend who was so supportive to her participation in the *Reverence for Life* organization that had espoused animal rights. And now this? "You can't even be sure he's the one," she blurted out.

It was like a red flag. Kevin's anger now included her. "No, of course not. He's the only one who's ever threatened me like this, but that's just a coincidence, isn't it? And the subtle interaction between two people that helps one recognize the other, including . . . yes . . .

alterations in voice; that's not to be given any credence, is it? Just wait around like some sitting duck or sacrificial lamb. That's the thing to do, huh?"

Her tears were flowing. "I don't want to talk about it anymore," she said.

"So I'm not the mild-mannered Clark Kent you thought I was?"

"Is there anything I can get you?"

"No, thanks. I think I should get to bed early tonight." His voice had become detached and withdrawn.

"Okay, I'll go along then. I'll call you tomorrow." Linda felt absolutely empty as she left. In the several years of their relationship, they had sometimes disagreed, but never really argued. It wasn't her style.

On the following day, she called and then went out to visit Kevin. For the first time though, they avoided a subject of their disagreement. Communication has its limitations. Sometimes, the only way to avoid termination of a relationship is not to talk too much about an irreconcilable difference.

CHAPTER 15

Another phone call, and Kevin recognized the muffled voice right away. "Third week-iversary. You made it through the last one, but the third time never fails."

"You're planning to kill me next time for real?" Kevin spoke the words coldly.

"I don't know. That just might be too easy for you. I may let you squirm a while longer." And his voice broke into that horrendous laugh once more.

Kevin wanted to discover whatever clues he could, so he tried to keep the conversation going. "What do you plan to do?" he asked, though he recognized the question's inanity.

"Just think about that a while. But don't worry too much, will you?" And the voice broke off again into loud, diabolical laughter. Then *"click,"* and the conversation stopped as abruptly as it had started.

* * *

Kevin returned to work a week after the injury, using a temporary leg splint at first, a device that somewhat limited knee motion but allowed sufficient flexibility to operate his new car. More than two weeks had passed since the most recent threatening call, and on this particular day, he had for the first time gingerly tried his knee out in a squash game. Bernie hit with him in friendly fashion so he could begin to loosen up. Afterwards, he headed home, constantly on the alert—the tremendous energy expenditure involved was bringing him close to emotional exhaustion.

After coming off the main highway nowadays, he drove as fast as he needed to make sure no car passed him. He helped out Boston Edison by keeping his home fully illuminated—a dozen new timers turning on houselights and deck floodlights at early dusk. As he turned from the back road on to his long and gently sloping driveway, he would stop his new wagon at various points outside the circle of light on different nights, then reconnoiter the area like an army patrol unit. He kept the car's interior light doused so it wouldn't betray him when he opened the door, and he carried his shotgun in the car, covered by a loose-fitting scrap of rug so its presence wouldn't be obvious.

He had little experience with armaments but had gotten a shotgun some time back for varmints and general home protection. Shooting a pattern, he'd easily been able to knock off a Coke can at thirty yards with no previous practice. At present though, he had a pistol permit in process. Meantime, he was making do.

Circling the frozen ground around his house, he found no evidence of hostile forces. He quickly passed through the floodlighted area on the deck and up onto the back porch that he'd purposely left in its penumbra—no point in forming a stationary target in full light at the back door while fumbling with keys.

Whether the early stench or darkened sight hit him first on this particular evening was hard to say. Lacerated entrails hung down to the floor from the still body. Large nails impaled the flailed hind legs that had been spread-eagled near the top of the door as in some bizarre crucifixion. A gaping laceration, hacked through the entire abdomen, ripped across the battered chest cage along the sternum. Pendulous organs were still weeping from multiple tears, with mixed drainage of blood and intestinal seepage emitting a rank fetor through the night's chill vapor.

Stunned, Kevin felt his hand move wet down the carcass, along the once fine body to its head, which he lifted by the Ammon curve of its horns. Where eyes had been, he noted in the semi-dark a crisscrossed lattice work of what had once been ocular tissue. His prized ram, sire to most of his growing flock, doubly castrated and forever gone.

Numbed beyond words—even had there been another person present to share his pain—Kevin wiped his bloodied hand thoughtlessly across the tan corduroy surface of his new fleece-lined car coat, and half ran along the wintered crispness of meadow, over the fence, and down to the animal shelter. Within the penned area, sheep's bodies were cast around in a ghoulish slaughter. All had been painfully disemboweled and left to die. In the full moonlight, they appeared like shadowed figures beyond the natural. One of the pregnant ewes had been lacerated deeply in the area of her vulva, and the handle of an old garden hoe had been pushed deep within her like some wantonly thrusting phallus.

Kevin started to count the bodies, and as he did so, he suddenly vomited. He started the count over again and reached a count of twenty-three. Only eight skittish sheep had escaped the massacre, hiding out now within the tangled brush that formed the farther recesses of the twenty acres through which they ordinarily foraged. With a sense of apocalyptic doom, Kevin half-walked, half-stumbled, back to the house. Almost oblivious to his external surroundings, he was naked in his vulnerability and would have been at the mercy of any external predator. But none came forth.

His whole being in fact was having difficulty making distinctions between outside and inside. He kept wanting to vomit again, as if the devastating scene he had taken in through his eyes could be expelled like spoiled food from his stomach. And the turmoil that was heaving up created a sense of disintegration, as if he himself was being ripped and shredded into dissolution.

Without explicit attention to his actions, he unnailed the ram's corpse from its crucifixal moorings and placed it within a twenty-gallon Hefty bag. He filled a bucket with hot water and Lysol, then scrubbed down the back door and surrounding porch area mindlessly—mindlessly, that is, except for an obsessive thought incessantly repeating itself, a broken groove emitting its message with constant clarity: I am the good shepherd, thou shall not want. . . . I am the good shepherd, thou shall not want. . . . I am the good shepherd, thou shall not want. . . . I am the good shepherd, thou shall not want. . . . I am the good shepherd, thou shall not want. . . . I am the good shepherd . . .

No matter how benign a thought may be, its constant and unbid repetition—its relentless intrusion—forms a torture not fully appreciable by those humans forever spared such monomaniacal ideation. Kevin stepped outside his own mind to observe this occurrence within, intellectually identified the manifestation as an obsessive thought, and emotionally gathered a greater empathy for those victims of obsessive-compulsive states whom he had seen professionally for many years.

I am the good shepherd, thou shall not want. And Kevin distracted himself by thinking of Linda. Of some of their conversations. An animal lover to the extreme, she had always enjoyed these African sheep and had befriended them easily despite their skittish nature. Too bad they weren't even more skittish tonight, Kevin thought. But they've learned to go to that penned area around the shed for their special horse checker treat. Polito would have had little difficulty enticing them within by means of this delicacy. Then slamming the gate, he would have had them completely at his mercy. Nimble as they are, within a space not much larger than a boxing ring, they could run but they couldn't hide.

Kevin had seen his sheep panic in response to even trivial stimuli, leaping and throwing their bodies at barriers they could have run around, even springing up on top of other sheep whose herd closeness had coalesced them into one large mobile form, or at least as close to one form as the moving school of neon tetras within his large fish tank. The image came to him now of Joe Polito traversing the pen, catching hold of first one body, then another, and sadistically slashing them.

In response to the vivid image, Kevin rushed to the bathroom with a revulsive wave of nausea, threw himself down on all fours like an animal, and tried to wretch into the toilet. His salivation increased profusely, and he felt his body moisten with a cold sweat while he made voluntary expulsive motions. Nothing would come. He stuck his index finger into the rear of his mouth and wiggled it against his uvula, at which point he gagged convulsively.

Still he could not vomit. Getting up, he stumbled down the short hallway back to the living room, noticing only then that the white duck covering of his favorite easy chair was swatched with blood and other less identifiable stains—he had earlier thrown himself down there, oblivious to the animal juices he'd accumulated on his clothing. *"I am the good shepherd; thou shall not want. I am . . ."*

Kevin distracted himself again, turning his thoughts back to Linda and recalling her love for his sheep and all animals. He pictured her as Francis of Assisi has so often been depicted, sitting on a sylvan rock with hand outstretched toward a Bambied fawn, songbird perched gently on one shoulder, the absolute antithesis of the necrophilia he had just witnessed. *"I am the good shepherd . . ."*

He recalled a conversation with Linda, one of those half-in-jest, totally-in-earnest talks. "I dreamed from childhood of having my own children. I was going to be the ideal father, unlike my own. And then, everything went wrong. But this time, I'm going to get it right with the sheep. I'm going to be *the Good Shepherd.*" Intellectually it was absurd, and humanly it was pathetic. Yet emotionally it had still worked.

His wounds had been to a degree soothed, even if they could not be healed.

He recalled then the time Linda and he had agreed to disagree about the place of animals in the food chain. That was the first occasion he had one of the lambs butchered for meat, and she'd been visibly upset. "You can't do it, Kevin. You just can't do it!"

He had replied with conviction, "They're not pets. They're farm animals. Modern city people are out of touch with the cycle of life. They think meat grows under little transparent covers in refrigerator cases at the supermarket. But every time they buy a piece of beef or a breast of chicken, some animal has been killed for that purpose. In fact, that is the *raison-d'etre* of meat animals, without which, they would not have had their moment of life in the first place."

"Well, in that case," she'd answered, "they would have been better off not to have existed."

"You're not coming to terms with Nature in general and Human Nature in particular," Kevin had replied. "As with the *Lord of the Dance,* that Hindu depiction of the Deity, life is summoned into existence by the throbbing drum in His upper right hand, and back out of existence by the consuming flame in His upper left hand. That's at the same time an obvious fact and a profound mystery. And we are animals, omnivorous animals to be exact. That includes carnivorous. It's our nature to eat meat animals, and their nature to be eaten. It's not against Nature, it's part of Nature."

"But man isn't just an animal. It's his possibility to rise above the purely animal, to transcend his previous nature." The passion in her voice had told the depth of her feeling.

Kevin's memory subsided as quickly as it had come, and he returned to the sickening immediacy of the present. Linda had been able to accept their differences of view on the cycle of animal life, but would be revolted by the humanly caused abortion of this cycle that he had just witnessed. He dragged himself to his bedroom, pulled off his clothes, which he left in an unaccustomed heap on the bedside chair, and threw himself onto the caressing oblivion of the percale-covered mattress. His brain plunged almost immediately into the surcease of sleep, accompanied by his usual plethora of troubled dreams:

A lamb came toward him, but stood out of reach. He tried to move toward it, but could only reach his arm out impotently. Then the lamb seemed to be growing sessile, from the ground like a flower. Kevin's voice as in an echo pleaded, "I did my best—I did the best I could." The lamb said nothing in the sadness of its stare but, slowly, unfoldingly, metamorphosed into a small child—boy or girl, there was no way to know. Again the echoed voice, but no answer, only the silent tears of a sad-eyed child.

And as the tears flowed, the pink-skinned body grew progressively smaller, whether washing away or shrinking he could not tell. With an unspeakable effort, he managed to reach the child, enfolding its now diminutive form in a new white handkerchief. Caressing it gently with both hands, he felt it slipping through, slipping away. Tears welled in his eyes through a moment's surge of his consciousness to an almost waking state, before another plunge into the purgatorial depths of his twilight dreams. It had never even occurred to him to call the police.

CHAPTER 16

Kevin woke the next morning with a decisiveness suggestive of carefully thought out plans. Yet he could consciously recall only a few frayed fragments of some graying dreams. Though it was a work morning, he unhesitatingly dressed in old clothes, grabbed a quick bowl of cold cereal, and sat down by the telephone. He called his answering service to leave word for Frances to cancel office hours. Then he called the police to report the massacre.

Bad vibes started almost immediately when the receiving officer, in Kevin's mind, trivialized the described atrocity as "vandalism." A police cruiser came by later, driven by a familiar-faced man in his mid-forties, an officer whom Kevin had seen occasionally around town. As is characteristic of police, the man did not introduce himself, letting his uniform speak for itself. Trim and winter-tanned, he proclaimed a nonverbal message with his close-cropped hair (a few gray hairs starting to show around the temples). Striding rightly to the deck past the large planter that formed its front margin—and that in warmer times hosted yellow marigolds—he asked directly about the problem and listened intently to Kevin's explanation.

Together, they walked down the slope to see the dead sheep, whose carcasses Kevin had not yet disturbed. The officer whistled quietly, almost under his breath, and inquired if Doctor Kiley knew anyone who might want to get back at him for any reason.

"*Of course,* I know," said Kevin impatiently. "The same man who almost killed me several weeks ago when he ran me off the road, the same man I took to court for firing at me with a gun, the same man who's been harassing me since last summer—the same man who's eventually going to kill me if you guys don't stop him!"

"Christ! I remember now hearing about that auto accident," said the officer.

"That accident was no *accident*." Kevin shook his head, aggravated for the second time today by a policeman's choice of words. "They found the hit-and-run truck later. It had been stolen just for the job."

"What's the guy got against you?" The officer's tone conveyed a mixture of curiosity and professional searching for motive.

"I sent in an unfavorable disability report on him," Kevin replied.

"Geez, seems to me this guy's pretty sick." And the officer nodded his head toward the carnage they stood in the midst of.

"That wasn't the *issue,* Officer. It wasn't whether he was sick, but whether it was his job that had disabled him. The Department of Labor used my report as a basis for taking away his equivalent of Industrial Compensation, and he held me personally responsible for his resulting financial difficulties."

The officer smiled broadly and without warmth. "Oh, my brother-in-law ran into someone like you." Then, after a pause, "I guess you shouldn't have taken the poor bastard's pension away, Doc."

Kevin turned back toward the house, playing for time to control his anger. The thought occurred to him that all people resent the power exercised over them by others, because it deviates so often from their sense of fairness. It contributed after all to his own assessment of the petty and not-so-petty abuse of police power. And now this officer, with his own axe to grind, was twisting a doctor's tail in regard to a physician's use or abuse of the power entrusted in him by society.

Kevin also thought about that inevitable split within people, between their generosity toward the individual supplicant and their niggardliness toward the impersonal masses—especially when their generosity toward a particular person gives them emotional pleasure and seems to cost nothing (the Insurance Company or The Government will pay for it), whereas the giving to faceless numerals provides no emotional pleasure and causes a detectable pain at tax time.

His anger still strong but now cold, Kevin asked matter of factly, "Well, what are you going to do about this Polito fellow? I already gave you the information about him after he ran me into a tree."

"We'll keep a lookout for him, and we'll check your home every day. But one thing you've got to realize. We know, like, a number of guys who are ripping off houses in this town. But that doesn't mean we can prove it. So we keep our eye out, and we wait. They'll trip themselves up eventually." A full professional tone had reentered the police officer's voice.

"That's consoling to know," said Kevin "especially if he trips himself up before he kills me rather than afterwards."

* * *

Their work together finished, the officer drove away in his black and white police cruiser. A few minutes later, Doctor Kiley's new Subaru drove along the slanting asphalt driveway and turned onto the road outside. He stopped first at the Longfellow Bank and cashed a personal check for three hundred and forty dollars. Adding additional cash from home, this would amount to five hundred dollars—enough to make things interesting, because he knew it wasn't enough. Stopping in the nearby drugstore, he then bought three current magazines, a cheap pad of paper, and some unmarked envelopes.

Returning home, he set to work with scissors and glue, assembling an anonymous note from the newsprint words he had clipped out:

You win.
Enclosed is first payment.

He placed the cash in its paper sheath, and slipped the entire bait into the plain envelope to Joe Polito (with no return address). Then he drove to a different locality to mail the letter—humming out of context (and slightly out of tune) a duet from Mozart's *Marriage of Figaro*: "And the rest he'll understand. . . ."

After that, he drove home to bury his sheep or, rather, since he knew the ground was still frozen, to transport their bodies to a back area of his woods near the swamp line. It took seven slow trips, using the front-end loader of his tractor, a device usually needed only for plowing snow during the winter season.

CHAPTER 17

An eighty-gallon tropical fish tank sat in the partition between dining area and living room. With each new morning, before walking outside to feed the other animals, Kevin fed the fish—mostly a large school of diminutive neon tetras, a luminescent red stripe along their entire length highlighting the bright blue of their bodies. Taking a pinch of phytoplankton between index finger and thumb, he released it on top of the water and watched the fish swim avidly to the surface. Rising to the bait, he thought today, though in their case, he had no wish to hook them.

Four days had elapsed since he'd mailed the letter to Joe Polito. His experience with local mail nowadays told him that cross-town delivery might take anywhere from one to four days, seldom longer. Today, he hoped to hear the whir of the reel playing out.

Yet nothing happened on that day or the next. Still, Kevin thought he knew his man, so he continued to wait. The call came on the sixth evening.

"Doctor Kiley?" The opening mildness of voice did not surprise Kevin.

"Speaking."

"I gather you're feeling guilty about what you've done."

Incredible how a person can turn things around one hundred and eighty degrees, Kevin thought. Outwardly, he replied, "More frightened, you might say."

"I hear you've had your troubles . . . too bad." And for the first time, a detectable trace of sarcasm entered the voice—a voice thus far unidentified, though both parties knew its owner.

Kevin was not sure at this point, however, how far the owner would own up. So he went slowly. "Look, I want to see that no more trouble happens to me. Let's say I want to make amends."

"I can understand how your conscience must be bothering you." The voice now sounded like a father-confessor.

Kevin read this, not just as hypocrisy, but as a sign of growing confidence on the other's part of having the upper hand in their relationship. Trying to foster this sense further, he replied, "I just don't want anything else to happen. Please. I'm really scared."

An ice-cold laugh rang through the telephone receiver, and for a moment, Kevin thought he was about to experience the full hysteria of the Avenger's maniacal roar. But the voice stayed in full control.

"Please," Kevin repeated. He was acting, and yet he was not. He really *was* scared. All he had to do was let it come out naturally.

"After all you've done to me—robbed me of more than fifteen hundred dollars every single month, and you think you can make amends and ease your conscience by donating a few hundred crummy bucks?" The familiar voice now spoke in naked anger, the voice that was one in Kevin's mind with Joe Polito and the Avenger.

Though taut with tension throughout his body, Kevin was pleased. Pleased because he'd been able to predict his opponent's response to this point. The ability to predict, he knew, was one of the cornerstones of true power. With appropriate supplication in his voice, he answered, "Please . . . please . . . that was just a start. I'm sure we can work something out. Look, let's get together and talk this whole business over reasonably."

"Yeh, I think you'd better learn to be more reasonable. When someone commits a crime like yours, he shouldn't expect forgiveness for three Hail Marys."

Assessing the situation so far, Kevin was impressed by his opponent's caution. Not one damaging admission made—probably convinced the phone was being bugged—and not even formally identifying himself. His options were still open to use his own name or his alias. No doubt, his caution also extended to calling from a pay phone rather than from home.

Kevin decided he'd test that hypothesis, as well as nailing down his adversary's identity, so he continued, "I can see that better, Joe, now that we're talking. Just give me a chance to work it out right with you."

And at that point, Kevin flicked the control of his beeper off and on, producing an attention-calling sound pattern. Interrupting himself then with a tone of surprise, he said, "Oops, the hospital must be trying to reach me. I'd better call. Look, I'll call you right back."

"I think you'd just better let that wait." It was the voice of authority, feeling in full control now—also avoiding the need to give out any call-back number.

"Sure, Joe, whatever you say." Again, Kevin slipped in the name obsequiously. "Look, I'll bring you over a check right now for double the amount."

"No, I don't want you over here, scum. I'll meet you." The tone was arrogant.

"Okay, Joe." Kevin breathed a quiet sigh of relief. The last thing his plan called for was a meeting at the Polito house, but he had suggested that rendezvous immediately to throw his opponent off guard. He knew that Joe would be leery of such a close link, and though it hadn't been mentioned yet, of receiving a personal check.

"Drive over to Franklin Park by the golf course and stop your car up at the pro shop." Joe spoke now in a tone of routine command.

"Right now? *Tonight?*" Kevin asked with the querulous tone of a child given extra work.

"Right now," said Joe, appearing to enjoy his newfound position of authority. (Power corrupts, but it also can make its wielder careless.)

"I can't, Joe. I can't do that. I'm too frightened. I'm just too scared to meet you all alone. I'd meet you out someplace, like at a restaurant or a bar." He was not about to take any extra risks with this madman.

"I don't see why you're frightened of me," the voice replied with earnestness. Then turning to scorn: "But I guess I should have known. You're nothing but a yellow-bellied cur, the lowest form of life, with all your bullshit airs."

"Don't go so hard on me," Kevin said plaintively. "Look, what about the Howard Johnson just off the west expressway? That's about halfway between us, so we'd get there about the same time."

"Okay, Doc, whatever you say." The voice was patronizing. "See you there in one hour."

"Okay, see you." Kevin hung up the phone, and made his last minute preparations.

CHAPTER 18

Reaching the Howard Johnson before his opponent, Kevin thought, I've got him more than halfway there. If he shows up. Still, he was uneasy. His mouth felt dry, and a tightness ran from his breastbone to his abdomen. His arms and legs felt tingly and heavy.

The restaurant was populated with its usual late night lack-of-crowd, though there were enough customers and staff around to discourage any attempt at an unwitnessed assault. As an insurance policy, Kevin approached the young sandy-haired man at the register. "My name's Kiley. I'd like you to remember the name of the guy I'm with. His name's Polito, as in polite. *Polito*, got it?" And he gave the puzzled young man a five-dollar bill for his troubles.

Like flight insurance, Kevin thought. You don't expect to collect. In any case, you wouldn't be around to collect. But it's comforting in the here and now to envision your loved ones better cared for after you're gone. In this instance, it was comforting to think that Joe Polito wouldn't get off scot-free if he chose this time to kill. Though Lord knows what the law would do about it nowadays, even with a positive identification.

He sat at a booth, ordered a cup of coffee, and waited. He noticed the sandy-haired helper looking over from time to time. I certainly succeeded in wetting his curiosity, thought Kevin. Seven additional minutes went by with exceeding slowness. It was hard for him to sit still. His body wanted to get up and pace about, like an expectant father in the waiting room. Except that death was at this doorstep, not life.

Then the glass entryway over by the milk bar opened, and a heavyset man entered. Kevin would have recognized his swarthy face anywhere. Now. The man stood leisurely, still half-obstructing the doorway, and scanned his dominion with those prominent eyes until they met Kevin's. Then, smiling, he sauntered over to the table.

"You beat me here, Doc. I guess rabbits run fast, huh?"

"I guess so," said Kevin. "How're we going to do this?"

"Not so fast, Doc. First, it's time for you to make a confession."

"A what?"

"A confession . . . you know . . . an apology and an explanation."

"Oh, you mean about the disability report?" Kevin had not been purposely obtuse. It had taken him this moment to understand.

"Really smart, Doc. You're *really* smart—must have gotten all A's in school."

"Well, what do you want to know?"

"You know what I want to know." And anger entered Joe's voice for the first time this meeting, accentuated by a widening of his palpebral fissures that gave his already protuberant eyes a distinctly menacing quality. "I want you to tell me why you falsified my report, why you took away my disability!"

"Look, Joe. I didn't set out to do you wrong. That really was the way I saw it—that your nerves had caused a lot of difficulty for you, including troubles with the job."

"If you're going to stick to your lies, then we have nothing more to discuss." And Joe started to rise and leave in one motion.

"Hold on—wait a minute." Kevin stretched his arm out sincerely. For he sincerely did not want to let Joe get away when he had him almost hooked. "Okay. What do you want to know? I'll tell you."

"I want the truth. That's what I want. Why did you falsify your report? What was your motive?"

"Joe, don't leave in a huff, but let me ask—how do you absolutely know that I lied in my report? I mean, could I have possibly made an error for instance?" If Kevin had been doing psychotherapy with a psychotic patient, he might have countered a delusion in this manner, first by a direct effort at reality testing, then by a more indirect approach of trying to open up a closed delusional system to other possibilities. But right now he was simply trying to understand where his opponent was at. For the present, his money-bait was being ignored, like a brightly colored lure flashing by unattended, while the trout broke surface for some unknown prey.

"Don't stall me, Doc. One way or the other, you're going to have to 'fess up. I think someone at the Department of Labor paid you off, and I'm going to get to the bottom of it. I want you to tell me who it was."

"I'm not trying to be difficult, but you have taken a possibility there and treated it like a certainty." Kevin used his most diplomatic tone.

"You're a real son of a bitch, Doc, you know that?" A rim of anger hiding just below his matter-of-fact tone, he continued, "I suppose you'd like me to believe, for example, that the Department wouldn't send you more cases if you saved them money by calling the shots their way."

"You've got a point there. I think they would use me or any other expert more, if the expert's point of view did favor their position. But that's different from saying they *bought* his opinion in the sense that he changed it just to please them."

"So you knew they'd use you more if you played ball with them, but that didn't influence you at all? Come on, Doc. What do you take me for, a sap? Just because I didn't have all those years of school and the fancy title?"

"Well, I can see I'm not convincing you much."

"No, you're not. You're not very convincing at all. As yellow as you are, you must be more scared of the people you're trying to protect. You're impossible to deal with in any reasonable manner." And, again, Joe started to rise and leave.

"No, please don't, Joe. Let me make amends. You know, sort of a private disability fund."

Joe sat back down. "You mean with that sort of pittance you sent along?"

"No. I just wasn't thinking clearly enough. I could give you fifteen hundred a month. That would help, wouldn't it?"

"What's this? A bribe you're offering me so I won't unmask you?"

"No . . . I mean . . . let's say I want to stay healthy. I want to live out my life. I want to go home safely every night. I want to raise my animals in peace."

"Pretty hard for a guilty conscience to ever have peace, Doc. You should know that. That's why you've eventually got to confess this whole thing to me."

At this point, Kevin felt so guilty about his present intentions that he involuntarily hung his head. As it turned out, he could not have planned a more effective ploy, because Joe seemed satisfied for now with the involuntary act of contrition he'd extracted. Breaking the long pause with sudden abruptness, he said, "I want some real money, *big* money, right now!"

The surge of aggressive cupidity brought Kevin back to life. "Sure, Joe," he answered. "I'll write you out a check right now," and he reached into his coat pocket.

"I don't want a check, jerk! I want *money*."

"All right . . . all right . . . I have money at home. I have to keep it there. You know, the IRS. I'll get some for you now."

Joe looked at him suspiciously. Why would an intelligent person be so stupid as to keep a bundle of cash stashed away in his house? Kevin resolved his opponent's suspiciousness with a brilliant non sequitur: "Look, Joe, you don't have to trust me. You can watch me all the way. We can even decide how much you need of it tonight."

Joe's facial expression remained taut for what seemed a long time, then relaxed into a macho grin. "Okay, Doc," he said, "you lead the way and I'll follow." Standing then, he gestured politely like a *maitre d'* and patronizingly followed Kevin out the door.

CHAPTER 19

Driving home, Kevin had a hard time feeling it was all real. His plan, despite the slight setback, had been working so well that he kept looking for the hitch. Maybe secretly hoping for one. He was driving stiffly, having to think consciously of not driving too fast or too slowly. He could see the headlights of Joe's old Montego following about thirty yards behind. At that hour, there were few cars on the road.

He thought for a moment about Joe's interpretation of the disability report. Funny how paranoid thinking will generally have a basis in truth, or at least in plausibility. It sounded sensible to suppose that a person would tend to slant his opinion in favor of the party paying him. And yet Kevin felt confident that he'd been subject to no such bias. Why? He immediately cast aside the high sounding motives of professional objectivity and altruism as so much polite pooh. He did accept, however, in himself and in most individuals an immediate enjoyment in doing something well. Then too, he valued the esteem of his peers (though, for other reasons, he wanted not to), and the thought of being seen as a "hired gun" who would prostitute his professional opinions to the highest bidder revolted him. There was not even any significant financial temptation in this direction, since he did not need these consultations. It's easy, he thought, to be virtuous when a situation doesn't really tempt you.

Turning off the highway at his exit, Kevin glanced again in his rearview mirror to make sure the Montego's headlights were still following. He became aware of an increasing tension, half-apprehension, half-excitement. A vibrant tingle of energy surged through his arms and legs, alternating with waves of weakness, like an intense fatigue, though he had done nothing.

Now, his mind became bereft of all but the most inchoate of thoughts. Visual impressions of light and dark flashed by on the road. The butterfly sensation in his stomach gave way to an unbearable tautness that surged downward to a restless electricity in his feet and upward to a heaviness in his arms so severe that a substantial effort was required to manipulate the steering wheel. He smacked his tongue on his lips, and it sounded like the high-pitched crinkle of dry grass. No saliva.

Pulling into his driveway, Kevin thought he was going to pass out. Animal fear started to enclose him. He felt desperate about the enemy from without (and the enemy from within). Yet his actions went on ineluctably, like the swallow-reflex once set in motion, or an orgasm beyond the staying point. Getting out of his wagon, he was amazed that he actually stood erect, not collapsing like a stringless puppet. "We're here," he called back to Joe, and his own matter-of-fact tone struck him eerily because it was so different from the porcelain fragmentation he felt within.

As Joe neared, Kevin turned to lead the way onto the deck, knowing by premeditated plan that he had to show this evidence of complete subjection to the other's control—yet all the time spastic with fear that his opponent would use this unguarded interval to deliver the final blow in his increasingly vicious series of personal assaults. The vision of a bullfighter flashed in Kevin's mind, and he thought of that sadistically noble athlete moving his cape by ordained prescription. The bull would do its thing and follow the red billow in its harmless surge. But if some suddenly erratic tendency caused that bovine brute to deviate course, the matador would bear the knowledge of having behaved correctly, even in his mortal agony.

In the present moment, Kevin knew he was correct. His thunderous opponent would sweep along with him to his final goal, certain of the intimidating power he held over his foe and anxious to receive the initial spoils of war. Yet some mistimed surge of angry paranoia within the next few seconds could alter the whole outcome in another fatal direction.

Floating as in a dream less real than our ordinary reality, Kevin fumbled momentarily with his key at the door. Feeling as though he were gasping for breath under an ethereal sea, he nevertheless managed to make a banal remark about his lack of door-opening dexterity, further lulling his adversary by his clumsiness.

Then the door opened, and the two figures seemed to flow inside as by suction—otherwise Kevin would have collapsed on the back hall linoleum in a perfect paralysis of fortitude. Lifting the latch of the inside door, he abruptly bolted four feet to his side, grabbing the shotgun he'd left standing in the angle between refrigerator and wall.

Shaking with relief at having traversed the previous seventy feet intact, he had the gun turned and beside him at hip height before his surprised adversary showed any adequate reaction. Joe started to leap forward, eyes bulging more at the sight, then stopped his lunge as abruptly as if he'd hit a glass wall. He stood instead, a little over a yard away, and his body slowly relaxed. Then he said, almost with nonchalance, "Come on, Doc, put the goddam gun down. You might hurt someone with that thing." His tone still hadn't lost its earlier sense of having attained supremacy in their relation.

"That's exactly what I'm going to do, Joe. I'm going to shoot you dead." Kevin heard his own voice speaking in cold control.

"Come on, Doc, let's get serious. In the fist place, you're not a killer. In the second place, you'd never get away with it. Right in your own home?" And the prospect started to seem so implausible that another explanation jumped into Joe's mind. "Oh, I get it, you're trying to frighten me." And he laughed at the ludicrousness of that effort. "Forget it. It won't work."

Kevin took a step back toward the kitchen sink and let the gun rise a few inches as his elbow joints became more relaxed and less strained. "I'm not trying to frighten you, but I am going to kill you *before* you kill me."

The unemotional tone finally seemed to make a more serious impression on his adversary. "Hey, wait a minute, Doc. Take it easy. I'm not worth killing. I mean, I'm not really going to hurt you. And besides, they'd lock you up for a lifetime if you ever did anything like that. And a lifetime mightn't be all that long if they sent you to Walpole. You know how dangerous it is there, especially for someone like yourself."

"I know," said Kevin. "But you see, you made the mistake of invading the sanctity of my home just now. So get moving, down the hall there to the end." And he nodded his head in the direction around the brick fireplace toward the hallway across the living room.

"What do you want me to do that for?" Joe spoke now with the concern of awakening fear.

"I'll tell you as we go." They marched carefully in tandem fashion, Kevin directing his now captive tormentor into the bedroom. "For purposes of emotional impact, I believe a person's bedroom is the most private and sacred part of his home. Our state law that allows self-protection at home, even to the use of deadly force if necessary, will be most understandable there."

"But I'm not a marauder or some B & E man. I came here with you, at your invitation." Desperateness had completely replaced arrogance.

"Aren't you? You're worse than a marauder, worse than a mere plunderer. You're a sadist. For months now, you've tortured me beyond endurance—not just out of illness but out of willfulness. Eventually, you would have killed me, but I'm not going to stand still for that. I have a brief span of existence ordained by nature. And within its limits, I plan to live out my days by means of every rightful act at my disposal. If society in its inertia won't protect me, I'll protect myself. *If it's meant to be, it's up to me.* I'll take that saying from words to action. And as far as society's concerned, you forced me here through intimidation, to complete your predation and render the final blow under my own roof. But I managed to momentarily outwit you, grab my gun, and shoot you in self-defense."

"For God's sake, don't do it! My family—think of my family. My God, you're a doctor. You're supposed to save life, not take it. And you won't get away with it. Honest, you really won't!"

BOOM! BOOM! OOM . . . OOM . . . oom . . . oom. The bedroom convulsed in deafening fulmination as both barrels emptied with echoing reverberations. Like a bucket of red paint, Joe's face, jaw, and left shoulder disappeared in a carnage that splattered onto the off-white bedroom wall behind, peripheral elements of the shotgun blasts adding holed crescents through the plaster board matrix. Lifted up, down, and back in one continuous motion, Joe's body landed on the wide pine boards up against the wall, blood gushing outward still, and flowing with a speed enhanced by capillary action along the crevices in the floorboards.

Kevin half collapsed into a sitting huddle on the bed, the smoking shotgun lying diagonally across his knees. He felt his heart pound with a strength and rapidity that astounded him, forcing him to experience the reality which otherwise he could not have fully grasped at that moment. He could not bear to look at the freshly bloodied corpse, nor yet to look away. Shaking uncontrollably, he stood to walk out of the room and heard the noise of heavy metal on the floor as the gun heedlessly fell from his lap as he rose.

In the kitchen, he took a large carving knife out of its place in the butcher-block holder and forced himself back down the corridor to the room. He grabbed hold of the right arm that had once been Joe's and placed the handle within the fingers that he shakingly encircled around it. The arm and hand fell limp. The knife fell loose. Kevin looked and tried to decide (he hadn't thought that detail through carefully enough), then concluded that the knife would have fallen out anyway when Joe was shot, so he left it on the floor.

Legs growing weak again, he half-stepped, half-fell back, sitting on the bed. For moments or minutes, he tried to collect himself. Finally, he managed to make his way around to the bedside table along the opposite wall. Lifting the receiver of his telephone, he dialed the police and listened for the ring to be interrupted by the official voice of authority.

"Hello. This is Doctor Kiley. I've been attacked in my home. Please hurry. I've shot him, and I think he's dead." Kevin had absolutely no need to act into his voice any of the anguished horror that his words conveyed.

CHAPTER 20

Still shaking without and quaking within, Kevin met the whirling blue light as it came to a silent stop at the driveway's terminal loop. Almost wordless, he and the police officer (the same one who had extricated him from the wreck weeks before) mounted the front deck and entered the house. With Kevin leading the way, they walked through the back hall and kitchen/dining area, across the living room and down the hall, roughly the same route he and Joe Polito had traversed just a short while before. Turning into the master bedroom, he thoughtlessly kicked the fallen carving knife out of his way, then went to pick it up.

"Don't do that, Doc," said the small town officer, his dry-mouth voice managing an involuntary remnant of professionalism in the face of this unaccustomedly brutal carnage. "We'd better try to leave everything pretty much as it was at the time."

"Oh, yes, of course," said Kevin distractedly. And the weird part was, he actually felt distracted, though he had consciously moved the knife in case his original placement had turned out to be forensically implausible. "Shall I put it back where it was?"

"I guess not. I'll remember that it got moved." Then another pause and the officer looked at Kevin with concern. "You were pretty lucky, Doc. How'd you manage to get him?"

Feeling weak again, to the point of faintness, Kevin met the officer's question with a question. "Can we go in the other room and sit down?"

"Of course," said the police officer solicitously. Then he shepherded Kevin down the hall, arm stretched forward to Kevin's waist in case he were to pass out en route. "Sit here," he said, guiding his charge to one of the easy chairs, "and I'll call the chief." Looking through the opening toward the kitchen/dining area, the officer saw a wall phone beside the pine-framed entryway. Approaching its old-fashioned dial, he chugged out a number and waited for a sleep-filled voice to answer.

* * *

The chief was tall, very good looking, and also managed to keep a ruddy winter tan. Kevin had never known him, except from a distance at the occasional town meeting, and then he'd never been favorably impressed. The fellow had struck him as an arch politician, flashing his amiable smile indiscriminately while he vagued out his responses to any questions about police activity in the town. I'd never buy a used car from him, Kevin had thought, though he admitted to himself that there was no solid basis for his intuition.

Tonight, however, when the chief turned out during sleeping hours, he seemed competent and experienced in his questioning, and appropriately concerned in his attitude. Kevin related his carefully thought-out account: the intimidation, the meeting arranged through fear, and the hope of dissuading his deranged tormentor from perpetrating further harm, the nightmarish trip home before the watchful beams of his psychopathic adversary, the verbal abuse to which he was subjected as he sat in the dining area with his heavyset and explosively taut companion, the drawing and brandishing of the knife, the forced march to the bedroom for God-knows-what indescribable purpose, his frantic lurch for the bedside gun—kept loaded in recent weeks through desperation—the sudden discharge, the horror, and the phone call to notify the police.

Chief Blakely shook his head in silent sympathy at the gruesome ordeal from which the doctor had just emerged. "You'd better not stay here tonight," he said compassionately. "Is there family or a friend you could go to?" He glanced at his watch and noted the time: 1:40 a.m.

"Yes . . . yes . . . thanks. I do. That's a good idea." This was another detail Kevin had not considered beforehand. But in his ravaging distress of the moment, he thought immediately of Linda.

"Fine," said the chief. "Give us the number where you're going to be so we can contact you tomorrow in case there are any further questions."

Repeating Linda's number, Kevin put on his outer coat from the closet off the living room, picked up his car keys, and left with no thought of reentering the bedroom to pack anything. His new car turned over effortlessly in the cold of that early winter morning, and he headed up the gentle slant of drive. To Linda's.

CHAPTER 21

He drove straight over, not thinking to call, and announced his presence only by a middle-of-the-night ringing of her doorbell. "It's Kevin," he said, in response to her sleepy, "Who is it?"

While he was mounting the stairs to her third-floor apartment, Linda quickly brushed her hair and looked at herself in the mirror. Then the door sounded with a quietly insistent knock, and she let him in. Closing the door behind him, Kevin embraced her clingingly. Linda seemed to know instinctively that there'd been some crisis. She said nothing for what seemed a long time, holding him, soothing him with her caressing hands. After a while, she led him silently to her bed and lay beside him. Only then did she speak: "Dearest . . . what's wrong?"

Kevin's attempt to speak was interrupted by a sob, and another. Barely detectable at first, they gradually grew in magnitude until his whole body started to shudder. The effort he exerted to silence the convulsive sounds succeeded only in tautening his vocal cords, causing a high-pitched moan like the pathetic call of a dumb animal in extremis.

Aching with a compassion that sent shivers down her legs, Linda clung to him tightly. At the same time, she rocked him back and forth, fondling the hair on the side of his head and repeating over and over with a gentle coo, "I know . . . I know . . . I know." But she didn't. She could not even imagine.

Finally, no more sobs would come. Kevin puffed the double pillows up and sat against them at the head of the bed, enfolding his arm now around the still cuddling body of his partner who had followed him up as he went. "I did it," he said with anti-climactic matter-of-factness.

"Did what?"

"Killed him."

"You *what?*" She sat up straight.

"I killed Joe Polito. Tonight."

Linda suddenly bent forward as if someone had punched her in the stomach. Her face winced in pain, leaving the sides of her mouth to quiver like ripples spreading outward on a pond. "I don't understand." And the desperation in her voice indicated rather that she did not want to.

Kevin, looking for a miracle of acceptance, knew in that moment he had not found it. Yet he continued hopelessly. "I told you I was going to do it! I told you I couldn't go on living like this."

"But I never thought you *meant* it! I never even dreamed . . . I mean, you're not like that! You can't . . ." And her voice trailed off. A pause, oppressive this time, and she started up again. "The police . . . the police will get you. You'll have to go to prison. Oh, Kevin, *why?*"

"That's not the problem. I've already informed them. I got Joe to come out to my house, then I killed him in self-defense, so to speak."

Linda was huddled on the edge of the bed now, knees up under her chin, arms on her legs, rocking back and forth inconsolably. Her whole world had crashed, and at that moment, all she could do was whimper.

Kevin's composure had returned to him like ice. "You can't accept it. You can't accept me now." He spoke with the calmness of the truly sad.

"Oh, Kevin, how can I?" she whimpered piteously. "You were so good. You were so wonderful. You helped everybody. You were everything to me . . . and now this? How could you?"

"No. I never was wonderful," Kevin continued to speak calmly, reflectively. "You only thought so. And I guess I enjoyed having you think that of me. It came across all the time. It took me out of myself, out of my own sense of smallness. I basked in my own reflected glory, I guess. In my own myth as it bounced off you." He was rising to his feet now and putting on his car coat as he talked. "But I'm no martyr. I wanted to live out my life. I refused to be bullied when I could prevent it. I was *not* going to turn the other cheek and get it blown off." Turning, he started to walk out of the room.

"Where are you going?" Alarm entered Linda's voice. She jumped up suddenly off the bed toward Kevin, arms outstretched, then pulled them back like arson-withered shrubbery as she shrank within six inches of him.

He shook his head slowly. "Can't even bear to touch me now, can you? Someone who couldn't even stand the killing of one small laboratory rat in the interest of medical science, and now your boyfriend goes around killing human beings, no less." He walked out of the room, across the vestibule, to the apartment door.

Linda followed, her shoulders huddled and arms folded with hands up under her sagging chin. "Where are you going now? Where will you stay for the night? Stay here!"

"You had to really gather yourself to offer that, didn't you?" The anger in his heart hardly showed in the observational tone of his voice. "Don't worry, it's almost morning now anyway. Besides, I'm used to fantasies ending. It's just . . . I seem to have a hard time learning from experience."

Linda sank to the floor along the wall, folding up as naturally as a collapsing stool. Tears flowed silently down her cheeks, and her eyes, straight ahead, focused on nothing. She trembled at the coming dawn.

Kevin returned to his car and drove, with no special goal, in the general direction of his house. On the way, as if by plan, he stopped at a motel. Once in his room, he phoned the police to leave his new number and his answering service to leave word for Frances to cancel another office day. He felt less soft, less vulnerable, less human in his isolation, which at that moment seemed absolute. Taking off his clothes, he pulled down the covers without bothering to remove the bedspread. If he had his usual troubled dreams in the comatose sleep that followed, no recorder was hitched up to the mnemonic aspects of his brain. He remembered nothing.

CHAPTER 22

Kevin slept uninterruptedly till late morning. On waking, he went over the facts of the preceding night in his mind—almost to make sure they were real—to orient himself for the new day as one might do by checking out the date in one's first morning thoughts. Then he walked over to the coffee shop and ordered bacon and fried eggs, sunny-side up. At the cashier's counter, on the way in, he had picked up a morning paper. Only then did it dawn on him that the killing might be news. He looked all over the front page, and with great relief saw nothing. It occurred to him that the event had happened too late. They don't say "Stop the presses" anymore, he thought. TV and radio take care of the instant stuff.

After breakfast, he returned to his room before one o'clock check-out time and phoned the police. The body had been removed. He could return home. Then he phoned Frances and told her to cancel the rest of his week, also to ask Doctor Johnson to cover for him at the hospital and with any emergencies. On arriving at his house around two o'clock, he felt overcome by a strange listlessness. He could not concentrate enough to read, nor involve himself in any of the physical projects to be done around his homestead. He paced back and forth, going from one thing to another. Walking into the bedroom, he experienced a generalized malaise as he looked at the gun-pocked wall. He decided that he'd sleep in the other bedroom for a while, a room he had used till now as a combination guest room and storage area.

When dinnertime came, he went out to a fast-food outlet rather than cooking for himself at home in his usual fashion. He avoided radio and TV, figuring that he did not need the extra stimulation of hearing a news story about himself. And that night he slept poorly, with what seemed like a continuous sequence of troubled dreams whose contents he could not remember.

*　*　*

Late the following morning a police cruiser came down his drive, and the officer walked up to his door. "We've been trying to reach you all morning, Doc, but you haven't been answering your phone."

"Sorry. I didn't think of that. I unplugged it when I got home yesterday. Just didn't want to talk to any of my acquaintances who might have called, not to mention any reporters who might want to rehash the thing." Kevin still felt listless.

"We got a call at the station this morning requesting that you come to the DA's office."

"Okay, where's that?" Kevin asked.

"I'll drive you. We're supposed to ask for the assistant DA, Mr. Miller."

"Thanks anyway but I don't want to tie you up. Just give me the directions."

"No problem. They asked me to pick you up and take you over."

Kevin's negative feelings toward the police were triggered off once more by the way the officer had said "pick you up." Resisting an urge to ask sarcastically if he were being arrested, he replied simply, "I'll get my coat." He felt no suspicion.

CHAPTER 23

Mr. Miller turned out to be a brown-haired, brown-suited man of about thirty-five, well built, with a tailored moustache above prominent white incisor teeth. He had darting, hazel eyes, and his hairline, receding at both temples, gave him an appearance of growing maturity.

He greeted Kevin by name as Doctor Kiley, nodded to the police officer, and introduced himself as Thornton Miller. Then he excused himself, evidently to finish up some odds and ends of work, returning after several minutes with a pleasant smile.

"Come on in the office now," he said to Kevin in Hail-Fellow-Well-Met fashion, and they walked together through the translucent-glass door from the sparsely furnished waiting room into an equally plain but manuscript-laden area that formed his bailiwick. The whole ambience, and especially the wooden door with its upper half opalescently screened, reminded Kevin of the principal's office at high school.

"There's something I'd like you to listen to," said Thornton, dropping a mini-cassette into the tape deck on an adjoining table. "Have a seat, won't you?"

As the assistant DA pushed his thumb down on the playback lever, Kevin felt a sudden sinking in his stomach. The familiar voice of Joe Polito crackled from the machine, then his own. It was the conversation at Howard Johnson resurrected electronically. No wonder, he thought, Joe was making such a big deal about a "confession" and being so noncommittal himself. Whether or not he could have used the recording in court, it might conceivably have been introducible before a medical board.

His smile now evaporating, Thornton Miller asked if the voices sounded familiar. Kevin didn't have to wait for the other shoe to fall. He already knew he'd been caught in a sting originally intended for less fatal goals. He replied simply, "Go on."

Pressing the eject lever, Mr. Miller replaced the first small cassette with a second one. Eyes now riveted firmly on Kevin while his hand performed the tape deck maneuver blind, he started the new tape from a strategically placed position:

"For God's sake, don't do it! My family—think of my family. My God, you're a doctor. You're supposed to save life, not take it. And you won't get away with it. Honest, you really won't!" *BOOM! BOOM! OOM . . . OOM . . . oom . . . oom*, then a series of crumpling and rustling sounds as Thornton Miller took his time in turning off the apparatus.

Looking at Kevin evenly, he said with a professional tone, "You should have frisked the body, Doc." After a pause, he continued with an almost sympathetic tone, "Would you like to talk about it?"

Kevin was dumbfounded—literally struck dumb—by the disclosure. A long pause ensued as he could find no mind, let alone words, to speak. At this point, Miller started to recite, without benefit of a printed card, words that made Kevin feel more like an actor on some TV drama. "You have the right to remain . . ."

Without conscious deliberative effort, Kevin interrupted decisively and said, "I guess I'd better call my lawyer." Inside, he imagined himself dressed in a dark gray pin-striped suit with wide silk tie, chomping on a cigar and jutting his chin out defiantly with the words: "I don't got nuthin' to say. Speak to my mouthpiece!" It's crazy, he thought. I even have one to call.

His mind began to buzz, and he wanted so much at this minute to tell the DA with the sympathetic voice all about it—to explain himself, to have another person understand his point of view, to overcome his isolation.

The image of his sheep came to mind, and he saw them herding together, startled by some sound into a rapid flow like loosely knit cells of a single creature, or drifting more leisurely from pasture to pasture, always together.

Why doesn't one of them strike out on its own? Because it's their nature, of course, he thought. Human consciousness imposes enough exclusion from the Garden of Eden that a man can choose to rail against nature, but he can never win the struggle. Though subject to a more subtle bondage than sheep, he needs community with his fellows every bit as much. And for most members of the species, this requirement is experienced more as a joy than a burden.

Kevin had to fight his way back from these internal ruminations in order to return to that outer world impinging from his periphery. He had scarcely heard what Mr. Miller was saying, but got the gist of it sufficiently to use the desk phone for a lawyer's call. When Michael Grady's secretary tried to put him off (like a good secretary), Kevin responded emphatically, "But this is an emergency. You tell Mike I'm being held *right now*, by the *police*, at the *DA's office*!"

"Certainly, Doctor Kiley. I'll tell Mr. Grady right away."

Thirty seconds later, Mike's voice came on the line: "Doctor Kiley, what's up?"

"I've just been arrested," he answered, "for murder."

PART II

CHAPTER 24

First time ever in a jail cell. Kevin sat on its cot, stood from time to time, walked a couple of steps to the far wall, turned around, and sat down again. He kept shifting positions, lying with his head at the top of the cot for a while, then sitting up with his body curved uncomfortably against the near wall. Or he'd lean forward as he sat, cupping his chin in his hands. His inner life—the thoughts and reflections that usually occupied him with more interest and appreciation than what was going on outside him—seemed as aseptic as his surroundings. He experienced a constant flickering of dull impressions and an ill-defined ache of tedious impatience.

After finishing at the office, Mike came over to see him. They met in a spartan room furnished principally with a shellacked hardwood table, possessed of two drawers side by side and plain brass handles to match the brass caps covering four sturdy square and squared-off legs. The details of the table, down to specific elements of the wood grain, fascinated Kevin. It was like a melding of all the tables in all the classrooms he had attended from Miss Hart's first grade on through. And always, in those educational enclosures too, he had experienced the vague feeling of being trapped by his own unfathomable turpitude.

"How're you doing?" Mike inquired with his usual energetic concern.

"Okay . . . last time I checked, which was about an hour ago," Kevin quipped with a deadpan expression.

They reviewed the recent events, and Mike listened carefully to the whole story, even tolerating Kevin's fairly frequent digressions into why he had to do what he did. Finally, the lawyer put down his pad and pencil. "This is a tough one, Doc," he said. "You've been through a lot, and right now I don't think you've got your head on straight. I'm going to ask the court that you be sent to a hospital for evaluation."

"You mean a psychiatric hospital to determine my competency," replied Kevin, calling a spade a spade.

"Yep," replied Mike, "that's what we've got to do."

"No way!" said Kevin. "I killed him before he killed me, and society had neither the will nor the way to protect me. It's as simple as

that. If public hypocrisy puts me behind bars for taking the law into my own hands after society showed itself bankrupt in effecting either justice or safety, so be it!"

"Look, I'm not trying to tell you your own business, Doctor Kiley, but I do know that a person can't effectively be his own doctor, especially when it comes to matters of the mind. We're all too close to ourselves. I'm not trying to make a judgment on the issue myself. That's a medical matter. And for that, we've got to have a solid medical opinion."

"What even raises the question in your mind?" Kevin asked with exasperation.

"Have you ever used violence before in your life?" countered Mike.

"No . . . except for the usual schoolboy skirmishes. But I've never been put in this position before. Have *you*?"

"Well, let's look at that position, Doc. You were convinced that this particular fellow, Joe Polito, was *absolutely* the one harassing you. Furthermore, you were convinced that he would progressively up the ante until he eventually killed you—"

Kevin interrupted, "Wait a minute. You don't have to draw diagrams or make speeches. I can see where you're going. In the first place, I killed a mere suspect—*in your view*. And in the second place, I did so with the premature conviction that his behavior would extend beyond aggravating harassments to actual murder—that, in short, I grossly overreacted by taking a human life. Well, you weren't in my car when I got forced off the road, or you wouldn't talk in such a stupidly hypothetical way. That act *was* lethal. I could well have been killed or, worse than death, I could have been rendered quadriplegic. And the diabolical destruction of my sheep that followed; that wasn't *just* harassment. It was a sadistic statement of my own destruction that was to follow!"

Ignoring the passion in Kevin's voice, Mike continued evenly, "I'm not going to second guess the symbolism you saw in that unbalanced action. And I certainly agree, the truck incident most definitely represented assault with a deadly weapon. But neither of these episodes could justify to a reasonable man the vigilante excess of murdering a likely culprit. And *ordinarily* you are a reasonable man."

Kevin interrupted hotly, "God damn it, I don't need another prosecutor on this case. When you really need help, that's when no one's around. Thanks for coming over after hours, and thanks for your candor anyway." His tone had shifted as he spoke, from anger to resignation.

"Wait a minute," said Mike, "not so fast! Hear me out! You just want to listen to the good things, and when you have to hear something different, you want to shut the other person out. That's why you're such a loner in the first place. Well, I'm not trying to kiss you off now that you're in trouble. That's just the way you'd like to see it, so you don't have to face the facts.

"Let me tell you something. When that young lawyer made a monkey out of you, you thought he was diabolically clever, and that somehow he had perverted the Halls of Justice. Now he's going to be a real good lawyer all right. He already *is*. But he didn't have to be brilliant. All he had to do was point out that your case had more holes than swiss cheese. He was *right*. Any number of screwballs whom you must have met over the past twenty years could have decided to get you. I defended a guy once who shot a doctor walking home across Huntington Park. The guy had been nursing a grudge like aging wine. He hadn't even seen that doctor for sixteen years.

"In your case, of course, there was this coincidence. You started getting harassed shortly after the time when Polito started bitching. I grant it makes him the number one suspect. It certainly justified our taking him to court to put him on notice. The probabilities are that he was the one. Maybe the odds were seventy-five or eighty percent, maybe ninety, who knows? But it was nowhere close to certain.

"No one in his right mind," and Mike gave particular emphasis to the phrase, "would have considered him to be guilty beyond a reasonable doubt. Would you want our courts to put people behind bars on such probabilities? Would you—*reasonably*—want the courts to exercise the death penalty in such cases." There was no question mark at the end of his question.

Kevin felt an odd combination of reactions. On the one hand, he grasped the apparent sensibleness of the lawyer's statements. On the other hand, he was totally convinced that he himself was right, though he also believed it might be a hopeless task to convince others.

After a pause, Mike was continuing, "Doc, I really do know the way you feel, and I realize you've been through an absolute nightmare the past several months. But that's my point. The sort of stress you've been under can upend a person, can twist his thoughts. And if we get to thinking something's so, we fill in the blanks without even being aware of it. Once we get the conviction that some particular person is doing something, we can end up interpreting everything that happens to fit our beliefs. Isn't that what you guys call a self-fulfilling prophecy?"

Kevin didn't think that was exactly the right term, though he knew what Mike was getting at. But feeling hopeless and totally alone, he just kept silent. As Mike headed out the door, however, Kevin spoke up, "Oh, would you do me a favor, Mike, and call Frances for me? Ask her to get in touch with Jimmy Fowler. He's a neighborhood kid who fills in for me sometimes when I'm away and takes care of my animals. For a while."

CHAPTER 25

On the following day, the judge readily agreed to Michael Grady's request that his client be hospitalized for psychiatric evaluation. It hadn't been easy for Mike to make the actual arrangements. He wanted to avoid the State facility for the criminally insane at Bridgewater, but it was hard to find placement in a private hospital. Two of the hospitals he might have used were having *Certificate of Need* problems, one because of new construction and the other because of change in ownership. Though both institutions had been in operation for more than seventy-five years, and though it was generally understood in the community that both places provided essential services, they would have to close immediately if their certificates were withdrawn.

It was the same old story. Everyone recognizes the need for such facilities—but in someone else's neighborhood, please. Though virtually all the neighbors had moved in long after the hospitals had started, abutters saw the *Certificate of Need* hearings as a potential opportunity to extrude the "loony bins" from their midst. Both neighborhood groups had hired lawyers, and they took advantage of TV news' thirst for visual spectacles by parading around with the compulsory placards and bullhorns.

Very much on the defensive, neither facility wanted to risk the additional outcry that would certainly be forthcoming if a murderer were placed within its walls. So they respectfully declined access. It would have been out of the question for Kevin to be placed in the facility where he hospitalized his own patients, some of whom were still there under Doctor Johnson's care. While a physician struck down by a more narrowly biological state like acute appendicitis would be welcomed with open arms by his own staff hospital, a doctor with psychiatric illness—especially with the complication of grossly deviant behavior—becomes a pariah in his own land. Those lower in the medical hierarchy cannot comfortably shift to a supervisory roll, and his peers tend to lose any semblance of objectivity.

A bed was finally located at Hamilton Hearth, a small psychiatric hospital set in a countrified area south of the city, and Kevin was delivered there on the following morning. His first view of the institution was of its long blacktopped driveway, winding up a gentle slope through lawn plantings that had once been formal, to a large old mansion on top of the rise. This structure had received a great deal of attention—an ugly tower of concrete blocks on the far end, for example, forming an awkward prosthesis against what might otherwise have been esthetically interesting structure. No doubt, the tower had saved this central building from being condemned as a fire hazard to its enclosed patients. But to Kevin, it evoked only the macabre association: Tower of London.

Inside, the furnishings of the reception area were grandly informal, as in one of those early resort hotels. He met a blur of faces, culminating in his introduction to the admitting doctor, a young psychiatrist with longish brown hair and a rounded face blemished by the continuing vestiges of adolescent acne. Kevin gave as his reason for being there the directive of the court, otherwise declining to give any history, except as he said facetiously, "name, rank and serial number." He submitted to a cursory physical examination after which he was taken upstairs to roost.

The intensive care unit consisted of two bedrooms with four cots each, one day room with TV set and long table for eating, and a small nurse's office behind which was located a fixed-bed Quiet Room. Also, there was a bathroom with two sinks, two stalls, one urinal (to be used by human persons of the type with built-in external catheters), and a shower. A hallway about four feet wide and just short of thirty feet long, gave access to the rooms and provided a walkway for one back-and-forth pacer at a time.

No privacy could be had in such a setup, which no doubt constituted the lesser of two evils when managing a suicidally depressed or acutely psychotic patient until the gravest of his symptoms were brought under control. For Kevin, however, the arrangement caused particular duress, since he was so used to solitary living. At least it's safer than Walpole, he thought, referring to the maximum-security prison where rapes and murders occur too frequently to count on making the newspapers. Some of the murderers, already serving life without parole, have little to lose.

At that moment, Kevin's ruminations were interrupted by screams curdling from the other room, as a man in T-shirt and poorly fitting brown slacks ran down the hall, banging himself against the exit door with the abandon of an all-league linebacker plugging a hole. In his mad dash, he had upended an elderly man in lumber jacket and suspenders who had just walked out of the nurses' station after demanding to see his wife.

"Get them away. Let me out!" screamed the younger man, evidently referring to his own private demons that none of the others could see. Warding off three mental health workers, he showed a determination as great as might be expected if his life had in fact been immediately endangered. He looked upward and to the side, terrified by Lord knows what images, allowing one of the workers to slip behind him. Then all three converged simultaneously, restraining him physically without further injury to himself or others.

As they took him to the Quiet Room where he was placed on the bed, temporarily in padded wrist and ankle cuffs, Kevin was impressed by the virtuoso performance of the nonprofessional staff. As a doctor immediately on the scene, Kevin went over to check the elderly man, who was miraculously getting to his feet. His body was still pretty resilient, having unfortunately outlasted the useful functioning of his brain.

"Are you all right?" Kevin asked.

"These bastards are trying to kill me," was the old man's initial complaint, ". . . and they won't let me see my wife!"

"But from the fall . . . did you get hurt?" Kevin persisted, noting as he asked that there was no obvious injury or favoring of one part of the body. The man seemed mollified for the moment by this attention, though he didn't seem to grasp the meaning of Kevin's question. "This isn't my home, you know," was all he answered.

CHAPTER 26

Kevin was called to an office downstairs the following morning to see his psychiatrist, Doctor Wilfred Lofgren. Though originally having no intention of speaking to this doctor, Kevin was by now feeling a bit stir-crazy, so he welcomed the opportunity to get off the ward. The room where they met had oak-paneled walls with a built in bookcase at one end, a solid but not obtrusively large desk, comfortable chairs, and an Oriental rug with red motif. At first glance, Kevin found the setting congenial and warm.

"Hi, I'm Bill Lofgren," said a friendly enough voice.

"I'm Doctor Kiley," Kevin said noncommittally, warding off the other's effort at first name informality.

"I gather you're not too happy to be here." Doctor Lofgren's tone was matter of fact. He was a man whom Kevin judged to be maybe five years older than himself, somewhat on the short side, lean, with prominent nose, frontal balding, a low-key smile, and gentile manner. His two-piece beige suit fitted him comfortably.

"You're right," answered Kevin, "I'm not."

"Well, as you know, the court sent you here for legal purposes . . . to have an opinion rendered as to your competency to stand trial, and also for a determination as to whether you were responsible for your actions on the night of the murder." Doctor Lofgren's tone was businesslike but cordial.

"I guess the court has the power to send me any place it chooses," said Kevin. "I am a prisoner."

"Do you consider yourself competent to aid in your own defense?" Doctor Lofgren was sticking to business.

"I know what the charges are, and I want to help myself so I won't be sent to prison, though I doubt I can avoid that. In terms of the killing, I was aware of what I was doing and that my action was against the law. From my point of view, The *Law* was unable to protect me, and I was exercising legitimate though illegal self-defense."

"Tell me more about that." Doctor Lofgren seemed interested.

Kevin had the strong impulse to relate his side of the story, but stifled it. "What's the point of talking about it here? You're not on the jury, and if you were, my point of view wouldn't be relevant anyway. The judge would define society's law, which wouldn't be mine."

"But your point of view might at least differentiate you from a malicious murderer," Doctor Lofgren countered.

"So I'll be eligible for parole in time to go to the retirement home?" Kevin replied cynically.

"You don't seem too happy with our laws," Doctor Lofgren said.

"Neither our laws, nor our rules," Kevin added enigmatically.

"I'm not sure I know the distinction you have in mind."

"The distinction between rules formally codified into laws and those that express the unspoken attitudes of most of the citizens. Even the trivial ones, like the rule of dress you obeyed this morning in donning that suit for white-collar professional work."

Doctor Lofgren smiled. "I never even thought about it—that I was obeying a rule this morning in the way I dressed."

"So what? I don't suppose you've given any thought to following the Law of Gravity either. Yet you haven't risen up to the ceiling as we've been talking. The only difference is, the Law of Gravity is ineluctable. That Law of Professional Dress is transient, bendable, subject to human whim."

"And the law against killing?"

"That depends on where, when, how, and why. Given our direct involvement in Vietnam, our role as munitions maker for the bombardment of Beirut, our complicity in San Salvador, I'd say there is no hard and fast rule about killing. It's true we do have laws constraining individual citizens like me."

"Is that bad?"

"Depends on the situation. If I killed a person to rob him, that would be horrendous. If I killed an attacker to save my own life, I would call that legitimate self-defense."

"That rule of yours seems to reflect the attitude of our society pretty closely."

"It should. I'm a victim . . . I mean . . . a member of our society."

Doctor Lofgren smiled again. "You certainly don't seem to be a fan of our society. But getting back to the particulars, my understanding is that the police investigators believe you lured Mr. Polito to your home and then killed him."

"That's right. But that was to make my lifesaving need for self-defense squeeze into society's laws of legitimate self-defense. After all, here's this guy who's onto me like a bulldog. I can't dislodge him, and he's determined to maim or kill me. But he's so sadistic he's going to string it out and make the torture prolonged and progressive before the final blow. And despite or because of his illness, he's intuitively clever enough to put society on his side, at least insofar as it defends him from any effective comeback on my part. So we end up playing a deadly game of wits, in which I try to maneuver him into a position where society would no longer protect him. But as it turns out, he outmaneuvered me—posthumously."

"He sounds like an evil genius."

"Cut the bullshit, Doctor Lofgren. You don't have to be an evil genius in our society right now to wrap yourself in the flag of your civil rights. You just have to be evil. And you don't have to be a genius to get away with murder, judged from the number of unsolved homicides each year. As a matter of fact, insofar as I'm accused of murder, you'd have to say I'm a dunce as murderers go. But that's because I wanted the act to be seen by society's law as it truly was, an act of necessary self-defense."

"If it really was legitimate self-defense, why did you have to make it seem that way?"

"Laws have to be generalities, but it's the specifics of a given case that determine what must be done in real life. It's like that old children's story—I can't even recall its details—a mother in India or someplace sends her young son to the store to buy butter. He puts it in his pocket where it melts. She explains that he should never do that. Instead, he should carry it on his head where, open to the air, it will stay firm. Next time, she sends him for eggs. Not much luck there either. They roll off his head and break. So she has to give him another rule to take account of the difference between butter and eggs. That rule, in its turn, creates more problems—and so it goes."

After a pause, Kevin continued, "That's the way it is with our laws. 'Don't kill!' But what about killing in order to avoid being killed? So another law allows for legitimate self-defense. Well, is it right to kill a man who is attacking, not to kill you, but to rob the loaf of bread you're carrying from the store? So there's another law made to cover that. And what about a situation where one man is going to kill another, but he hasn't done anything illegal yet? Reminds me of the movie, *High Noon*, where Gary Cooper yells out 'Frank Miller' so the villain will take the first poorly aimed shot. Well, I wasn't safely able to maneuver the situation around into some equivalent of yelling 'Joe Polito.' But since the current law has no adequate provision to handle the particulars of my case, I tried to arrange the details of my self-defense so they'd at least seem to fit what the law would allow."

Doctor Lofgren, listening intently, nodded affirmatively at this point and said, "I can follow your reasoning perfectly." Then he said reflectively, without any trace of argumentativeness, "There's one point that bothers me though. You know yourself, as a psychiatrist, that future behavior is a chancy thing to predict. That's why *first strike* defense, if I may use a pejorative term from international parlance, is generally frowned upon. It would be too easy to conclude that the other country—or fellow—was going to attack, although he might well show some forbearance when the chips were down. Otherwise countries and people might end up killing each other on the mere suspicion that someone was going to do them harm. I mean, once it was allowed, where would it end?"

"That's raising a generalization again, leaving out the specifics of the case." Kevin leaned forward in his chair. "Where it would end, where it *should* be allowed to end, depends on the particulars of a given case. Take yourself right now. You're sitting alone in a room with a murderer. Yet I've seen no trace in you of fear or discomfort. Why? Is it that you're such a good poker player? Or is it that you in fact feel no threat from me? Yet you have to make a report about me that might well harm me. Why not a *first strike* defense of myself against you? Why don't I try to kill you? Well, of course, that would be absurd. You, Doctor Lofgren, are not about to kill me, and that particular point is crucial. Joe Polito was going to kill me. He had in fact run me off the road in an event that might *already* have killed or maimed me. Then he further showed his ongoing malicious intent by the sadistically symbolic slaughter of my sheep!"

"Yes, I heard about that." Doctor Lofgren's words came across with genuine compassion. "Let's get together again tomorrow."

CHAPTER 27

Kevin felt disappointed the next day when he got the message. Doctor Lofgren had been unavoidably detained and would not be there until the following morning. Strange, he thought, that he should look forward to talking with this unknown man, a person whom he had not wanted to meet in the first place.

Confined to the ward because of the legal constraints, he felt restless. When the other patients went over to "The Old Barn" for Activities Therapy, only Kevin and two others were left behind. The old man had become even more confused at activities on the previous day, unpredictably assaulting one of the occupational therapists with a leather-working tool when she would not allow him to see his wife. The T-shirted man who had run screaming from his demons yesterday appeared perfectly lucid now. But the staff had evidently chosen to keep him under close observation for an additional time to make sure his condition had stabilized. He turned out to be a pretty pleasant guy (with a pretty unpleasant alcohol problem) named Joseph Green. The old man's name was Steven Walsh.

The young mental health workers were pleasant and respectful, except for their habit of addressing everyone by first name. He had winced at being called "Kev" and had said to the worker, "My first name is for friends, and you are not a friend of mine. Please call me Kiley when my name is in order." From that time on, all the staff had called him "Doctor Kiley."

As for friends, Bernie visited that evening, though he appeared uncomfortable in doing so—probably in part because of his unfamiliarity with a psychiatric ward. But also, Kevin thought, I've certainly become an embarrassment to him. They quipped for a short time about playing squash in the day room and such; then Bernie left. It was his only visit.

Later that evening, Linda came. She smiled broadly when she saw him, then immediately burst into tears.

"You'd better shape up," Kevin said humorously. "If they see your emotional lability, they'll keep you locked up too."

She threw her arms around him without hesitation or embarrassment. "Oh, Kevin," was all she said.

In response, a lightness gripped his head, and he seemed to levitate without effort. In that brief moment, she was literally everything to him—the wonder, the power, the receptiveness, the grandeur of the whole universe, refracted through the soft convexities of her body. Yet had she not rejected him when he'd needed her most? On the outside, none of these responses were evident, and his words came across only with a disengaging humor: "Hey, take it easy. . . . How've you been?"

She looked up into his eyes from where she had buried her head on his chest and said, "I'm sorry, Kevin. I'm so glad to see you."

"Well, I guess I do look more like one of the stray dogs down at the pound now than some wanton marauder." The words were spoken in a good-humored tone, yet their hostility and reproach were immediately evident.

Linda slipped her arms around front to his chest, holding his loosened blue sport shirt below the lapels with both her hands. Softly, she repeated, "I'm sorry." Then after a pause, she looked up—Kevin liked the anatomy of nature that usually caused women to look up to men—and her expression brightened happily. "I brought you something." She went over to the long, common-room table where she'd set down a bag, and uncovered a chocolate frappe and a big piece of cake wrapped in aluminum foil. "Here," she said.

Old Mr. Walsh, looking on from one of the day room chairs, commented, "Bringing your son his demmin."

"Well, she's bringing me a snack anyway," said Kevin good humoredly. "Come on over, Steve, and I'll give you some, and I'll introduce you to Linda."

The distance wasn't all that far across the room, but Mr. Walsh chose to continue the conversation from where he was already seated. He directed his next remark to Linda. "My wife's coming to see me—Mary."

"Oh, isn't that nice," she replied.

A pause followed, and his expression turned bitter. "They won't let her come. The bastards won't let her come!"

"Steve, don't bother her with that stuff." It was the voice of Joe Green, intervening tactfully. "Let's let them visit. Come on, I'll show you something in my room." And gathering the old man up, Joe guided him in friendly fashion out into the hall and into the multi-bedded room beyond.

Meanwhile, Kevin had unwrapped the large piece of chocolate layer cake and was making a big production out of examining it. Then he took the plastic fork from the enfolded paper napkin and made two or three preliminary passes down through the substance of the cake. Looking puzzled, he said to Linda, "I can't find it."

"Can't find what?" replied Linda. She tried to think what she had forgotten.

"You know—the file," said Kevin.

"The file?" Linda didn't know what he was talking about. *"Oh!"* And the light dawned. "Oh, yes, the file. I forgot the file." And she laughed happily, mostly out of relief that she'd gotten Kevin's attempt at humor. "Actually, I heard the bars here were made of krypton so you couldn't file your way through anyway," she quipped.

After a while, Linda noticed old Steve Walsh wandering around again, going no place in particular, and with no sign of recognition when his eyes caught hers. Turning to Kevin, she asked quietly, "Why doesn't his wife visit?"

"That would be pretty hard," answered Kevin. "I heard Tom, one of the mental health workers, saying that she's been dead a good twenty years."

"Oh, that's so sad," gasped Linda.

"Sympathy for another ole stray dog, huh?" said Kevin. "Well, I don't know if, on balance, it's so bad. At least it gives him the sense that he hasn't really lost her, that all he has to do is overcome these outside forces of evil and he'll have her back. And after all, there is some truth to it. What difference does it make really whether some evil men are keeping her away, or it's the evil in nature that's robbed him of his other half? Not to mention robbing him of the better part of his own half, with his brain cells shrunken like the mosquito population in a drained marsh."

"You mean, the way he thinks about his dead wife as still living comforts him?" Linda spoke, more to digest this consideration than to request an answer. Then she reflected, "It's still sad though. It's all just an illusion."

"Well," answered Kevin, "one way or another, all women are illusions in the lives of their men."

CHAPTER 28

The following morning, Kevin met with Doctor Lofgren again, right after breakfast. "Sorry about yesterday," the doctor said.

"That's okay. I know the feeling," said Kevin.

"Now let's see. Where'd we leave off?" The doctor took up a manila folder from his desk and surveyed the last page of his notes.

"With the killing—where else?" said Kevin.

"Yes," said Doctor Lofgren. "You had been explaining to me your action of self-defense. But are you absolutely certain you defended yourself against the right party?"

Kevin flushed. "Are you *absolutely certain* you're talking to the right party?"

Doctor Lofgren smiled disarmingly. "Who else but a psychiatrist would answer a question with a question?"

"Well, how do you know with *absolute* certainty," Kevin persisted, *"which* psychiatrist I am?"

"What's your point?" asked Doctor Lofgren seriously, though with a lack of any obvious counter hostility in his voice.

"Now it's your turn to answer a question with a question, huh? Well, let me repeat mine. How do you know with absolute certainty who I am?"

Doctor Lofgren scratched his head, like someone pondering his next move in a chess game. "I suppose, from a strictly philosophical point of view, I don't. But I do think, beyond a *reasonable doubt*, that you're Doctor Kevin Kiley."

"Why?"

"Because you were brought to the hospital by the court officers, so identified."

"You were here at the moment when they arrived?"

"No" said Doctor Lofgren quietly. "But the nurses recorded that fact."

"And how did *they* know for certain that the self-identified officers were actually what they purported to be?"

"Because the court had phoned ahead, saying that you would be coming at that time."

"Oh, you were absolutely certain that the voice coming across the telephone wire emanated from the court?"

"The newspaper stories, the call from your lawyer, the later call from the court, your arrival on schedule, your identifying yourself as Doctor Kiley. It all fit together, if not with absolute certainty, at least with probability beyond a reasonable doubt." Doctor Lofgren continued to speak calmly and patiently.

"Well, you didn't ask me about probabilities *beyond a reasonable doubt*," said Kevin. "You asked if I were *absolutely certain* I had the right party."

"Well, I'll say one thing, Doctor Kiley. I really am getting to understand your viewpoint a lot better. Let me tell you though why I asked about your certainty. I was reading the transcript of the probable cause hearing and noticed that Mr. Polito's defense lawyer cast some doubt on the identity of his client as the one who was perpetrating these crimes against you."

A long pause ensued. Just as the space at the end of a series of alphabetical letters communicates something specific—word ends here—the silence after Doctor Lofgren's statement coded a definite message: "Please comment on what I've just said." But Kevin felt ornery enough not to break the silence. Finally, Doctor Lofgren took the bull by the horns. "I was hoping you'd tell me your reactions to that court hearing—what you made of it."

"I made of it that I came out looking like an ass."

"But did it shake your own sense of certainty at all?" Doctor Lofgren persisted. "I mean, when the defense lawyer tricked you into misidentifying Mr. Polito's brother as the defendant, did it diminish your own sense of being sure?"

"*Sure*? Well, I was sure I'd been tricked. That's what I was sure of. No, I knew that Joe Polito was the one with the vendetta against me. I knew then. I know now. And I know that, if I hadn't been arrested, if I had been free to resume my life, the dangerous harassments and the constant threat of assassination would be over."

"I understand your subjective state of certainty," said Doctor Lofgren with his apparently unflappable calmness. "But could you give me the steps that led you to that inescapable conclusion? What was the *evidence* that convinced you?"

At this point, the obsessive side of Kevin's nature almost welcomed the opportunity to detail the data, perhaps to reassure and reconvince himself. He paused to recollect, then proceeded. "First, in over twenty years of practice, having seen well more than two thousand patients, Joe Polito was the first and *only* person to ever explicitly threaten me. When I, early on, noted that he was threatening me, he immediately denied that fact, indicating his awareness that such threats were against the law. In perfect time sequence, right after that, he accelerated his threats, but now without identifying himself. During this transition, however, there was only a gradual change in the quality of his voice, so that at first it was quite recognizable. I'm convinced he wanted me to recognize it, to know who was threatening me. Eventually he constantly used this angry semi-falsetto voice, but I could see the continuity. When you get calls like that, you find yourself paying pretty close attention.

"Oh, yes, I forgot to mention. *Motivation!* He had strong motivation, subjectively speaking, for his crimes. He held me responsible for everything, from the loss of face he experienced at not being considered a worker injured in the line of duty, to the impending starvation, as he put it, of his family.

"Well, back to the sequence of events. And I emphasize *sequence*. If some other persons had coincidentally decided to take a vendetta out against me, they would have done so at the precise moment in all these years when Joe had come out against me. He seemed to almost stumble on the word *Avenger*, in one of our conversations. From then on, that's what he used.

"He went from phone harassment to spiking my tires. And after that, frightening me half to death with those gunshots. Though his lawyer made me look silly, I *did* recognize his voice at that time. After our progressive series of telephone conversations, I would have recognized that voice *anywhere*. In fact, it *was* primarily by his voice that I recognized him, his voice and the subtle nuances of his not so subtle manner. That's why I was tricked so easily by his lawyer. I had seen him only one time before, in my office.

"But that court appearance gave further proof. Not that I needed any. Not the happenings in the courtroom itself, but right afterwards outside. A lot can be said in the moment of meeting between two people's eyes. He caught mine and fixed them for a sadistic moment with a telling leer. I should say perhaps a foretelling leer, because it foretold clearly the events to come.

"Then with perfect orchestration came the attempt on my life while I was in my car, and the slaughter of my sheep. When he agreed to meet me after that to take the money, he *knew* without hesitation what was motivating me: desperation from the mortal fear he had produced. That accounted for his sense of complete mastery in our relationship. I must admit I was a bit puzzled at the restaurant by his coyness in coming right out with all the facts. It's clear in retrospect that he wanted to force damaging statements from me about my disability report for whatever use he could make of them later. And probably, since he was recording me, it would be easy for him to believe I might be doing likewise."

As Kevin stopped for breath, Doctor Lofgren leaned back in his chair, pursing his lips slightly in indication that he was about to say something. Then he spoke speculatively, as if he were considering the cause of some event remote in history. "Do you think there's any other hypothesis that might explain the data?"

"What?"

"Is it possible that this Polito fellow, under the subjective stress of his circumstances, might have developed an acute dissociative state, a series of fugues during which he took on another personality, that of the Avenger?"

"Doctor Jekyll and Mr. Hyde? Two Faces of Joe? Another fictional thriller for our bookshelves?" Kevin's tone was heavy with sarcasm.

"You don't seem to think too much of that hypothesis. Don't you believe such states exist?" Doctor Lofgren's voice was almost cajoling.

"Two personalities? Two sides to a person? I'm sure there are more than a thousand and two. And I'm sure we sometimes literally don't let our left hand know what our right hand is doing."

Kevin, who taught as well as practiced, didn't hesitate in lecturing a fellow psychiatrist. "I've had many examples in my own life. One time years ago, for instance, when I was in the Navy and stationed in Philadelphia, I was preoccupied with some problem as I set out to drive. Ten minutes later, I realized I was well on the way to the Naval Hospital where I went each day, though in the opposite direction from my destination on this particular occasion. Who was driving the car all that time while 'I' was consumed elsewhere in my thoughts?

Who was negotiating all that traffic, stopping at streetlights, and avoiding pedestrians? Some other personality? Some other 'I' within me? And who is 'I' anyway? I can never seem to strip me away from some particular experience, or viewing some mental experience, or viewing the view, or the view of the view. It's like trying to peel off all the layers of an onion, closer and closer, until you get to what's left—nothing.

"But I'm getting off the point. Dissociative states occur. I've just illustrated that with myself. However, psychiatrists have sometimes shown such a fascination with their occurrence that they've at times unwittingly reinforced their prominence in their patients. After all, a patient is likely to develop whatever interests his doctor . . . once his doctor's attention becomes important to him.

"But from a practical point of view, suppose I had crashed my car while 'I' was elsewhere on that day's drive? Should I be held *not responsible* for the damages? After all, 'I' had not consciously chosen to leave the helm. Why not punish this unknown pilot within me who caused the wreck? Fortunately for me, my unknown inner pilot must have performed with attentiveness and skill, considering the traffic in that fair city. I would thank him now, if I knew whom to thank.

"And Joe Polito? What if he *did* have another pilot within his ship, steering him from time to time on his sinister course, rousing him from the lethargy of his home and bed to perform his diabolical tasks? Perhaps this alter ego was the *real* Joe Polito, and Joe himself was the everyday Clark Kent facade. Put all the facets together, whether or not they communicate consciously with one another, and they still add up to *one individual, one body*. I had to defend myself against this one body!"

"I hope you got the right body." Doctor Lofgren's words slipped out almost involuntarily, his tone quietly sad. A facet of him had gotten too involved. Then he seemed to recover, and he said with matter-of-fact brightness. "I'll see you again tomorrow."

CHAPTER 29

Kevin returned to the ward with a distress he could not identify. He felt strangely heavy in his chest, and each step felt burdensome. It was an effort even to stand upright, so he made his way to the cot assigned him and sat down. He could feel the nubby wool of the tan blanket (no bedspreads here) as he supported the weight of his torso with the angle braces formed by his two arms.

"Can I get you anything?"

Kevin looked up to see one of the workers standing in front of him, trying to be helpful. "No, thanks, Tom. Nice of you to ask. I'm just going to rest for a while if it's all right."

"Sure, Doc. Let me know if you need anything."

Kevin hardly heard. Stretching out on his back, hands folded behind his head, he stared at the ceiling's whiter shade of pale and tried to gather his thoughts. He wanted to account for the oppressiveness he felt. Why? Certainly Doctor Lofgren had been cordial enough to him, considerate, interested, not just going through the motions. Maybe *that* was it. Another human being, a doctor whom he had come to like, obviously doubted his action. "I hope you got the right body." . . . "I hope you got the right body." . . . "I hope you got the right body." It was the way those words just slipped out, inadvertently, but with concern.

Christ, he asked himself, did I kill the wrong man? And that thought erupted more vividly within him than the spoken word! No, came his replying thought, I am sure. Yet the oppressiveness remained. First, Mike Grady and now Doctor Lofgren, two people whom he respected, and they both doubted the certainty of his opponent's identity.

And the newsreel of memory suddenly played back a sequence that had been stored in the archives of his brain years before: Susan Eliot, an attractive woman with a dynamite figure, divorced after seven years of an unfortunate marriage, struggling to support herself and her young children. She came to see Kevin because of anxiety and depression. To his surprise, she had unveiled a delusion that spoke to the psychotic intensity of her disorder. She'd been involved in an affair with a well-known public official and had become convinced that he was sending his men around to follow her, to take care of her, and to keep her from any harm. Kevin had rendered support and medication to his patient. In their meetings, he had cast gentle doubt on her delusions. Gradually, her symptoms of emotional distress improved and, one day, she abruptly expressed insight into the delusional nature of her convictions. He had been pleased (prematurely, as it turned out) at the progress of his patient. Then she relapsed, not into psychosis but into a depression so profound that hospitalization became necessary.

Later, when she felt better again, she had provided the following account: "I came to realize that the affair which was so important to me was to him a casual dalliance outside of his marriage, and that my conviction about his men always helping me and protecting me anonymously was absurd. It's hard to explain the effect this had on me. Before that, I had been worrying about all my problems, but I didn't let them get me down. I knew he'd bail me out if I reached some point where I couldn't handle them myself. I was like some trapeze artist, walking fearlessly across a rope stretched over Niagara Falls—fearlessly, because I was holding on to a pole suspended from a firm guide-track above my head. Then as I got halfway out, happily hearing the roar of whitewater thundering over the falls immediately below, I looked up to find that I was holding on, not to a secure safety cord, but to the handle of a delicate parasol, balancing daintily in the breeze. . . ."

As usual with Kevin's vivid memories, this one subsided abruptly into the mysterious recesses from which it had just emerged. But it left him agonizing. Have I been deluding myself? Have I misidentified the evil that came my way? Have I killed the wrong man? Am I, in truth, a reckless murderer? And if so, could I possibly live with myself? He turned over restlessly onto his stomach, clawing at the sheets around his head, pulling the pillow down to his side, finally rocking his body back and forth, the balls of his feet pressing recurrently against the lower bed board, trying vainly to push himself away from his misery. But no way could he outdistance its dreadful intensity.

CHAPTER 30

"I saw from the nurses' notes that you didn't sleep too well last night." It was a preliminary remark by Doctor Lofgren. Like athletes on a field before the game, the participants in a psychiatric interview have to warm up a while too.

"No, the new fellow in the corner bed snored all night." Then Kevin smiled ruefully. "Besides, you've got me wondering. It boggles my mind that I actually killed another man. But I can live with that, since I know I had to defend myself. I know he would have killed me. But when you kept doubting who *he* was, it really upset me."

Doctor Lofgren nodded in understanding, but said nothing directly on the point. Instead, he changed the subject. "There's something I don't understand about you. You're intelligent, good looking, and charming. You're highly successful by the standards of our society. You're witty and have a feel for what goes on between people. I know from your background that you have in the past been elected to posts such as president of your hospital staff and, when you were in college, captain of the track team. In short, you have all the social skills necessary to be in the lively midst of everything. Yet you're really quite a loner. You're in solo practice. You live alone. You socialize little. And in your thoughts, you seem to be very much out of sympathy with our whole society. Why is that?"

"I don't really know," said Kevin.

"It's obvious that you want to share yourself, and you certainly must do so in your work," Doctor Lofgren continued supportively.

"Well, I do think the best part of me has gone into my work. I always wanted to be a doctor, from as long as I can remember. Going to medical school at a time of super specialization got translated into becoming a psychiatrist. I achieved my childhood goal, and I still felt empty. Of course, there were some other goals that sort of fell by the way. . . ." Kevin paused for a moment, then broke off the subject. "Well, that's got nothing much to do with my legal competency or sanity now."

"Please go on. I did, after all, ask you about yourself. I want to understand."

"Why? I'd say you already have enough of a mental status examination to render your opinion to the court." Kevin could observe his own walls involuntarily rising again. It's not the disclosures of intimacy that hurt. It's their aftermath, the vulnerability to rejection.

"I don't fully know why," answered Doctor Lofgren. "I do think I see in you an extreme form of myself, partly at least. And you can see things more clearly in their extremes than when they're mixed in more subtly. So perhaps by getting to know you, I'll get to know myself better."

"But, Doctor, that's not why we're here." Kevin spoke facetiously, knowing, however, that the point was a valid one.

"I know." Doctor Lofgren laughed. "But I thought you'd be less suspicious if I started with my most self-centered motivation. Fortunately, that goal's in the same direction as the need to understand what happened within the total context of *your* life."

Kevin continued to banter, "Why is it pertinent to understand the killing in—what did you say—the *total context* of my life? What difference does it make?"

"It'll help us understand why it happened."

"Doctor Lofgren, the scientist, huh?" said Kevin ironically. "Know all the antecedents and you can predict the outcome. Add hydrogen to oxygen, two parts to one, under known circumstances, and you will always get water. Bring pure water to a temperature of one hundred degrees Celsius at standard pressure and it will always boil. Arrange the precise series of events in the life of Kevin Kiley, and he too will boil over, killing such and such a person at exactly such and such a time in a thoroughly predictable fashion. Yes, sir, the ideal of scientific determinism lives on."

"That might well be so for any of us," replied Doctor Lofgren genially. "But of course we would never be able to discover or grasp the virtually infinite number of factors involved, not to mention the incredible complexity of their interaction. All we can hope to do is understand a rough outline—to make plausible what otherwise might seem incomprehensible."

"It seems incomprehensible to you that I'm a killer?"

"Well, you're not the most likely candidate, on the surface of things anyway."

"That's funny," replied Kevin, "I've always thought it harder to understand, given the raging passions I've seen smoldering beneath the surface of my acquaintances and patients, why *everyone* isn't a murderer. But anyway, your position seems as anomalous to me as the theologian who belongs to the God-is-dead school."

"What do you mean?"

"You keep looking for the psychological determinants of an action. Your ideal, granted that it's unattainable, would be to comprehend all the factors involved that determined my action. The court, on the other hand, is moving in the entirely different sphere of voluntarism. Its underlying assumption, and my own also, is that a man voluntarily chooses to do what he does, and that he could have done otherwise—in short, that his action has not been ineluctably determined by forces that impel him along the precise course of some final vector.

"I must admit that *free will*, like *love*, is one of those concepts whose meaning recedes the more you try to grasp it. I certainly have no wish to go to prison. But to think that I'm only the passive observer of my own acts, that I'm not responsible for the things I do—at least in regard to those major decisions that shape my life—is from my perspective a more chilling prospect still. In my opinion, all the court wants from you is a statement that there was nothing gross and obvious impairing my decision. That I didn't think, for example, that I was passing Joe an ice cream cone instead of the contents of a shotgun shell in rapid transit. Beyond that, a psychiatrist's concern about psychic determinism is about as meaningful to the law as is conversation after the second round of martinis at a cocktail party."

Doctor Lofgren listened patiently, then responded, "I understand the sensibleness of what you're saying. But each of us has to proceed in his own way through this controversial area. I still am very interested in the question I asked you."

"What was that?" Kevin turned from serious to jocular again. He realized that one function served by his effort to engage Doctor Lofgren in debate was to avoid personally painful investigation. He had observed that phenomenon frequently—from the other side—in his own patients. Yet he had not consciously chosen any such strategy. And he saw vividly at this moment the connection between conscious choice and the *sense* of exercising free will.

Doctor Lofgren had just summarized his question again, but Kevin, preoccupied with his own thoughts, had not even heard. "I'm sorry," he said. "My mind was somewhere else. Could you ask me again?"

"Why you're such a loner?"

Kevin laughed. "That's a pretty brief summation of your question, now that I recall. You're not taking any chances this time at overwhelming my attention span."

"It does seem like an emotionally charged subject for you."

"That's just an inference on your part because I keep getting off the subject you want to talk about. Actually, I don't know why I am, so I can't explain it to you."

"Maybe if you try to explain it to me, you'll get clearer on it yourself."

"Why, Doctor," said Kevin sarcastically, "that sounds to me like a definition of psychotherapy."

"I guess it is." It was Doctor Lofgren's turn to laugh.

"But we're not doing psychotherapy. You're examining me for the court, and anything I say may be used against me. I have no confidentiality with you."

"That's right," said Doctor Lofgren. "On the other hand, you don't seem to be denying the fact of the killing. And from your own point of view, you were responsible for your actions. Under those circumstances, I don't see how my report could possibly jeopardize your case further. And if the subtle data of *your own* justifications is to see the light of day in court, I might be a useful conduit for you in that regard.

"As to the issue of therapy, you would be the first to say that the labels we use hardly encompass all the dimensions of an activity. I understand you're a squash player. Well, I could say then that you're playing a game. But that certainly wouldn't mean that squash couldn't at the same time be described as getting exercise or as a way of socializing."

"You're right."

"You were starting to tell me about you're being alone so much."

"I was telling you about my difficulty in telling you, but tell me. Do you do much forensic psychiatry?"

"Not too much. Why do you ask?"

Kevin laughed, no longer unkindly. "You don't seem to know what you're doing."

"I figure that the court wants an opinion, from a person whose job it is on an ongoing basis each day to understand the mental and emotional determinants of human behavior."

"You understand the catch-22 of your position?"

"What's that?"

"My defense lawyer or the prosecutor, depending on which one doesn't like your testimony, will hammer home the limitations in your forensic experience. Of course, on the other hand, if you did a great deal of legal work, they'd attack you as a hired gun, an expert who sells out for money."

"Well, since the judge asked for my opinion, rather than the defense or the prosecution, I should be helped a little on that score."

"True . . . and judges, of course, are unbiased."

"No comment. As I recall, you were starting to tell me more about your somewhat solitary life."

"Right . . . but I notice I've just about used up my hour, Doctor."

"That's very nice of you, Kevin, to be so solicitous of my schedule."

Both participants knew the truth without having to verbalize it that Kevin was happy not to have to talk any more on this day. And as he left the office, he was glad that Bill Lofgren had chosen just this moment to address him by his first name.

CHAPTER 31

Kevin started right off at the beginning of the next meeting, "I've been thinking about that business of my being a loner. One of the keys is my *sensitivity*."

"Sensitivity?"

"Yes."

"What do you mean?"

"I'm too sensitive about things."

In order to illustrate what he was getting at, Kevin then recounted an early memory. As a small child, he'd been raised in a beautiful old house that featured, among other things, a formal wood-paneled dining room with fireplace. In the room's center stood a circular table, whose top had been fashioned from a horizontal slice taken from a mahogany tree of tremendous girth. On this table, his mother would from time to time place a vase of cut flowers.

On the occasion in memory, Kevin, who was probably about five years old at the time, had just come indoors and had walked into the dining room. But then a strange event occurred: instead of feeling happily appreciative as one might expect when gifted with such pleasant surroundings, he gazed at the freshly cut flowers and experienced a momentarily overwhelming sense of *melancholy*—a feeling for which he did not even possess a verbal label till later in his young life.

His memory also provided a clue as to *why* he'd experienced this rather odd response. It seems that the emotion had been accompanied by a thought that went in the direction of: those beautiful flowers will soon wilt and die. And it was this *sense of transiency* about all that he cherished, himself included, that had evoked his curious response.

"I think," concluded Kevin, "*that's* the sort of thing that made me a loner: my *sensitivity*. The day-to-day rubbing of elbows with other people that gives them more joy than pain, has so often given me more pain than joy. Factors you mentioned, such as my intelligence, have simply enabled me to have more control over the situation . . . to limit and structure my contact with others."

* * *

In subsequent interviews, Kevin continued to respond to the issue of his being a loner—an issue that Doctor Lofgren apparently considered of considerable importance, since social isolation can encourage the type of idiosyncratic thinking associated with paranoid behavior. It's the continuing feedback from others that helps keep an ordinary person's thoughts from straying too far from the beaten path. By contrast, the socially alienated person lacks much in the way of this corrective input.

* * *

During the session immediately following, Kevin revisited yet another painful memory of his childhood, an episode of personal cowardice that had hung over him for many years. In discussing the episode, he compared himself to Joseph Conrad's fictional antihero, Lord Jim.

"If you recall," said Kevin, "the story had to do with this idealistic young man who had all sorts of gloriously heroic fantasies about himself. He became a ship's officer, but during a horrendous storm at sea, he panicked and abandoned ship with the rest of the crew, leaving the passengers behind to perish. When a calm following the storm allowed the ship and passengers to be towed into port, that fact renewed a devastating storm in his own soul.

"Most people in his position would, of course, have felt terribly ashamed. But ultimately, they would have come to terms with the fact that they weren't such big deals after all. They would have told themselves that nobody's perfect. They would have put the past behind them and would have gone on to the next thing, sadder and wiser as the saying goes. But not Jim! He virtually *insisted* on an official inquiry with a public excoriation, then exiled himself to the boondocks where he became a hero—so terrified was he of his own cowardice, so cowed was he by his own humanity with its inherent limitations.

"When I first read the novel," Kevin continued, "I thought Conrad's character was an ass! Why didn't the fellow just accept his cowardly act—his less than superman status—and get on with his life? But I should've known: so often when we get impatient with another's ways, we're reacting to the same disowned traits in ourselves. Sometimes, I wish my incident had been as dramatic as his. But after all, that's what fiction does; it takes our own little private agonies and writes them large. At any rate, given the fact that my cowardice was trivial and that my overreaction therefore even more absurd, you'll have to bear with me.

"I'd say I was about eleven years old at the time, and since there were no boys my age in my immediate neighborhood, I had joined up with a group about ten minutes away. I was a reasonably good athlete, and I could more than hold my own with the others. They saw that in playful skirmishes, so I never had to get into fights the way they did along the way to establish the necessary pecking order. I say *necessary*, because it always seems to be necessary, whether it's trees striving upward for the sun's light, hens working out the order in which they'll have access to the available food at the trough, or young boys unwittingly—or half-wittedly—asserting their ontological importance before a peer group.

"For reasons that I'm still not clear on, I despised people throwing their weight around, and I tried never to do so myself. I sort of like that, by the way, about the young boy who became me. On the other hand, it may have been simply a more presumptuous form of arrogance on my part—that I was above all that.

"At any rate, this more or less satisfactory state of affairs was thrown into instability when a new boy moved in. Joe Doyle. He was smaller than most of us, though perhaps starting to mature early. Within weeks, the initial miscalculations of the group had been corrected. Based on size, the members would have figured him at the lower end of the pecking order—that is, if they had ever explicitly thought of such things—but he put them all down easily. He had fast hands, and, I heard, his father had taught him how to box.

"Well, one day when I wasn't even expecting it, he took me on, first with some trash talk. Then WHAP! The punch came so fast I didn't even see it, right in my bread-belly. That was all. That was the whole thing. It was all over. I wasn't knocked down. I wasn't knocked out. I wasn't maimed. The wind was knocked out of me a little bit, but I wasn't doubled over. He did have a hard punch though.

"We talked back and forth for a while after that. The other kids had all gathered around, shouting out their comments, like 'Let's get going.' . . . 'You've gotta fight.' . . . 'Let's get it over with.' Then they started saying: 'He's afraid of you, Joe. He won't fight you.'

"Completely beaten, crying abjectly, I walked away. And I never went back. I would circle blocks around to avoid any of them. But I couldn't walk away from myself, from my own shame and cowardice.

"You know, it still rankles me now to bring it up. And when I *do* think of it, the whole matter's still a puzzle to me. Why, for instance, could I never get myself to go back and challenge him alone? I could certainly see that, fast as he was, he *had* sucker-punched me. And later I learned that he had just fought to a draw with another boy whom I had, at the very least, held my own with in friendly roughhousing. This boy had wrestled Joe off his feet where his boxing skill was no longer such an advantage. That's what I should have done myself, of course.

"Or why didn't I come to terms with the defeat and just move down a notch on the pecking order? Most people have that much strength—the strength to adjust to their weaknesses. So why didn't I? The best answer I can come up with is my *sensitivity* again, which made my injured narcissism intolerable—made it unable even to risk further defeat.

"But I tell you one thing," Kevin had concluded emphatically at the session's end, "I sure wasn't about to let *that* happen to me again!"

CHAPTER 32

"What the hell's wrong with you, Doc?" It was the following day, and fellow patient, Joe Green, was asking the question—not in his usual jovial fashion, but with a measure of pique.

"Nothing, Joe. What's up?" Kevin spoke not altogether candidly. He'd been preoccupied with frustrations and misgivings about his childhood cowardice ever since his session with Doctor Lofgren—troubled by a sealed-over scar from childhood rubbed freshly raw.

"When I said *hello* just now, you didn't even answer."

"Sorry, Joe. Guess I was preoccupied."

"I want to talk to you."

"What's on your mind?"

Joe sat down at the day room table directly across from Kevin before he continued, "You're a doctor, and there's something I've gotta talk over."

"I'm also a patient," Kevin said with a smile. "But go ahead."

"It's my wife. She's leaving me. She just brought over some divorce papers for me to sign."

"I'm sorry."

"I told her if that's what she wanted, she could have it. I signed the goddam papers and threw them back at her, then walked out. Good riddance."

Kevin nodded. "Well, it's true, you did mention a couple of days ago that she was such a flaming bitch, she drove you to drink."

"You'd better believe it. I'm better off without that cunt anyway!"

"I know *goodbyes* are always hard though. How long'd you say you were married, fourteen years or so?"

"It'll be *fifteen* this spring."

"That's hard."

"*Hard*? I just can't do it! Here I am trying to straighten my life out, trying to get off the booze, and she comes along and throws a monkey wrench in the whole fuckin' works."

"It's tough."

"What a bitch. What a fuckin' bitch." Joe slammed his right fist on the table. "How the hell does she expect me to survive? Get a room somewhere? Visit my two kids on Sunday mornings? Well, she can just go fuck herself! That's what she can do." Joe spat the words out in bursts of angry phrases.

"It's a bad situation all right." Kevin's words evoked a continuing tirade from a man whose anger toward his wife was surpassed only by his emotional dependence on her. Meanwhile Kevin's own anger swelled, as he attended mostly to an inner rage at Joe Polito for threatening his life, and even at Joe Doyle for devastating his childhood self-esteem. He hardly heard what Joe Green was ranting on about, though he did register a pause in the barrage of words and then recognized he was being called upon to speak.

"What d'you think I ought to do?" Joe was asking.

Kevin resented the intrusion at this inopportune time, but tried to stay with it. "Well, maybe it's for the best right now," he heard himself saying.

"For the *best*? How the hell can you *say* that?" Joe was obviously not going to take any disagreement on the subject lying down.

"Well, Joe, you want to give up the booze. But from your point of view, she's always aggravating you and driving you to drink. If that's really so, you're going to be much better off, because she won't be around to accomplish that. If, on the other hand, you've been using her as a scapegoat, you'll find that out too, and it should help you in the long run."

"What? You some sort of crazy doc or something? You're off in the wrong direction! The thing here is *trust*. I promised her that I'm *not* gonna drink again. She's got to *trust* me, and she won't. She won't take my word for it! She thinks I'm lying."

Kevin felt impatient, just wanting to end the whole conversation. "Look, Joe," he said, "I'm sorry you're so upset about your wife leaving. But from what you told me, it may be the first sensible thing she's done in the past two years. You've been in three detox centers already in the last year and a half before coming here. If she'd been a *saint*, which she apparently isn't, she'd have been out of her gourd by now. You can't legitimately promise her *anything* at this point. And you can't even promise *yourself* that you're not going to drink. All you can do, which I hope you will do, is take it the AA way, one day at a time." Kevin accentuated the last phrase with pauses, then continued, "Words in themselves are empty containers until they're matched up with actions. You're asking your wife right now to take the equivalent of a promissory note for a million dollars, with absolutely no collateral. What you've got to do is build some up. Go six months or so without drinking. Show her, don't tell her."

"You're sick, you know that? You're really *sick*! I've got to be some sort of asshole for even trying to talk to you about it." Joe was livid. "You goddam shrinks are all the same anyway. You're all crazy. That's why you went into the business in the first place, to cure your own fuckin' problems. Well, let me tell ya, you haven't made much progress. In fact, I'd say you've gone downhill pretty fast. You get a crazy notion that some guy's bugging you and ya blow'm away! Jesus. I'm glad you don't have a gun with you now. My brains would be *splat* on the wall. But I'll bet you're a yellow bastard when you don't have a gun. If you tried anything now, I'd cold-cock ya."

Of the entire fusillade, only the part about being cowardly hit home. Kevin got the urge to swing at Joe in order to prove he wasn't yellow. Instead, he cussed inwardly at his own ridiculousness. Then he shifted into his professional persona, his suit of armor. He saw how much Joe was hurting right now. And he realized that, through his own impatience, he had just added to Joe's hurt by clobbering him with insight. The angry striking out in return was reflexly predictable. So Kevin didn't say anything for the moment, which gave the other man's cauldron a chance to simmer down.

Joe still needed to talk. Desperately. "You don't understand. I need that woman. I can't live without her! I can't just walk away and pretend that was a part of my life that never was. We've been through thick and thin together. We have two children together. We were supposed to spend our whole lives together."

"I know," said Kevin. He could feel the hurt from his own personal memories reach out empathically toward Joe. And at the very same time, he could hear in his imagination the strains of an old ballad triggered by Joe's repetition of the word *together*. That old love song started playing melodramatically in the background of his mind, giving testimony to the repetitive pinings of brokenhearted lovers from a previous generation.

"No, you *don't*!" Joe's angry retort interrupted Kevin's inner musings once again. "You don't know *at all* how I feel! You've never gone through anything like this. You're a doctor. Everything's gone smoothly for you up to this point in your life, so you just sit there like a goddam dodo bird. You really are sick, ya know that, Doc? In fact, you didn't even try to disagree when I said you went into psychiatry to cure your own problems."

Back from no problems to mucho problems again, Kevin thought. With a smile now, he said, "Why should I, Joe? You were right. I don't think anyone would be attracted to the field unless he had had to deal with lots of emotional pain himself. But a psychiatrist's own emotional problems can give him insight and empathy into his patient's difficulties, as long as the psychiatrist is more or less on top of things in his life at the time he's trying to help his patient. That's what went wrong for you just now, Joe, when you needed some help. I was too tied up with my own can of worms."

"Yeh, that makes sense. Hey, Doc, I'm sorry I unloaded on you."

Kevin smiled. "You sure were angry." Then, after a pause, he asked, "Say, has anyone ever called you Mean Joe Green?"

Joe smiled back. "That's really young, Doc. Oh-riginal! Ever think of writin' some stuff for Johnny Carson?"

Their eyes meeting, Kevin and Joe laughed out loud. They were friends again.

CHAPTER 33

Perhaps because Doctor Lofgren's professional background had been in psychoanalysis—or possibly because he shared the common-sense view that a boy's relationship with his mother significantly influences his subsequent outlook on life—the doctor spent significant time in trying to understand this aspect of the murderer's background.

And when asked to say something about his mother, Kevin had responded immediately in a serious tone, "She's the one who's responsible for all my troubles."

"Why?"

"Without her," Kevin answered, "I wouldn't be here to be in this mess." Only then had Doctor Lofgren realized that Kevin was kidding him about the perhaps excessive tendency of psychiatrists to make a great deal over this primal relationship.

Nevertheless, the doctor had persisted in his inquiry, and the following picture had gradually emerged: Kevin had been his mother's odds-on favorite, a position in life that had made the young boy feel rather like a conquistador. Yet his very good fortune had its downsides. For since his mother always seemed to be standing on her head for him, his tendency toward a grandiose overestimation of himself became enhanced—not to mention his natural aptitude for being excessively self-centered.

And in more recent times, Kevin had noted a subtle downside accompanying the upside of his attendant degree of self-confidence. Here's one of the ways he illustrated the point: "My mother and I were walking along the sand of Nantasket Beach near the water's edge. I might have been in the second or third grade at the time. Anyway, we came across a neatly constructed sand castle with moat and wall, and with its owner not there to protect his work. For some reason, I got this awful urge to crush it underfoot. But just then, an inner voice cried out DON'T—loudly enough that at the last moment I neatly stutter-stepped around, leaving the castle intact.

"My mother applauded. 'Kevin,' she said, 'you're so good. Another boy would've wanted to smash the sand castle, and that would have made somebody very sad.' I beamed. And the lost pleasure of my destructiveness was more than compensated for by the reflected joy I felt in my saintliness. What a good boy was I. And my mother loved me! Like a rock. Yet I had this uncomfortable feeling underneath. I *was* that other boy who would have smashed the sand castle and reveled in its squishing."

"If I understand correctly," Doctor Lofgren had subsequently summarized, "your mother idealized you to such a degree that it became difficult for you to develop a realistic appraisal of yourself, particularly in regard to accepting your limitations and imperfections. Also, I gather, your excessively idealized relationship has been associated with some problems between the two of you in more recent years?"

"When I look back," Kevin had continued, "I can readily see that my un-choice of mother led to my choice of wife."

"How's that?"

"Adriana was a nice average girl, with one exception. She thought I was some sort of god. She stood on her head for me. I couldn't figure out afterwards why I hadn't courted one of the foxy ladies, but it's easy to see now. They all have a bunch of young bucks huffing after them. They have the disadvantages of their *own* narcissism to attend to. They need to be chased. But that wasn't in the game plan I'd been trained for. The woman in my life was supposed to recognize all of my *wonderful* qualities spontaneously. No crass salesmanship from me.

"Adriana filled that role. Except for the fact that the honeymoon was over even before the honeymoon was over—though we staggered along in a series of poorly comprehending compromises for almost twenty more years. Though she must've been standing on her head for me during our courtship, all the time she had a private image of chiseling me into some finished product of her own sculpting efforts.

"During one of her later harangues, for instance, she was complaining about my lack of sociability, my refusal to go to cocktail parties, my reading every night instead of watching some program on the boob tube with her, and a whole bunch of other stuff. Summing up, she said almost wistfully, 'Kevin, when we married, I was hoping you would change.' With equal plaintiveness, salted with a pinch of sarcasm, I replied, 'That's funny, Adriana. When we married, I was hoping you *wouldn't!*'

"But I could no more have solved my marriage problems at the time by divorce than I could solve my financial problems now by robbing a bank. As a strict Catholic, divorce was unthinkable. So I staggered along, trying to accentuate the positive. My veneer of matter-of-factness told me that no marriage was perfect. I guess I told myself a whole bunch of other compensatory half-truths too. But the veneer got to rubbing very thin.

"The ironic thing is, I think our religious subculture's law about the *indissolubility* of marriage ruined the best chance at solution. After marriage, Adriana didn't really change, I suppose, any more than the used-car salesman does. It's just that the conditions of your relationship are changed, once you've bought the car. The conditions of the relationship between me and Adriana were drastically changed, once she got the 'no-cut contract.' She had *security*. She didn't have to stand on her head anymore. She could go on to the next item on her agenda. Ironic though—just when no-cut contracts were coming into football, they were going out of marriage!"

Kevin, who'd obviously given the matter considerable thought even before Doctor Lofgren inquired about the issue, spontaneously linked the relationship with his mother to the one with his wife. Here's how he expressed himself:

"It wasn't until I left my wife for another woman that the *fantastic* nature of my relationship with my mother became apparent to me. 'Don't think you can walk out on your wife,' she said, 'and still maintain your relationship with me. Go home where you belong, to your wife so she won't divorce you, to your child who needs you. You won't be welcome here again until you do that!'

"I walked out of her house . . . just walked away. I didn't say anything about my side of the story. I wasn't about to go into personal details. Anyway, from my point of view, the reasons weren't relevant. It didn't matter *what* I did. My mother was supposed to love me *unconditionally*. Well, of course, she didn't. Nobody does. It's just a nice fiction, a happy idea.

"What human beings can accept another unconditionally, when they can't even accept themselves in that way? And I could immediately see that fact in reference to my mother. I just hadn't ever thought about it before. And, after all, my behavior to a devout Catholic of her generation was so gross that it had temporarily removed the blinders from *her* eyes. She saw me more as I was—more as I *am*—than as her fantasies had constructed me.

"And as the scales fell from her eyes, my scales fell away too. She had never been challenged before. Why shouldn't she have accepted me? I had made her proud by my achievements, and I had never really done anything much wrong. She wasn't *bad*. It's just that she wasn't all that good either. In my *mind*, I can understand and accept her limitations. But in my *heart*, I've never been able to. Like Adriana, she promised something that wasn't there to give, and I can never forget the fact that, when I was *down*, she was *out*."

CHAPTER 34

That same evening Linda arrived at the closed ward, on time as usual for the beginning of visiting hours. "*You* look cheerful," she said.

"Why shouldn't I?" replied Kevin. "Another visit from Florence Nightingale to the wounded animal ward." Though the words were said in jest, they hurt. (Sensitive people can sometimes be maddeningly insensitive to the feelings of others.)

But Linda managed to muster a smile and say, "Look what I brought!"

Kevin laughed. "Just what I always wanted, Mallomars and milk." He really did feel pleased, not as much for the snack as for her continuing thoughtfulness.

"How did everything go today?" Linda asked.

"Fine. How about yourself?" He had opened the milk carton and was inserting the plastic straw.

"Okay. Did you see Doctor Lofgren?"

"Yes."

"What did he have to say?"

"Not much. You know what shrinks are like. He mostly listens." The trace of a twinkle entered Kevin's eyes.

"Do you think he's going to be helpful?" Linda asked with obvious concern.

"He already has been. He really *does* listen, and it's been a good outlet to talk."

"I mean, do you think he'll be helpful to you in court?"

"How could he possibly be? He knows I'm as sane as you are . . . well, maybe a little bit more."

"Still, Kevin. That wasn't like you." Linda's voice trembled ever so slightly, even though she tried to remain matter-of-fact.

"Let's not go through that one again." Impatience entered Kevin's voice. "It wasn't like me because I was never put in that position before."

"Well, Doctor Lofgren might think that the terrible time you'd been through upset you to the point where it temporarily disturbed your judgment. I mean, that sort of thing *can* happen!"

"That's great," Kevin replied sarcastically. "If I'm really lucky, Doctor Lofgren will think I'm crazy. Oh no, not crazy so they'll lock me up for life. *Temporarily* insane. Then they can let me back on the street again—until my next relapse. Yes, what a wonderful prospect to look forward to." His voice had taken on a bitter edge. "One of the most severe crises of my life, one that I meet head-on without flinching, one that I take step by step, trying to handle with the least force necessary, one that leads ultimately to the coolly premeditated decision that I've got to defend myself to the extreme or accept the premature termination of my life, and I'm to be told officially by the society in which I live that I'm not responsible? That an action I consider a supreme human choice was no choice at all? That my carefully considered act lacked human freedom? That my behavior was as determined as that of an arch-building termite? What a wonderful prospect! But no thanks. I'd just as soon be sane, if it's all the same to you."

Linda felt swept up by a counter agitation, and her voice turned pleafully louder. "Kevin, *please*! Don't get carried away on one of those philosophical trips about existential freedom or whatever. You always said it was important in life to be practical. Well, this is a time to be *practical*. It's not for you or me to decide how a severe stress might have influenced your actions. That's up to the doctor and the court, and, I guess, finally the jury. The way you're looking at things right now, you'll have yourself in a no-win situation."

"No win. That about sums it up all right," he said without emotion.

"Kevin, Walpole isn't like here." She spoke apprehensively.

"What's your point?" Kevin replied. "What am I supposed to do about that right now? Dwell on it? Make myself sick worrying about it? Maybe act sick with Doctor Lofgren? After all, a psychosis has no objective signs—no x-ray changes, no diagnostic blood tests. Should I make up a couple of delusions, sprinkle in a few voices from God, throw in some random acts of bizarre behavior, practice talking ragtime, is that what you'd want me to do?"

"I'm sorry Kevin. I shouldn't have said that. I'm just worried."

"I've thought about Walpole too," he said, more reflectively now. "I can't really imagine what it's like, though the newspaper accounts are horrendous. That scares the bejesus out of me. Not the prison cells. Did you know, when I was in college, I had fantasies of becoming a Trappist?"

"No." Linda smiled as she thought of a womanizing monk.

"Well, I did. I think it started after I read Thomas Merton's *Seven Story Mountain*, an account of his life leading to the Monastery at Gethsemane. It did leave out a few details, like about his out-of-wedlock child who later died in the London blitz. Imagine the emotional impact of that on his life, and his superiors wouldn't let him put it in the book. Too racy, I guess. They probably would have censored *The Confessions of St. Augustine* too."

Linda smiled again and Kevin got the message.

"I still have a way of rambling off the point, don't I? At least I'm no stranger to you in that respect." Kevin laughed. "Well, a prison cell might not be that far from a monk's cell, and that part of it I think I could take. A religious order of one, with no founder to revere, no organization to write bylaws for, and no need to proselytize for new members to achieve the illusion of permanence. No need to fast, just eat the prison food. No need to seek penance, just endure the whips and scorns of prison life. No need to escape the distracting allurements of the world, just gaze at the small dull walls enclosing fifty-four square feet and turn inward—inward to the infinite reaches of the human soul, window to the Godhead.

"But back to reality," he continued. "It would be the other people, that pure distillate of all the Leroy Browns in Massachusetts, meaner than junkyard dogs, either lacking a moral sense to begin with, as thalidomide babies lacked proper arms, or having that highest human faculty beaten out of them by the meanness of their life experiences. I would be subject to the physically strongest or most aggressively sadistic of them. Living in constant fear of their physical brutality and emotional domination. My punishment would be the return of one hundred Joe Politos, and with far fewer resources to protect myself. No, I just don't think I could hack it. I'd have to find some other option."

"What could you do?" asked Linda.

Kevin laughed. "*Fortunately,* we always have one option left, though we're cleverly programmed by nature to dread it."

Not knowing what he meant, or at least reluctant to face it, Linda asked, "What do you mean?"

"To shuffle off this mortal coil."

"Suicide?"

"Right."

"You wouldn't!"

"Seems to me we went through this before the last killing."

Linda shuddered. "No, I don't even want to talk about it."

"Okay."

A short pause ensued. But Linda couldn't let the subject go. "Would you *really*?"

Kevin laughed coldly. "Well, you've said yourself I'm pretty much down to a no-win situation. It's comforting to know I always have that ace up my sleeve—or in some other aperture—for when I really need to opt out."

"But you're the one who's always dreaded death so much. You've always regretted how short life is. How can you even *think* of such a thing?" Linda was taking his implied threat quite seriously this time.

"You know what the Elusive Dreams said."

"Elusive Dreams?"

"Yeh, the country group in their song 'Blue Cowboy'—terrific song."

"What are you getting at?"

"One of the verses goes: 'Ride, cowboy, ride, though you can't find your place, Ride, cowboy, ride, though you're losin' the race, Lookin' for something that won't have to end, You'll prob'ly find that death is your friend.' "

"I remember now." Linda shook her head. "It figures that's the part you'd recall. But the ending went something like: 'Meanwhile, I'll tell you, *Life* is your friend.' "

"Yep, it's your basic human ambivalence again," Kevin said, as lightheartedly as if he were discussing the merits of a Caesar salad. "When you die, you miss all the pleasures of life. But you miss all its pain too. In modern medicine, with our incredible yet low-level technology, we can keep life going at subsistence levels long after its flame would have been naturally extinguished. But to what end? Doctors talk about the *quality of life*. If the quality gets bad enough, life's no longer worth sustaining. I think, for me, Walpole will probably do the trick in that respect. Unless I retreat to the cowardice of my childhood."

"You mean, if they sent you there?" To Linda, the conversation was half-frightening, half-just talk.

"No, before that. Though I try to be independent of others, I'm a herd animal in my basic nature. I'd want to make a public statement in front of an official audience."

"What do you mean? Where would you do it?" Linda thought she knew what he meant, but she wanted to be sure.

Kevin laughed lightly again. "That's my secret. I'm not going to tell you everything. Statements are more effective when their format is not fully predictable."

"How would you do it?" Linda paused. "Not with a gun?" The tone in her voice slid once more from matter of fact to distressed.

"Where would I get hold of a gun? I think my jailers would take a rather dim view of my carrying one. Besides, though I have no dread of my decomposing body after death, I seem to have emotional qualms about its state at the moment of my demise. I wouldn't at all mind my carcass being dissected by a medical student. In fact, I would welcome the opportunity to be of help, as a nameless benefactor once helped me in my anatomical studies. But at the very moment of death, it repels me to splatter my body around. No, I would prefer a more subtle derailing of my organism's activities. Lock the cytochrome systems up sub-microscopically in all my cells, and the motion I call life will grind to a halt within minutes, consciousness maybe within seconds, while breathing out the sweet aroma of almonds."

"Cyanide?"

"Hey, that would be an idea, wouldn't it?"

"I hope you can't get any!"

Kevin laughed again. "That's too bad. And I was hoping you'd help! But I suppose the truly prudent person would have prepared himself for a contingency like that beforehand. He would have laid away more than enough, in a container that could be cleverly secreted."

Linda shook her head back and forth, as if she'd just eaten something revolting. "I don't want to talk about it anymore."

Kevin smiled agreeably. "Okay, what do you want to talk about?"

"I guess I can't let go. What sort of message would you be wanting to give if you . . . if you did . . . ?"

With apparently high spirits, which stood in marked contrast to the pathological conversation, Kevin asked, "Do you remember our visit to Puerto Rico?"

"Would I ever forget?"

"I hope not. Well, you remember our driving down along the east coast and then over to Ponce on the south shore. And though the old Capitol had lost luster, its Art Museum was truly wonderful."

"Oh. That large painting you stood and stared at?" Linda was getting keyed in on Kevin's train of thought, thanks to their shared life experiences.

"Right. *The Suicide of Seneca*. I don't even recall who did it. But I remember you thought I was being morbid as I was trying to take it in. The impact has stayed with me. Though for the life of me, I can't picture the painting all that clearly in my head. I've never wanted to look for a copy of it since, because I've been afraid that would lessen its effect. You remember, the painting had to be several feet high. Miniaturizing would destroy the power it exerted over me. Besides, my mind has no doubt worked the thing over so that it's far distorted from the author's original vision." Kevin added facetiously, "But, I don't want anyone straightening me out now with the irrelevant details of the original work.

"Anyway, I remember Seneca sitting alert and purposeful in his final moments of consciousness, ashen white in his color as the blood drained from the self-inflicted lacerations of his extremities. Scribes and students earnestly surrounded him to write down his final words of wisdom. He'd been condemned for plotting Nero's overthrow, but had been given the opportunity to take his own life. And he did it. He, who must have loved life and who lived it so successfully in the eyes of the world, chose the right moment to die. That's what I think intuitively attracted me. And the gathered scribes, with quill pens busily at work? Their impact lay in the futility of their written words. His message at that point rested in his action, not in his words, trivial or profound as they might have been. The artist could capture that message visually perhaps, but the writer would fail."

"Well, Kevin, what choice did he really have? They were going to kill him anyway."

"Of course, he had a choice! Most people would have clung to each miserable moment of life until they were dragged kicking and screaming to a more miserable death at the hands of an executioner. He knew the moment that was fitting, and he exercised his choice. You know, people have pooh-poohed Socrates along similar lines— that he was old and beginning to fail, so it wasn't as if he was magnificently giving up the fullness of life for a noble cause. He was just opting out of a decrepit old age at the moment of greatest dramatic impact. Well, fine. I salute him for choosing his time and place! We are all condemned to die. Not just Seneca or Socrates.

"Reminds me of the old story about the general who was sentenced to death for trying to overthrow the czar. Since the fellow was such a decorated officer, the czar told him that he would be given the right to choose his means of execution. Reflecting on the matter carefully overnight, he finally told the czar his choice: old age!"

"At least your sense of humor hasn't changed," Linda said, lifting her eyes ceilingward.

"Well, you just think," said Kevin, "how many patients in the hospital cling to every last miserable crumb of life. It's fashionable to blame the doctors. And Lord knows, they deserve their fair share of abuse for having lost sight of the forest for the trees. But more patients and families than not opt for pulling out all the stops rather than for pulling out the plug. I hope I'll have the courage when my time comes . . . when the moment is right."

"If that means *soon*, I don't want you to. I'll visit you, Kevin. I'll help. You're important to me. And Mike can probably get you out of Walpole to someplace else."

Kevin's face darkened. Was it that being important to somebody weakened him, weakened his resolve? "Sure, Linda. You can be one of the prison groupies—one of the women flirting with cons because she can have her romantic fantasy without the aggravations of living with the reality. The *Redemptoress Fantasy* of saving the poor wretch from his sins. That'll be just great. And when reality calls you to a new relationship, think of the exquisite agonies of inner conflict you'll be able to experience. Which one of the stray animals tugging on your heartstrings could match that one in poignancy?"

"You're trying to hurt me now," exclaimed Linda, "in order to save yourself pain. The pain of your closeness to me. You've got to forgive me. Even Christ forgave Peter, not one, but three denials, because he knew Peter was a human being. Human beings stick with each other despite their lapses. If Christ who's supposed to be God could forgive someone letting Him down, you've got to do it too."

Kevin laughed, half in bitterness, the other half in affection. "Your reasoning's a little off. It's not just the magnitude of any offense against the Almighty. 'To forgive's Divine', remember? And that doesn't fit me, unless you want to put me back up on my pedestal again."

"I don't need a pedestal for you. I'm committed to you and that's that."

Kevin was silent now. He felt oppressed. And unexpectedly—to him—his eyes went wet. "You're really nice, you know," is all he said.

CHAPTER 35

Every societal grouping that has managed to extend itself for even a single generation has done so by forming a harbor where its constituent vessels may be moored in orderly fashion. And woe to that individual who loses his moorings, because then he is subject to aimless drift. Or worse. Such were the reflections of Doctor Lofgren as he continued to interview the unlikely murderer in his charge. The doctor noted that, one by one, Kevin seemed to have lost the multiple moorings that work in concert to fasten the normal individual to his society's ways. And once untethered from his moorings—or so Doctor Lofgren judged—Kevin's susceptibility to an idiosyncratic and paranoid mode of thinking had relentlessly taken over. It is after all not for nothing that ardent voices in our society decry the loss of "family values," or "religious values," or "patriotic values," since these three are amongst the ordinary individual's central moorings in life. And Kevin seemed to have suffered key losses in each of these areas.

The loss of family had extended beyond separation from his wife and estrangement from his mother to involve both children—though the loss of his only son had occurred years before. When John, not yet turned four years of age, managed to unclasp their front gate and wander onto the street, he'd been hit by a passing automobile. Modern medicine saved his life, but his severely injured brain could provide no more than dimly fluctuating consciousness housed in a spastically discontrolled body. On good days, when he was capable of limited eye contact and the production of inarticulate sounds, his parents read glimpses of recognition into his reactions. On bad days, they struggled to take care of him, for whom he once had been.

Following a year and a half of almost total care, John developed fatal meningitis, contracted by way of a tiny fistula that had developed between the fluid surrounding his brain and the inner passage of his nose. Perhaps because at that point Kevin's irreplaceable loss was confounded by a guilt-provoking sense of relief, his grieving became prolonged, if not macabre. Here's a pertinent sample of his response, as he explained it to Doctor Lofgren:

"After John died, we buried his remains in an old cemetery right near our tennis club. The first few years I used to go over there a lot.

I'd park outside the gate and wander along the road that slanted up through rows of tombstones, looking like obstacle courses on grassed fairways. The gap just before the top of the rise and opposite the big oak was where his remains were buried. No gravestone. We were always going to arrange one, but we never seemed to get around to it.

"Some summer days, I'd sit by myself, shaded by the oak leaves, feeling the hot breeze off the blacktop mellowing as it wafted across the grass. I'd pretend John and I were in eternity together, and I'd try to think what it was going to be like when we were reunited. He would be made whole, of course, with a beatified body. But how old would he be? Would we be able to talk as you and I are talking now, as adults? Would some fast-forward time machine enter the Hereafter to run his body quickly through to the first bloom of young manhood? Or would we romp effortlessly through the fields of forever as man and young boy, snapshot frozen through all eternity at that moment which represented the zenith of our temporal relationship here on earth. But I didn't want *that* kind of forever. I wanted to be able to talk to him, man to man.

"So would I be fast-forwarded to, say, my present year, to keep the age discrepancy in proportion for all time—*beyond* all time? What then if he had lived till sixty? Would I have been transmuted to the age of eighty-plus, with wrinkles and white hair made lusterful in my beatitude? Not to mention the full restoration of gyri and sulci to my brain, all my nerve cells reclaimed in order to contemplate John and the Beatific Vision with the fullest human aptitude? Surely, if I lasted on earth into my dotage, I would not be required to live an eternity of senescence, albeit a glorified one! Only primitives held notions like that, and I'm told they sometimes went around knocking off their elderly loved ones to forestall such an eventuality.

"Maybe our bodies would be irrelevant. Maybe we'd really be disembodied spirits with ghostlike forms resurrected to represent the good old days in time, but changed just enough that Robert Redford wouldn't be better looking than I. These forms would never get sick, and could pass through distances at will, of course. Not to mention walls. So if John and I took a heavenly motorcycle ride together, we wouldn't have to worry if we wiped out on an old stone wall when we hit the turn wrong. But then, where would the excitement be without the risk?

"And if John and I contemplated the Vision of God, would we even notice each other except in passing. I mean, if a man leaves his father and mother to cleave to his wife, just imagine what would happen when he got a chance to unite his mind and his loins with the Ineffable! No, the more I thought about it, the more I realized that my life with John was gone forever; that is, the life with John that I longed for as a young father.

"I got to seeing in detail that what we really want in Heaven—what we humanly want in the vision of our own personal immortality—is the continuation of our earthly existence, with more of the pleasures and none of the pains. That gets pretty hard to achieve, even in principle, when you consider that pain is the other side of pleasure—and there'll never be a one-sided coin, even in the land of Zen."

* * *

A more ordinary response to loss also occurred within Kevin. He had taken to second-guessing himself, in spite of his best efforts to forego that self-defeating mode of picking at wounds: "If only I'd had a childproof latch installed on the front gate . . ." But perhaps the most bizarre feature of Kevin's prolonged response to his son's death was his latter-day effort to become, in his own words, "The good shepherd." This time, as he put it, he was "going to get it right." Little did the villain who massacred his sheep know—or so Doctor Lofgren later reflected—how frighteningly effective this sadistic act would prove to be in symbolically unhinging his victim.

* * *

Kevin's loss of his daughter had happened less definitively, albeit devastatingly in its own way. When he'd separated from his wife, Adriana had felt an overwhelming need for allies. The ordinary father under such circumstances would have fought to maintain the relationship with his daughter. But, unfortunately, wooing women had never been in Kevin's repertoire, and it was not destined to start at this point, even in the case of Jessica. Here's a brief sample from Doctor Lofgren's transcript, one that will indicate additionally that Kevin had never really gotten over his daughter's loss:

"A few days beforehand—she was eleven years old then—I told her I was moving out of the house. I'll never forget that. I took her for a ride and talked to her as we were going along. Her face had gotten serious, because, of course, my manner had indicated some difficult business. When I finally broke the news, she said nothing. Not one word. Her face stayed the same, no change. Then after what seemed an interminable period, her eyes grew moist, and a single tear formed. I watched as it moved slowly, endlessly, down her cheek, just missing the quivering corner of her lip and leaving a path like some evanescent jet trail in the sky. That was all. The most devastating understatement I've ever experienced. From that moment until the present day, she's never really talked to me. Since then, she's treated me like a cordial stranger. She never challenged me, never once asked why I left, never ever asked me to move back. She's just always been somewhere else, right now in Portland—west coast Portland, that is."

"Has she written, has she phoned . . . since this problem came up?"

"No."

"That must hurt a lot right now."

"No. The hurt's been gone for some time. All that's left is a little numb. It's funny how things turned out. When she was little, I felt so close that I could never even imagine us separated. Just shows you, you should never trust feelings too much. What I see better in retrospect is how my way of relating to my mother shaped my relationship to Jessie as well as to Adriana. You see, I had this absolute conviction that nothing could ever come between Jessie and me, that she would always understand me and accept me, unconditionally. There it goes again.

"I told myself at the time that I couldn't talk candidly to her. She was too young. And I really did try to avoid making her take sides, to choose one parent or the other. But Adriana showed no such compunction. I guess she was too desperately in need of allies. Of course, I could have fought for Jessie without having to down her mother. I see that now. Even though Adriana had told me before my affair that she was going to leave me for another man, a mutual acquaintance, two wrongs don't make a right. That wouldn't have explained what I did. In fact, regarding Adriana's earlier affair, I just thought she was stupid. The fellow was actually a good enough guy, with his own problems. And when the chips were down, he sure wasn't dumb enough to set up housekeeping with her.

"But getting back to Jessie, I think the most crucial reason I didn't fight for her was that I wasn't *supposed* to. Easy as that is for me to see now, I sure couldn't understand it at the time. She was supposed to continue the Deadly-Nightshade fantasy of my mother and me. She was to know that, whatever came to pass, I would always love her. And she would always love me, whatever I might do or say, *'till the walls will crumble in ruins, and molder in dust away.'*

"Of course, that wasn't the case. It never is, and never will be. But by the time I grasped this obvious fact, the floodwaters of her childhood had passed way downstream. *Too much water flowing underneath the bridge.* Distance from an event really does change perspective though. Therefore, it changes the events themselves.

"I think I can put myself in her place much more readily now. Let's say that she experienced my own kind of fantasy. Let's say she believed that I would love her and accept her, come what may. In that case, troubles with my wife or newfound passions for another woman would never interfere. I would always stay with her.

"You know, it's true. Children always tend to feel put down when their parents split. It's as if they're thinking: If I were good enough, they'd make all other conditions subservient to me. They'd use the energy necessary to solve the other problems. Or they'd just live with them. But they'd both stay together, with *me!*' That's why they feel guilty. That's why they feel to blame. And, of course, despite all the reassurances by mental health experts to the contrary, like 'Your mom and dad still both love you', that little grain of truth lingers in the child's perception. I no doubt shattered Jessie's fantasy, as I was in the process of destroying my own. And now we're both alike. She treats me like a cordial stranger, and I can see that's the way I relate to my mother—a real Harry Chapin ending, huh?"

CHAPTER 36

Though Kevin had been born and raised in the ardent tradition of Irish Catholicism, he also seemed to have lost this mooring along the way. When Doctor Lofgren asked *when* he'd lost his faith, Kevin answered, "I don't know. There was no exact point when my creed crumbled. Old beliefs don't tend to snap at specific moments like old clotheslines. Beliefs are more like socks hanging on the line. At what point does their elasticity give out? They just get a little baggier and fall down on you more readily, and finally you decide to throw them out or make dusters."

And when Doctor Lofgren pressed him for specifics, Kevin had added, "One problem was the Church's silly stand against birth control. That touched my life personally, and it affected the life of many of my patients. I'm not even sure though how much the Church's bizarre sexual doctrines contributed to my loss of belief. The most important thing may have been simply my growing sense of mortality. If you don't believe in the comforting story of life after death, then as Paul himself said, 'There's little point to Christianity.'

"And it's funny. My experience with Joe Polito this past year added an exclamation point to my fading belief in personal immortality. Catholic theology taught us that we had a soul separable from our bodies, and that this soul-substance not only underwrote our human consciousness, it was of its nature immortal. Yet when I dropped unconscious after Joe shot at me, this supposed soul-substance wasn't up to doing its job. Not, that is, until my brain got back to functioning. Meanwhile, there was *no* conscious experience whatsoever! So what's the point of postulating an entity that can't accomplish what it's been conjured up to do?

"I found that empirical failure decisive, even before one gets to the logical problem that defeated Descartes when he tried to make the hypothesis rationally consistent. For how were two totally different substances, a physical body and its proposed soul—an immaterial substance with, mind you, no material qualities whatsoever—to interact causally with its own material body? If it could, it would by definition have been physically measurable.

"The best first-aid that even the great Leibniz could provide was that God knew from all eternity what you and I were planning to do at any given moment, and that He provided a program of *Preordained Harmony*. According to this bizarre doctrine, though our *willing* to perform some action couldn't actually *cause* the necessary bodily changes, the Almighty would fix it so that our bodies will always move just when our souls tell them to.

"But back to my own experience—or rather *non*-experience. When I had my first flittering return of consciousness, it was like coming back from nothingness. Not from sleep or dreams. I came back from no experience at all. And if that happens from a temporary derangement of my brain function, imagine the permanence of that condition when my cerebral tissue turns to postmortem porridge."

Doctor Lofgren pursued the subject a bit, asking Kevin if he was familiar with what have often been referred to as after-death experiences. Here was part of Kevin's lengthy response:

"We're biologically built to fear death and long for more life. In fact, if those built-in programs hadn't been naturally selected, it's doubtful that our species would still be hanging around. Otherwise, who would've put up with *the whips and scorns of time*, as good ole Hamlet once put it. Still, hope does tend to spring eternal, so I used to read accounts of so-called after-death experiences.

"All I could find though were reports of what happened during intoxicated brain-states—you know, things like oxygen-lack with a temporarily stopped heart and the like. Highly altered states of consciousness, that's for sure, often pleasantly oceanic, and quite consistent over the centuries, be they from the ancient *Tibetan Book of the Dead* or from present-day clinical accounts. How they console the modern doctors who write about *Life After Death* is beyond me though. They've got to know they're dealing with intoxicated brains, not dead ones."

* * *

Doctor Lofgren belonged to none of our institutional religions, and perhaps was even a bit biased against them—at the very least, he believed ardently that no religion was worth killing or dying for. And he had listened to so many and so varied stories as to WHY a given individual had lost his faith, or found his faith, that the doctor had lost faith in his own ability to distinguish reasons from rationalizations. But at a practical level, he could see that people who espouse institutional religions become embedded in highly meaningful interpersonal networks, and that the presence of such meaningful involvement works strongly against the extremes of societal estrangement. To him then, the relevant factor in the present case was not whether Kevin's views were correct, but rather that the loss of his religion had removed yet another crucial mooring that might have prevented his overpowering sense of alienation.

And there was an additional religious factor that Doctor Lofgren singled out as highly pertinent, one that dealt not directly with the Catholic Church's teaching about birth control, but rather with Kevin's transference reaction in response to the interpersonal machinations that ensued in the Church's continuing identification of artificial birth control as sinful. Like most dynamically oriented psychiatrists, Doctor Lofgren had been greatly impressed by the strong tendency people have to react to current situations in accordance with similarities these situations may share with important early experiences. Given fortuitous circumstances, such transference may lead to happily adaptive responses. Unfortunately, transference of archaic response patterns to present-day circumstances can occur on the basis of a merely superficial resemblance to some current situation that actually differs quite markedly from its historical analog. An extreme response often occurs then that may be totally inappropriate to the case at hand.

Specifically, Kevin's childhood relationship with his father had been difficult and often punctuated by lack of trust. So years later when the Holy Father had claimed that the special Vatican commission on birth control had unanimously approved the Church's traditional stand, it was not just this bottom-line pronouncement that was at stake. Kevin, an ardent intellectual Catholic at the time, knew that Pope Paul was not telling the truth—knew this because he'd read the detailed views rendered by one of the commission members—long before the commission's actual report was leaked to the Paris newspaper, *Le Monde*. While other intellectual Catholics seemed capable of taking this misspeak in their stride, Kevin's archaic response to his own father set the stage for a totally repugnant transference response to this humanly understandable sin of yet another father figure.

* * *

Doctor Lofgren also made mental note of the fact that lack of trust had been a key issue in the case of Kevin's estrangement from his government, an institution that had once evoked in him the most passionate feelings of patriotism. When Kevin had been drafted during the Vietnam conflict (doctors could be called up until age 35, and he'd been called one month before that cutoff age), he'd been dismayed, especially since he disagreed with the war:

"The whole endeavor didn't seem to make much sense. After all, a metaphorical version of the San Andreas fault running in the border between China and Russia had by then gaped widely. Communism turned out to be far from monolithic. And Southeast Asia had been fighting against Colonialism for many centuries, long before the Chinese had translated the works of Marx, and certainly before the relatively recent times when Frenchmen tried to altruistically bear their own version of the White Man's Burden. Ink on the paper-line drawn after Dien Bien Phu was still wet with arbitrariness, and the actual battle-lines seemed to gyrate as complexly as the issues underlying. Considering this fact and the practical risks of getting sucked into the vacuum cleaner of a war on the Asian landmass, I considered the arguments of the Domino Theory less than compelling. In short, I was against the war, though my objections amounted initially to a more or less intellectual exercise.

"Then I got drafted. End of intellectual exercise. My dissent was now reinforced by selfish issues. I would have to leave my practice, disrupt my family, quarter my income, and subject myself to military law. That reinforcing of intellectual dissent by my selfish motivation led to maximum efforts to avoid service on the basis of community need or something, right? Wrong! Paradoxically, it made me distrust my own motives. Was I rationalizing the extent of my dissent just because it was so personally inconvenient to go? So I went off to war. But how could you play on a team when you thought the team was playing the wrong game?

"I tried to soothe my malaise by telling myself that our leaders were highly intelligent men of competence and judgment. They were *professionals* in the area. And furthermore, they were privy to detailed and private information that I had no way of assessing. I was an amateur in these matters, and I should avoid the arrogance of extreme dissent. As a doctor, hadn't I seen patients and their families going off half-cocked in the wrong direction after looking at some ill-informed article about their illness? If I could see the silliness of their untrained judgments in matters medical, why should there be any difference in matters military?

"Then came the Tet offensive. *That* did it for me! I'm not just referring to the terrible upswing in casualties we had to take care of. I'm talking about the complete collapse of *credibility* in regard to our leaders. You can fool most of the people some of the time, but come on! When you insist that a *foreign* army got within thirty miles of the Capitol city and no one knew that these outside invaders were there? Could I possibly imagine a foreign force coming within thirty miles of Boston and not knowing about their presence?

"Then, our Government's reflex response. Just up the ante by 200,000 more men and we'll have 'em where we want 'em! Half a million men there already and two hundred K more will do the trick? Well, we'd already been conned into upping the ante that way on a number of previous occasions. This time it was clear that our leaders had gone mad. I felt like a crew member on the Pequod, with that giant of a man towering over us, monomaniacally obsessed, nailing silver dollars to a huge mastlike crucifix, and calling on the crew to be steadfast—except that the ship he captained was no frail bark with a handful of sailors. He seemed intent on smashing the whole ship-of-State, that vessel stretching from Atlantic to Pacific, against a mystic white whale of epic proportions. Well, the people finally rebelled, and we ended up swapping one crazy leader for another . . ."

* * *

Having now obtained in considerable detail the information recorded in the foregoing chapters, Doctor Lofgren judged that he was in a position to provide the court with an informed opinion as to the defendant's competency. Thus, the stage was set for trial, and Kevin was expeditiously remanded to a jail cell.

PART III

CHAPTER 37

As the trial began, guidelines governing news worthiness came into play. An individual physician is much too commonplace to merit front-page attention for his personal doings; but let a doctor become involved in criminal activity, and the juxtaposition of this aberration against the noble ideals of his profession evokes intense community interest. Hence, the *Boston Herald* was to ask in its tabloid headline: IS DEADLY DOC DEMENTED?

It should also be noted that, at the trial's onset, Michael Grady had been pleased with the results of his initial strategy. A good defense lawyer is sometimes judged unrealistically by his record of acquittals, with the assumption—or fear on the part of law-abiding citizens—that he will miraculously produce a steady flow of *not-guilty* verdicts. Actually, the situation could be likened more to playing bridge. Occasionally the expert can steal an impossible slam, but he is judged highly proficient by his peers if he simply gets the most out of the cards he is dealt. In this instance, there was barely a face card in the whole hand. Mike's client had been caught red-handed, with motive established, and with his account of the murder transcribed magnetically for all posterity.

Still, it was strange behavior for a doctor who had been a man of peace rather than violence. The question could legitimately be raised, Mike had reasoned, that his client was not in his right mind. In fact, that possibility seemed so likely to him that he had taken the initiative in requesting evaluation by a court-appointed psychiatrist. The testimony of an expert witness, representing neither prosecution nor defense, would have maximum credibility with a jury. They would tend to see such an expert as unbiased. So when Doctor Lofgren's report to the court stated that the defendant was, in his opinion, insane at the time of the crime, the first step in *best defense* had gone according to plan.

The prosecutor, on his side, wanted to emphasize that the crime had been carefully conceived in advance by an intelligent and highly functional member of society—hardly the impulsive act of an irrational lunatic. To enhance his defense against the defense of insanity, the prosecutor had sought and found opposing psychiatric opinion (a procurement that is seldom difficult to arrange).

When it comes to expert testimony, there are a few hired guns in *any* field who will argue either side of a case. Their morals apparently allow them to look at the court procedure as a game, whose interest (aside from the money) comes from stating the strongest case for the assigned side. They are like forever ungraduated members of a college debating team, or like the sophists of old. Most hired guns, however, consistently take the one side of an issue that is consonant with their beliefs. Thus, Keynesian and Conservative economists will characteristically interpret the same data in a way that will lead to different solutions. Similarly, psychiatrists, whether or not they bother to categorize themselves explicitly, tend to be *Voluntarists* or *Determinists*. The Determinists will seek detailed information, tending to indicate that the event in question flowed inexorably from the confluence of preceding factors. Voluntarists, on the other hand, start with the conviction that a person is responsible for his actions unless the most extreme circumstances interfere with his free choice. For the Voluntarist, not even a psychotic illness with delusions and hallucinations would necessarily lead to a judgment of legal *insanity*, that is, a state of non-responsibility for one's actions.

Take, for example, the man who has the delusional conviction that his neighbor had been stealing his misplaced garden tools, and that the man also hears hallucinated voices telling him to kill the misidentified thief. Should this psychotic soul, in the midst of his craziness, be held responsible for the murder? A *Voluntarist* would say that, if the man knew he was committing the act of murder, and if he knew it was a crime to take the law into his own hands, then he was indeed responsible! So what if his delusion made him operate from a faulty premise? Even if the victim had *actually* stolen the implements, the theft would not have justified the murder. And so what if this man was being counseled by hallucinatory voices to proceed with the crime? Even if an underworld boss had *actually* whispered that command in his ear, the man would not be justified in following it. No, the illness might represent a mitigating factor, but it would not totally abrogate the murderer's criminal responsibility.

Thornton Miller, the prosecutor in Kevin's case, had come to use Doctor Ernest Koch for insanity testimony because this psychiatrist was, in the above sense, a *Voluntarist*. Doctor Koch saw Kevin for evaluation on one occasion, after reviewing data that included the transcript of the tape and the independent report from the court-appointed psychiatrist. This relatively brief appraisal was sufficient to convince him that Kevin was legally sane.

Doctor Koch's report indicated that Kevin certainly knew right from wrong in accordance with the law, and knew that what he was doing had to be altered and disguised because it was against the law. Furthermore, the carefully thought-out plan militated against any argument that his action was an impulsive one. As to Kevin's absolute conviction that Joe Polito was his tormentor, Doctor Koch did not consider that fact to represent a delusion. He said that the defendant gave very plausible reasons for his conclusions and displayed an intellectual arrogance toward those who would disagree with him.

In addition to bringing out this psychiatric data, the prosecutor planned to highlight the heinousness of the crime in order to undermine any sympathy that might be forthcoming toward Kevin as a beleaguered professional. To accomplish this, Mr. Miller intended to graphically portray the cold-blooded nature of the killing in all its gruesome, brain-splattering detail. Also, he would emphasize the likelihood that an innocent victim's blood had been shed, a victim whose grieving family still floundered in shock from his loss.

* * *

Meanwhile, Linda had her own decisions to make in preparation for the trial. She had berated herself earlier for not having taken Kevin's murder threats seriously enough. She did not want to repeat that mistake now, and was quite concerned that Kevin seriously planned another killing, albeit this time his own. From what he'd said, it seemed clear that he intended to use cyanide, and that he would commit the terrible crime (as she considered it) in public, almost certainly therefore at the court trial itself. She tried to put herself in his place and decided that he would most likely delay his action until the verdict was rendered.

What should she do about it? Perhaps she should tell Mike Grady, but what could he do? Probably he'd notify the court, and this would lead to increased surveillance and cell checks. She winced at the likely counter-productiveness of such an approach in Kevin's case. Even if they found his probably internalized container, he would be egged on to more determined action and would be further alienated from her. Instead, she decided to be in the courtroom for every day of the trial, and to prepare herself secretly for emergency treatment if this became necessary. But her first line of defense was to be her presence: to give Kevin something to live for (she afterall lived for him).

In addition, she obtained from a friend at the hospital pharmacy some useful chemical agents. Studying the toxicology of cyanide, she had learned that amyl nitrite, rapidly absorbed through the lungs when inhaled like smelling salts, would change some of the blood's hemoglobin to a form that would combine harmlessly with cyanide. Using her phlebotomy skills, she would then inject sodium nitrite intravenously to enhance the same effect. Finally, to accelerate detoxification, she would administer thiosulfate which interacts with cyanide to form the relatively non-toxic thiocyanate, a compound that is harmlessly excreted in the urine.

It all sounded good in principle. She hoped, if need be, it would work as well in practice—if she could find a vein after his blood pressure had fallen. A life depended on it, a life that was so much a part of her own. Linda packed the gear in her handbag (of size so ample that Kevin had always expressed incredulity that she could find anything in it) and began her daily pilgrimages to the courtroom.

CHAPTER 38

As part of his plan to establish concern for the victim and sympathy for his family, Thornton Miller first called to the stand Leonard Polito, Joe's youngest son by his first wife. Leonard, now nineteen and in his freshman year at Northeastern, came to court dressed in a dark sport coat and striped tie. No question that his forthright appearance and manner made a favorable impact on the jury. During testimony, tears came to his eyes as he told how his father, despite illness and current life expenses, had taken him out at the end of the summer and bought him new shoes in preparation for college. "He was proud of me," Leonard said, "and that helped. It was a little scary, starting college, but he gave me encouragement. He told me that I was going to *his* school, but that he hadn't had the chance to finish himself, and that it was important for me to stay with it all the way."

When asked by Mr. Miller if he intended to do so, Leonard looked straight at him and said with conviction, "Yes, sir, I will. I won't let him down."

"Thank you, Leonard, that will be all," Mr. Miller had concluded with an approving nod of his head.

Then Timothy O'Leary was called to the stand. Eighteen years old and a senior in high school, he was the second of Joe's three stepsons by his present wife. Dressed in an indigo V-necked sweater, he looked pale and unhappy. Speaking in a low voice, he told the court that Joe had always been around the house, especially since his illness, and that his presence had been a big help. Tim went on to say that he could barely remember his own dead father. "And now he's dead, too," Tim added with a sad shake of his head. "I was hoping to go on to college next year, but now I don't know how. We don't even have money to pay the bills we already have. For a while, they weren't even going to deliver the heating oil."

If Thornton Miller's purpose was to portray a demoralized household, he could not have done better than to present Timothy. The members of the jury had looked totally somber by the time he stepped down from the witness stand. Again, as in the case of his stepbrother, Michael Grady declined cross-examination.

Then Thornton Miller called Mrs. Polito. Bending his athletic frame slightly forward, he seemed to hover over her in unspoken solicitude as he personally conducted her to the stand. His continued concern as he asked that a chair be provided for her to sit down during testimony additionally communicated the terrible ordeal she had been through and the emotional pain that her present account of the horrible events would unavoidably add.

Clad in a black dress that buttoned down the front in the way of inexpensive clothes that may look satisfactory on the rack but that never seem to fit properly, she appeared older and even more frail than Kevin had remembered. Her brownish hair, now mostly gray, had been gathered into a bun at the back of her head. Worry lines creased her forehead, and the sadness in her eyes was reinforced by her lip line that alternately sagged at the ends or firmed into a pale thinness. The impact was inescapable. She'd been through hell.

After establishing her identity, Mr. Miller led her gently: "Mrs. Polito. I know this is very difficult for you, but could you tell the members of the jury about your deceased husband—what he was like?"

"My second husband? I lost my first husband too, you know." Speaking tentatively, in a low voice, Mrs. Polito almost seemed to have to orient herself to the present, to what she was going through right now.

"Yes, I know," replied Mr. Miller, his brisk assertiveness muted in gentle deference to this grieved widow.

After a pause, Mrs. Polito continued, "When I lost my first husband, I didn't know what to do. I didn't know how I'd ever survive. I mean, how I'd manage to get by with three small children. They were so sad about losing their father, and I was so broken up I couldn't be much help. He—their father—had left some life insurance, and that helped for a while, but it was running out.

"Then I met Joseph. He was wonderful. He saved us. He helped us out. He was so kind, right from the start—and not only to me. He was so good with the boys. Tommy was seventeen at the time, and you know how boys are, especially without a father. He got in with some bad kids, and one day they went into a house and took some things. Tommy wasn't even with them. He was outside. But the police got him, and they were going to arrest him because he wouldn't tell the names of the other boys. They were going to put him in jail. And

Joe—he came right over and went down to the police station, and he straightened everything out. I don't know what I would have done without him." Her voice had gotten a boost as she shared this positive memory of her late husband, then sagged with sadness in the words that followed the pause.

"Joe had a hard life. His father left him when he was still a boy, and they did everything to keep the family together. Joe was the oldest, and he was always working, working. Anything to help out. Paper routes, shoveling snow, bagging groceries, you name it, and my Joe did it. Then he was in the service, and he married young, and he had three kids. Three boys. She was a good woman, but they were young. She didn't understand Joe too good . . . no patience.

"So they broke up, and it was tough on Joe. Awful tough. Then he met this terrible woman, a barfly, that's all she was. And he tried to help her. Married her and tried to straighten her out. Joe was always trying to help. But finally he knew he couldn't, and he had to leave her. She was no good.

"Then he met me and, like I say, he tried so hard. He always tried. He helped us, and he helped all those people flying on the planes, people he didn't even know. He'd worry about them, about making a mistake or something, just like they was his family, and he didn't even know them. Sometimes he'd even brood about it. He lived his job, he really did, and he was so proud. He knew how important it was.

"Then his nerves started getting him about it, and he'd stay up half the night worrying. Or he'd wake real early and get up and pace, all because of that job. And it got so, if he didn't have a nightcap, he couldn't sleep at all. And then, like when someone made a mistake and there'd be a near-miss, he'd get so upset. And he said some of the guys didn't even care. They'd laugh and kid about it afterwards, like it wasn't even human lives that was at stake.

"He cared so much that he finally couldn't stand it anymore. He cracked up himself. He was a martyr, a real martyr." As she went on, Mrs. Polito's voice had become gradually stronger and more animated. By this point, she had become eulogistically emphatic. "Everyday, he had saved the lives of all those people walking in and out of the terminal. In and out. And they didn't even know it. Didn't even appreciate it. He gave himself for them, for all of them. And finally, he just couldn't do it no more.

"But he still helped us. He was still with us. He'd be awful tired . . . drained . . . and he'd have to stay in bed to rest. Or then he'd be nervous and have to get up and pace around. But he was with us, and he helped us, and he was so good, and he supported us.

"And then the Labor Department told him he wasn't disabled anymore! How did *they* know? They didn't live with him. That's when you really know someone. You don't know someone if you don't live with them! Then they got this doctor . . . this terrible man . . . to say that the job had nothing to do with it. That really killed Joe even before *he* killed him. I mean, all that he did for all those people all those years, going to work when he was sick, or when there was so much snow you couldn't get through, and staying overtime because there was no one to cover, and all those things. Then this doctor gets paid to write it all down fancy that the job had nuthin' to do with it.

"I tell you, he was a real martyr, because no one even *knew*. Did that doctor—how can he even call himself that—see him those nights when he was pacing and crying and worried about the people on the planes? Did he spend the time with him when he had all the ideas how they could do things better, and he'd write them down—pages and pages of them—and he'd try to tell them, and they wouldn't listen. And this monster sees him once in the office and chats with him like this, and then—" Mrs. Polito broke off in frustration and started to sob.

After allowing time for her ventilation to subside and for the impact of her tragedy to be digested by the jurors, Mr. Miller resumed gently, "I know this has been a terrible ordeal for you, Mrs. Polito. You know also that your deceased husband has been accused by the defendant of assaulting him. Now on the night of November fourteenth, nineteen-eighty-one, when your husband was alleged to have been the masked figure who shot at the defendant, were you aware of where your husband was?"

"Yes!" And now anger entered her voice. "He was home with me, in bed sick! He was always home with me!"

"And on the night of January eleven, nineteen-eighty-two, when the defendant alleged that your husband was the mysterious figure who drove him off the road, do you know where your husband was?"

"*With me!* He was home with me. And anyway, Joe wouldn't never have done anything like that. His job was to protect lives, not to take them. That awful man, I can't understand him. He's the one who was trying to get Joe all the time, not the opposite. He even called Joe at home after he wrote that wicked report, and he woke him up when he was sleeping—sick in bed. Then he had the police come to the house—throwing his weight around because he was a doctor. A big shot!

"Then he took him to court, and he made all those terrible accusations, and our lawyer made me sit up front with Joe's brother, and Joe came in with a bunch of people and sat in back, and he couldn't even recognize him. He couldn't even point out the one who supposedly shot at him. He fingered Joe's brother, Bobby, just because he was with me.

"Then he even had people following Joe around—probably was going to hurt him. But Joe was too smart. He said, if he could keep track of a bunch of planes flying through a fog, he guessed he could keep track of a few private detectives sneakin' around corners. But I was still worried, and I was right. They probably was going to harm Joe, but then they didn't because he finally done it himself! That awful man!"

At this point, Mrs. Polito broke down sobbing again, her body shaking uncontrollably in the chair. Thornton Miller walked deferentially to the witness stand and placed his hand comfortingly on her shoulder till she regained her composure. Then he said, "Thank you, Mrs. Polito."

Turning to the judge, he said in still quiet tones, "That will be all, your Honor."

The judge, looking down from his eminence, waited appraisingly to gain an impression of the witness' ability to continue. After she seemed to settle down, he asked her quietly whether she wanted to complete her testimony now, or whether she would prefer a break. When she answered softly that she just wanted to get it over with, the judge looked out toward the defense table. Peering over the top of his half-glasses so that a wrinkle creased his brow, he asked crisply, "Does the defense wish to examine the witness?"

"No cross-examination, your Honor," said Michael Grady matter-of-factly. That was all.

CHAPTER 39

Kevin was furious. Had he experienced less impulse control, he might have banged the walls of the smallish cubicle that made do as a conference room for defendants and their lawyers. Instead, he roughly dragged one of the wooden chairs out from under the flat desk, scuffing it loudly across the floor. "*Why*," he demanded, "did you just sit there?"

Mike settled down easily in an adjoining chair and seemed unperturbed. "What would you have done?" he asked.

"Well, to start with, I would have cross-examined the boys, or at least Tim. There was a reason, *some* reason, that none of the children contributed to Joe's alibi. Where was Tim on the nights in question? Okay, if he was out, make him say so. Maybe, in his confusion of the moment, he would even try to protect his stepfather. That's what he was there for today, posthumous protection. Maybe he'd make up some alibi for him that we could disprove because we could show Tim'd been out somewhere. But at the very least, we'd show that Joe's alibi consisted of one prejudiced person, his wife. If they had been going to add to it, Miller would have had them testify on the point. You can count on it!

"Then I'd have reacquainted Mrs. Polito with reality. Jesus, I know widows get to see their husbands with a golden glow as time passes. The good is often *not* interred with the bones, but harvested in memory and embroidered with fantasy. The aggravation their husbands caused them—like walking through a briar patch every day—that's all gone. So only the glow remains, or an afterglow. Like when the sun's just set, and it's far more attractive than the presence of its midday heat ever was. Widows get like that. But this fast? She's more motivated by a desire to save the family name, and perhaps to get some needed income.

"I'd cry too if I were in her shoes. But not at the loss of that bastard. I'd cry for all the heartaches he caused me by his drinking, by his not taking care of his health, by his brooding all the time; that is, all the time when he wasn't megalomanic and hyperirritable. I'd cry because I'd know that his drinking and his not taking his medicine made him unable to work and caused the whole family financial hardship. And I'd cry because, deep down, I'd know that his irritability and complaining all the time with me was the same thing that had gotten aimed at this doctor. Blaming the doctor for his own faults and problems as he was always blaming me. And I'd know how vicious he could be—how he used to beat up his first wife until she couldn't take it anymore, and how he would've beaten me up too except I was always pacifying him.

"I'd know how vindictive he could be, and that he'd easily be capable of harassing and bullying another man, and eventually bringing notoriety on the whole family. I'd cry for this. I'd cry for all these reasons, if I were she. And I'd stay out of his way even when he was home, and I'd be glad he spent so much time alone in his room. I wouldn't even check! And when he went out most nights—because I would know *that* more than the private detective who sampled just a few of his nights—I'd be half worried about what was going to happen and half relieved to think that he was gone.

"And if he got me started on the alibi route, I'd tell myself that I was being virtuous and loyal, rather than admit that I was always intimidated by him, and that, anyway, my own self-interest lay in the direction of protecting his. He wasn't going to bring home any bacon from the jailhouse, and I surely wouldn't need the embarrassment and vicarious shame of having my ole man in jail for assault with a deadly weapon."

Mike listened impassively as Kevin poured out his feelings passionately, though in somewhat disjointed fashion.

After a pause, perhaps to catch his breath, Kevin continued, "But if I was not Mrs. Polito, Mike—if I had been *you*—I would never have just let it all pass unchallenged. I would have tried to reacquaint her with some of the realities. I might have brought to her attention that his first wife probably understood him pretty well as a self-exculpating bully, and that she had indeed brought charges of assault and battery against him, and that sometime later she was finally granted a divorce for cruel and abusive treatment, and that the documentation of the reason for that divorce decree showed that cruel and abusive treatment in that case was not just a legalistic formula. I would have pointed all that out to her, so the jury could put her wonderful testimony about Joe in better perspective.

"Then I might have asked her more about her other poor little misunderstood boy, Tommy. He's twenty-five now, and he still doesn't have a regular job. I'd have asked her if she had ever heard of a lookout at a robbery, and what she thought Tommy was doing outside that particular house. Was it just by sheer coincidence, by a stroke of rotten luck, that he happened to be standing on that street at the wrong time? In short, I'd have documented for the jury her ability to distort things to protect her family.

"And as far as this vision of Joe as Helpful Harry, wanting only to aid others and contributing bountifully to the harmony of family life, how can that ever be when a guy's got an alcohol problem? I might have asked her how she felt when he drove home late at night intoxicated. How it felt to see the family car wracked up in the driveway one morning and her husband, fighting his way out of a hangover, having no idea how it happened, or how he even got home? That might help the jury see things in a different light!"

At this proposed line of questioning, Mike finally broke out into a head-shaking laugh. "Well, you're right, Doc. If I'd have done that, the jury sure would have seen things in a different light!"

Hardly stopping to process the amused feedback from his lawyer, Kevin continued, "And if I were you, I'd have challenged her alibi. He was at home, in bed, on the first occasion. Supposedly. Well, did she actually check the bedroom to be sure? And how often, and at what times? Could she be sure he hadn't left home part of the time? If that's her story, make her say that she was running into the room every half hour or so to check on him. And since he was in bed so much, that she was always doing that. Everyday, all the time. Make her say it! Make her sound less than fully believable.

"And the second time. She had to remember that one in retrospect. Well, how many people can remember in detail what happened on an ordinary evening a week ago Tuesday? How was she so sure? I'd pin her down. And if she went into that business again that he was *always* home, I'd take her up on it. 'Always?' And if she said, 'Well, most of the time,' I'd pin her down. 'Ninety percent of the time?' 'Seventy-five percent of the time?' 'How much of the time?' And if she chose some high percent, I'd contrast that with the sample from the private detective indicating Joe went out almost every night for at least part of the time. I'd make her try to explain that inconsistency. And once again, I think it would diminish her credibility.

"And then, the very way she answered the question concerning his whereabouts. She said he was with her and, anyway, he wouldn't do such a thing. That one would even be funny, if it didn't involve me. She might as well have come straight out with the old lawyer's joke about his client: 'In the first place, he didn't do it. And in the second place, you can't prove it.' "

By this time, Kevin's monologue, expressed against virtually no resistance on the part of his listener, had just about run itself out. Showing no outer sign of impatience other than a quick glance at his watch, Mike leaned back farther in his chair now and began to speak. "There's only one trouble, Doc."

"What's that?" asked Kevin.

"Joe's not the one on trial. You are. Even if he was the world's biggest bastard, even if he was out of the house on all those times when his wife's alibiing for him, even if he did take the shot at you, and even if he did run you off the road, that's not the issue. According to the law, Doctor Kiley, that would not justify *your* action. And that's why we're here. *You're* on trial for *his* murder!

"Now, let me ask you. You referred to the contents of his divorce decree. Did you actually read the testimony?"

"No," Kevin replied irritably, "but the private detective told me about it. I was just saying what I'd have done if I were *you,* and that would have included getting that testimony out and looking at it. I'm certainly paying you enough to prepare the case well." That last dig had a familiar ring to Kevin. He had sometimes been on its receiving end when a patient was disgruntled with him.

"Well, it's a peculiar thing about the law," replied Mike matter-of-factly. "When a person's on trial, you can't bring in legal findings from his past. There's a concern that this might prejudice the jury about the present allegation—that a person might be convicted of a crime he didn't do now, just because of crimes he did commit in the past.

"Now, if Joe Polito were on trial, the prosecutor would have to go after his wife. He'd have to attack her testimony. But we're in a different ballgame. You're in this thing for first-degree murder with your own confession of premeditation on tape for the jury to hear! If Thornton Miller has his way, they'll lock you up for life and throw away the key. I'm trying to provide you the very best defense I can." He paused to let that fact sink in, then continued, "The last thing we need to do is to alienate this jury by attacking the aggrieved widow.

"Of course, her testimony's damaging to you. And you know the main reason it's so damaging? Because it's *true*! Oh, I don't mean it's literally true. Maybe she's still protecting him in his grave, as you claim. I noticed that she was five years older than he was, and she probably always mothered him. But the point is, they were a family unit. He did provide income, and she did get to participate in a relationship that was meaningful to her, even if we think she was crazy to live with the guy. And his violent death had to be, in fact, pretty traumatic for Tim. And if Joe had been around with the chance of bringing income into the house one way or another, it would've made a difference as to whether Tim could go to college next year.

"The truth is, each one of us exists in a social network. Destroy one element in that network and you disturb other elements you haven't even thought about. I know, Doc, you did what you thought you had to do. And I'm defending you for it the very best I can. But it's also a fact that the killing seriously hurt a group of people you didn't even know. That's a truth, and the prosecution just saw fit to bring it out. Let's not make things worse by attacking these people indiscriminately now."

Kevin was silent. For what had to be more than a minute, he just sat there with no display of emotion. Then, without looking up, he muttered "Okay," and the conference ended. But during that quiet interval, he had experienced a veritable flood of feelings and thoughts that seemed to jump simultaneously into consciousness, sometimes on parallel tracks, sometimes with interlacing activity, and sometimes racing off in disparate directions. Their totality overwhelmed his processing ability of the moment, yet made a sufficiently enduring imprint on his brain that he was able to recapture many of the impressions— one by one—as he reflected on them for the remainder of the night in his cell.

Blue Cowboy, will you sleep tonight
Knowin' your memories are forever in sight
Dreams that will stir as the light leaves your eyes
Malevolent ventures and jagged goodbyes.

CHAPTER 40

Staring through the ceiling above his bunk, Kevin scarcely noticed the eerie patterns cast on it by the interaction of random light sources throughout the cell block. He was immersed almost totally within himself, analyzing the flood of impressions that had overcome him at the end of his meeting with Mike.

Kevin could see all too clearly that the quarrel with his defense attorney had to do with the fact that they were embarked on different courses. He wanted to defend his murderous action as reasonable under the dire circumstances involved; he wanted a jury of his peers to understand that he had been pushed beyond endurance by the escalating predations of this other man; he wanted them to realize that the machinery of society, in its effort to be evenhanded, was too cumbersome to protect him; he wanted them to empathize with his desperate straits; yes, that it might be legalistically wrong to protect himself by killing his tormentor, but that it was humanly understandable as a justifiable act of self-defense. He wanted them to become convinced, in fact, that he would have been both masochistic and cowardly to put up with more—to wait passively for posthumous retribution on his behalf by a ponderously laggard society.

If he had to be found guilty because he'd committed an illegal act, so be it. But he wanted the jurors to feel in their hearts: yes, this man was pushed too far. We would have done likewise in his position if we had the courage. His was a reasonable act, arrived at with the fullness of his will. Legally, he may have committed a crime requiring institutional punishment, but, ethically, he was innocent.

His lawyer, by contrast, was not at all out to prove the reasonableness of his client's actions. Quite the contrary! Mike would be content if the jurors saw his client's behavior as totally aberrant, so much so that it could not represent the doings of a previously reasonable and sane man. To argue for the understandableness and rationality of Kevin's act would be counterproductive. Better for the jury to consider it crazy. In short, Mike wanted the members of the jury to see the killing as non-ethical and non-free—the behavior of a man gone mad, at leave from his senses, not in his right mind. The lawyer could care less what these people thought of his client as a man, as long as they thought him not guilty of a crime.

Among the flood of reactions that had buffeted Kevin at the termination of his meeting with Mike had been the urge to fire his lawyer, to replace him with one who would follow a more compatible course. He had rejected this impulse, partly due to a strange anergia that had gripped him since his arrest—lethargy associated with a sense of pessimistic fatalism. A larger part of his decision to stand pat had to do with the anger he experienced toward himself, anger that he *cared* what these jury members thought of him. He wanted to ruthlessly uproot the concern in himself about how other people judged him.

He recalled his strangely rebellious nature from early years, the extremes of which struck even himself as weird. He had not been a childhood rebel against parental strictures, or an adolescent rebel in search of the perfect society. He had experienced a deeper sense of rebelliousness that he should be in servitude to the very laws of nature. Subjection to the law of gravity rankled him; that he could not fly like an eagle, soar like a condor, and hover like a hummingbird before all of nature's blossoms. And one day, when he saw a seaside gull working to make inchlike progress along the skyline against the severity of coastal wind, he realized that the birds themselves were scarcely freer from the laws that prevented his own transit to the stars. He had been undergoing an inner Lucifer-like rebellion against his own finitude, not realizing then that the very limitations imposed on his nature defined his being and separated his existence from the rest of "What Is." Destroy these outlining strictures that enclosed his being, and he would be no more.

No longer, as an adult, did he seek to be free from the fundamental rules of the universe. But perhaps equally quixotic, he still longed to be free from one of the fundamental laws of human nature; that we are gregarious animals, born into a group, and existing only within the matrix of other human beings who define our meaning, establish our significance, and secure our very existence. Kevin willed that not to be so. He did not object to doing for others, but he resented his *needing* them and his *caring* that they cared.

He reflected also on Mike's statements about the other people in Joe's life whom *he* had hurt. It was true that he'd given little consideration to the Polito family. His awareness had been more or less fully wrapped up in protecting himself from Joe. But what, he reflected, if I'd followed a more passive approach in the face of Joe's accelerating incursions? After a period of additional torment, he would have killed me. Probably at that point Joe would have finally been apprehended, and his family would have been seriously hurt anyway. No, there was no way Joe's family was *not* going to be badly hurt. In fact, this represented just one instance of an awful rule of nature: *In human interaction, one cannot not hurt others.* The best anyone can ever do is to choose a path that hurts one's fellows the least in the long run.

Wrapped in his thoughts, Kevin found himself hurtling through an inner universe of such vast dimensions that his outer six-by-eight enclosure of concrete became momentarily irrelevant. Eventually, he faded off to sleep, to wrestle once again with his dark dreams of night.

CHAPTER 41

When the defense finally took its turn at bat, Michael Grady's key witness was to be Doctor Lofgren. Like a jujitsu expert, Mike was attempting to use the strength of the prosecution's case against itself: *Yes, my client became obsessed that this probably innocent man was out to get him. Yes, my client then planned to kill him, and actually did so in a bizarrely mistaken act of self-defense. But my client, a lifelong man of peace, and an honored physician, would never have behaved this way if he were in his right mind. An impartial expert, chosen by the court and having no axe to grind for either the prosecution or the defense, will explain that fact to you.*

Mike had no intention of allowing Kevin to testify. The lawyer was convinced that his client's anger would alienate the jury, and that his intelligence and appearance of reasonableness might lead them to conclude that he was less crazy than he actually was.

Mike prepared Doctor Lofgren carefully so as to maximize the clarity of his information to the jury. While introducing the expert, he emphasized his fine psychiatric training, his years of experience, and his academic affiliation. He laid special emphasis on the fact that, unlike the prosecution's expert, Doctor Lofgren had been chosen impartially by the court. He also detailed the many hours of personal examination, which contrasted with the relatively cursory examination by the prosecutor's expert.

Then he came to the crucial question: "Now, Doctor Lofgren, did you come to a conclusion as to the defendant's sanity at the time when he committed the crime?"

Kevin's silent thoughts interpolated themselves here with sardonic humor: *Yes. He was crazy as a hoot owl!* An outside observer would have noted an amused expression on his face, behavior that certainly would have seemed inappropriate to the occasion.

After a slight hesitation—one that seemed to demonstrate an intuitive theatrical sense—Doctor Lofgren rendered his actual answer: "Yes."

"Doctor, what standard did you follow in arriving at your conclusion?"

"Whether the defendant could distinguish right from wrong, and whether he could adhere to the right."

"Now, in your opinion, Doctor, using this standard, was the defendant sane at the time he committed the crime?"

"No."

"Would you explain?"

"He was intellectually, that is, in his mind, well able to distinguish right from wrong according to the law; but in his actions, he was unable to adhere to the right."

"Why was that?"

"He had suffered a psychotic illness that severely impaired his judgment and that deranged his impulse control."

"This psychotic illness—does it have a name?"

"Yes. According to the current diagnostic manual used by the American Psychiatric Association, it would be called an Acute Paranoid Disorder."

"How do you diagnose this illness?"

"The essential feature is the presence of persistent persecutory delusions in a person whose brain functioning is otherwise intact. The delusions usually involve a single theme or series of connected themes, and are commonly associated with resentment and anger, which may lead to violence. The onset of this condition generally occurs in middle or later adult life and often in a setting of social isolation. Intellectual and occupational functioning are usually preserved, though often there is impairment in the social and marital areas." Doctor Lofgren, during this recitation, was speaking didactically, almost as if reading from a prepared text.

"Doctor, you referred to the essential feature of this illness as the presence of persistent persecutory delusions. Would you explain to us, please, what you mean by the word, *delusion*?"

"Yes," and at this point, having gotten over his initial nervousness at speaking before an audience in the not completely familiar role of expert witness, Doctor Lofgren turned his body a little so that he was now talking directly to the jurors as they sat diagonally off to his right. "A delusion is a false conviction that a person in a given setting would not be expected to have, and which cannot be corrected by any rational proof. You will notice then that there are *three* parts to the definition, and all three are necessary. *One:* A false conviction. *Two:*

which a given person would not be expected to have in his setting. *Three:* The conviction cannot be rationally corrected.

"A false conviction by itself is certainly not a delusion. For example, at the time of Columbus, most people thought the world was flat. That represented a false belief, of course, but one which was generally held. In fact, a person in such a setting would be expected to share that view.

"The third part of the definition is necessary also: that the conviction cannot be corrected by any rational proof. Let me illustrate the importance of that fact. Suppose a man develops severe chest pain and becomes convinced that he is having a heart attack. Suppose further that he does not actually have a heart attack. His conviction is false. Now he goes to his doctor who examines him, takes an electrocardiogram, and draws blood for some appropriate tests. After putting all the data together, the doctor concludes that there has been no heart attack. He explains this to his patient, indicating that his cardiogram and blood tests are normal. The patient feels relieved and is no longer convinced that he had a heart attack. His false conviction is *correctable* by rational proof. He is not delusional."

Mike listened intently, modeling for the jury what he hoped they would be doing. Then he summarized again. "So, Doctor, there are three parts to a delusion: First, that a person is convinced something is so that isn't so; second, that the ordinary person in his setting wouldn't believe it; and, third, that he can't accept any rational proof that his conviction is wrong."

"That's correct."

"Now, you mentioned *persecutory* delusion. What does that refer to?"

"To a delusion of persecution. That is, the person is convinced someone or something is going to hurt him when that's not actually the case."

"And after examining Doctor Kiley, you concluded that he was suffering from such delusions of persecution?"

"Yes, I did."

"Could you explain, Doctor Lofgren, what led you to this conclusion?"

"Yes. Doctor Kiley had experienced a series of increasingly traumatic incidents, starting with vulgar and threatening phone calls, progressing to vandalism like the puncturing of his tires, then being shot at, evidently with blank cartridges. Following this, he was run off the road by a pickup truck, an event that could have produced severe injury or death, though, fortunately, he escaped with some relatively minor wounds. The last incident, the one that apparently drove him to his act of desperation, was the wanton and sadistic killing of his sheep. His conviction that some person or persons were dangerously harassing him—*that* conviction seems more than amply warranted. What happened, however, is that he focused on one *possible* suspect who had, in fact, resented Doctor Kiley's unfavorable disability report, and he became *absolutely* convinced that this man was his tormentor."

If looks could kill, Doctor Lofgren would have toppled from the stand at that moment. Kevin, who'd been managing to stay more or less detached, now experienced a surge of rage. His body stiffened involuntarily as he sat, and he glared with head nodding negatively back and forth, half in disagreement, half in disbelief. After a brief period, he seemed to catch himself and returned to his previous impassiveness.

Doctor Lofgren was continuing, "The only real proof he had was the coincidence in timing. Mr. Polito's evaluation and report had been done shortly before the harassment started, and Mr. Polito had indeed phoned Doctor Kiley just before to express his disappointment and resentment at the results of the report.

"But once Doctor Kiley developed an absolute conviction as to who his assailant was, small bits of evidence were collected to justify his belief. The distorted phone voice, for instance, supposedly had a quality that he could tell *for sure* was that of Mr. Polito, even though they had met on but one occasion, and even though they'd had only two or three definite phone conversations after that. And when he had a chance to modify the extreme of his conviction—at the time in court when he mistakenly identified Mr. Polito's brother, Robert, as the person in question—he was unable to correct himself. He simply became angry that he had been *tricked*. Then, at the end of the hearing, he projected a message of vicious intent into a brief moment of eye contact from the other man.

"During my own conferences with Doctor Kiley, whenever I tried to assist him with some *reality testing* about the marked discrepancy between his conviction and his proof, he became angry. This sort of response is *fully consistent* with the behavior expected from patients with paranoid disorders. They commonly become very angry when their delusions are challenged.

"Be sure to keep in mind, the delusion did *not* consist in his belief that he was being assailed. It consisted in his *absolute conviction* that he knew *who* his assailant was. It is this extreme irrational belief, emphasized by the tragically extraordinary action that went with it, that constitutes the core of his delusion."

"So, with this delusion, in this psychotic state, the defendant could not help himself? He was not responsible for his actions?"

"That is correct," Doctor Lofgren answered evenly and emphatically, with a single affirmative nod of his head as he looked straight at the jury, his facial expression earnest and open.

"What caused Doctor Kiley's illness?" With the crime now explained by disease instead of depravity, Mike intuitively raised the defendant back to his professional status again.

"We don't know the cause of these conditions," answered Doctor Lofgren. "There are undoubtedly multiple factors that come together at a certain time. Often, severe stress seems to be a precipitant, and Doctor Kiley had certainly been under a great deal of that in the months preceding his loss of control."

"Are you referring to the repeated death threats, the being shot at, and the fact that he could well have been killed when he was run off the road?"

"Yes. Living in constant danger to his life was probably the biggest stress. And there were others also, of a much more subtle but of an emotionally telling nature."

"You mean, beside the terrible stress caused by the constant dread that he would be *murdered*, there were additional factors disrupting his mental equilibrium?"

"Yes. You see, by the time we reach adulthood, we experience everything that happens to us in the light of previous life events. Different people obviously have different experiences, which is why two people may react quite differently to the same sort of event happening in their current lives. They interpret it differently, they *experience* it differently, based on how they've been programmed, so to speak, by their past. Freud put it poetically when he said that people suffer from reminiscences.

"You notice, for example, that Doctor Kiley's final loss of behavioral control occurred, not following the experience of being nearly killed when he was run off the road. It happened after the sadistic slaughter of his sheep. As unnerving as that latter event was, it probably wouldn't seem as bad to the casual observer as the earlier one. Well, in a way, there *was* a last straw effect, the cumulation of severe traumata that finally broke him down. But there was something additional—something you couldn't understand without realizing the impact of a person's past experiences on the present, and how this impact manifests itself *symbolically* in events that on their surface may not even seem similar."

"This is getting complicated, Doctor." Mike wanted to slow the expert down so he would not outrun the jury's comprehension. He did not want them to be left behind, and he especially did not want them to feel dumb. Identifying the matter as *complicated* would help to forestall that eventuality.

Doctor Lofgren nodded sympathetically and without any trace of condescension. "Yes, it is complicated," he responded evenly "but there's no avoiding that. We human beings are very complicated creatures." He had scored with the jury. Attentive nods of affirmation could almost be seen. They could certainly buy that one! "But let me try to be specific in the case of Doctor Kiley. Two past events in his life are very important to introduce here. First, when he was a young father, he lost his four-year-old son in a pedestrian accident. He dealt with the accident and his son's death pretty well at the time. But he always had the tendency to feel guilty and, especially, to second-guess himself as to whether he could have prevented the accident in the first place.

"Then a number of years later, he and his wife divorced after a great deal of marital rancor. Unfortunately, as sometimes happens, his daughter who'd been the apple of his eye became estranged from him as a result, and this was extremely traumatic. He felt very hurt, yet guilty. Again, he second-guessed himself, thinking that if he'd been a good enough parent, he would have been able to avoid his family disruption and the associated alienation from his daughter.

"In short, here was a proud and in many ways successful man whose self-esteem as a parent—as a shepherd of his flock, so to speak—

had been severely injured. And remember, we literally cannot remain alive without any self-esteem at all. That's why we're always working at it. After his unsuccessful marriage, he was wary of getting too involved emotionally again, so he lived alone. He moved out into the country where a farmstead became his home and farm animals became his new *family*. With his sheep, he saw himself, literally, as the good shepherd.

"The malicious slaughter of his animals rekindled the overwhelming distress he had felt at the loss of his son and daughter. It brought back to the surface his rage against fate. It evoked an irrational guilt concerning fitness for his stewardship in life. In short, it demolished in symbolic fashion his flagging sense of self-esteem and his already damaged narcissism.

"No matter that he was not responsible for the death of his sheep. No matter that, in any case, it would be unrealistic to equate this event with the very different matters involved in the physical loss of his son and the emotional estrangement from his daughter. Emotions have a life of their own, and they make telling connections between events that our intellects may assure us are unconnected. All the anger from his losses and his injured narcissism became focused, as sometimes happens, on this one other person, as a sort of embodiment of those evil forces in his life that he wanted to stamp out."

Shifting in his chair, Kevin thought ironically: now there's an explanation with a familiar ring to it.

Mike intervened again at this point, trying to summarize for the jury Doctor Lofgren's complex symbolic excursion. "So the killing of the sheep really struck a nerve? In Doctor Kiley's vulnerable state, it brought back all the pain he had suffered in the past when he lost his children and focused it on this one other person, Mr. Polito?"

"That is correct."

"Were there still other factors involved?" Mike asked.

"Yes. And once again, in relationship to the impact of the past on the present. Once he developed the unshakable conviction that Joseph Polito was behind all the harassing behavior, Doctor Kiley logically felt that he was being bullied by the man. Nobody likes to be bullied, of course. But this had special significance to Doctor Kiley from his childhood. Partly because of his mother's extreme attitudes toward him—let's say, an enthusiasm that was unrealistically excessive even for mothers—he had developed an exaggerated narcissism. So when he was bullied as a child, as we all have been at one time or another, he experienced it as a profound defeat, an event that threatened the very foundations of his self-esteem."

"Doctor, you've used the word, *narcissism*, a few times, in referring to the defendant. Would you please explain that term for us?" Mike was continuing his effort to clarify the psychiatrist's psychodynamic explanation of behavior so that it would make sense to the jury.

"Certainly. Narcissism means self-love. The word comes from the Greek mythological figure, Narcissus, who fell in love with his own reflection in a pool of water. He became so entranced that he remained there, pining away till he died, becoming transformed then into the beautiful flower that to this day bears his name. We all, of course, have self-love. That isn't bad. It represents an appropriate appreciation of our own good qualities. But when our self-love becomes excessive, as it does from time to time in all of us, *that* causes problems, as symbolized in the myth by Narcissus getting *stuck on himself*.

"Narcissism generally has that connotation of excessive self-love. Doctor Kiley, albeit a talented person, developed an excessively inflated image of himself. At one level, this represented the picture he got from his doting mother. At a deeper level, it represented an intuitive recognition, never made fully conscious, that, *paradoxically*, he was not acceptable to his mother. That is, she accepted him only insofar as he represented this fantastically idealized figure. He had to approximate this figure in his own primitive mind, or she would reject him.

"So he had to live a lie to himself. And when something punctured this idealized self-image with the rudeness of reality, like a childhood bullying episode that most people shrug off or come to terms with, the effect on him was a quantum-leap more traumatic. His narcissism, or excessive self-love, was almost irrevocably bruised. In an effort to repair his shattered self-esteem, he vowed he would never again allow himself to be bullied—and achieved this for the most part by avoiding occasions where it could more easily happen. Of course, when he was recently bullied, he experienced it even more traumatically than the average person might have. He overreacted, focusing his defensive frenzy on the nearest likely suspect."

"So, Doctor, the defendant's childhood experiences with his mother gave him both an exaggerated sense of his own self-worth and an underlying feeling that he would be rejected by her unless he fulfilled in himself this fantastic picture that she had of him?"

"Yes."

"And *that* caused the bullying and the killing of his animals to be experienced as much more stressful than the average person would experience them—bearing in mind that those terrible incidents would have been markedly stressful to *anyone*?"

"Yes."

"Are there any other psychological factors that are important here, Doctor?"

"Yes. One of the predisposing factors to this condition is social isolation. Now we sometimes take that to mean *nobody else around*. But that's almost never the case. There aren't too many Robinson Crusoes, trapped all by themselves on a deserted island. Most socially isolated people languish within the midst of plenty. Their isolation may be caused by factors like living in a foreign country; for instance, the immigrant who can't properly relate to all these new people with their strange customs. Or the isolation may be caused by physical handicaps like severe deafness. Most commonly though, the isolation is caused by personality characteristics and life experiences that result in the person's estrangement from his potential friends and neighbors. Such was the case with Doctor Kiley.

"His unrealistic relationship with his mother resulted in a faulty marriage. We're all familiar with the tendency, expressed in that old song, to want a girl *just like the girl that married dear old dad*. Young men will be attracted to women who, in not necessarily obvious ways, resemble their mother, the first woman in their lives. For Doctor Kiley, that meant a woman who would adulate him and who would build her life around pleasing him. This immature fantasy was sustained through the courtship period, but, of course, not through the nitty-gritty of long-term day-to-day relations. He reacted by feeling progressively cheated, and the relationship gradually deteriorated. When, after more than fifteen years, he became involved with another woman who seemed to him better able to fulfill his unfulfillable fantasy, he left home. This action ruptured the relationship with his eleven-year-old daughter, Jessie, who'd been the most important person in his life since the death of his son.

"It also precipitated a falling out with his highly religious mother who could not accept this imperfection in his behavior—a falling out that was emotionally permanent, since he now became fully aware for the first time of the unrealistic nature of their relationship. He was likewise unable to make a full commitment to the new woman in his life, as he came to recognize that *all* his personal relationships were so heavily embedded in fantasy."

At this point, Linda, who'd been sitting in rapt attention as she listened to this psychiatric profile of the man she loved, shifted uncomfortably on the hard-backed spectator bench where she sat each day, inconspicuous but close. She clutched the large handbag on her lap, with its vital contents, and beat back a strong wave of feeling that all eyes in the courtroom had suddenly become focused in her direction. Her own eyes had as suddenly turned wet.

Meanwhile, Doctor Lofgren was continuing, "So he was estranged from all intimate and really meaningful relationships. Additionally, he'd lost the moorings formerly provided by his Catholic faith, and he'd become disillusioned with the processes of government in the country he loved, after having participated in the Vietnam War. Perhaps there was a parallel here with his personal life: exaggerated expectations leading to excessive disappointments.

"In the case of his religion, the increasing sense of personal mortality as he grew older was an important factor. After he'd been shot in his office parking lot, he regained consciousness with a vivid sense of his personal mortality. And he reasoned, if there is no immortality, all of the Christian sects are irrelevant. So he ended up profoundly isolated in the midst of plenty: bereft of family ties, lacking the consolations of his religion, and without confidence in the institutional workings of his Society. This isolation, brought about by the combination of his underlying personality in interaction with his life experiences, set the stage for his psychotic break—sowed the seeds, so to speak, of his vulnerability. For when we're under severe stress, it's the structure of the institutions with which we're affiliated, and it's the feedback from the important people in our lives, that helps to maintain our equilibrium, and tends to prevent our going off on an irrational tangent.

"A famous American psychiatrist, Harry Stack Sullivan, called this *consensual validation*. That is, we're ordinarily involved in a continual process of checking our views with those others around us—the *do you see what I see* sort of thing. The ongoing interplay, the constant feedback, is what keeps us from going astray. Lacking that, the isolated person becomes vulnerable. He can be victimized by his own distorted fears and uncorrected idiosyncrasies. Such, I believe, was the case with Doctor Kiley."

"Let me summarize then, Doctor Lofgren," said Mike. "You've testified that Doctor Kiley was *not* criminally responsible for his actions on the night of the murder. His behavior at that time, so unlike his ordinary state, resulted from the psychotic illness he suffered. This illness is called an Acute Paranoid psychosis, and is characterized by delusions of persecution that may lead to violent behavior. And while the cause of this illness is not fully known, it may be precipitated by severe stress, which Doctor Kiley was most certainly under. And social isolation, such as that evident in Doctor Kiley's life beforehand, also makes a person more vulnerable to this illness."

"Yes, Mr. Grady, that is correct."

"Thank you, Doctor Lofgren. That will be all."

CHAPTER 42

Mike was reasonably satisfied with the psychiatric testimony, though he always had reservations about this sort of evidence. In fact, he hated to have to depend on it, because psychiatric data seemed to him so *soft*. The reasoning left one with the uneasy sense of generalizations that might be applied after the fact to almost anything or anyone. And the psychiatrist's tendency to focus on the symbolic importance of a concrete life event reminded him of being back in college English, discussing the meaning of some modern poem. Still, he had done his best, and he believed the testimony had gotten across reasonably well.

* * *

In order to set the stage for his star witness, Mike had earlier called three police officers and had prepared them carefully for their testimony. He had drawn out of one the grossness of the scene that this officer had viewed on the morning after the sadistic slaughter of the sheep. He had listened to a second portray the twisted automobile wreck, the difficulty in extracting Doctor Kiley from the crunched-up cockpit, and the blood-splattering wounds from the crash.

The third officer, moustache still twitching, told about the eerie scene at the parking lot where the defendant had been fired at. He described the incredible apprehension one feels at staring down the barrel of a gun from the receiving end, and he empathized with the victim's emotional unraveling at the time—a state the officer went on to describe with details ranging from blanched face and incessantly rambling speech to urine-drenched pants and fetid odor. In short, Mike had used the same sort of testimony from this policeman that had been damaging to Kevin in the earlier court appearance, this time to his client's advantage. In fact, during preparation for the trial, the attorney had jogged the officer's memory continually in order to extract detailed embellishments of his client's emotional disarray.

Few witnesses, lacking something vital that they need to protect, will outright lie under oath. But since the truth is complex, and since a person cannot say everything, all testimony is false to some extent—

by both emphasis and omission. The effective trial attorney is seldom interested in soliciting perjured statements. Ethical concerns aside, they're too risky. Instead, he will try to size up the motivation of his witness and align himself successfully in order to elicit statements regarding those facets of reality that will be most favorable to his case.

Mike was a master at this art, reading his witnesses skillfully and helping them to articulate more vividly what they were willing to say in his favor. It was this interpersonal astuteness easily as much as his good intelligence that had brought him to the top of his field. And, of course. this ability was not reflected in his law school grades, because it's never tested. That kind of phenomenon in fact explains the great discrepancy between school grades and life performance in so many areas of work. For school grades measure some things that are of limited value in life achievement, and do not measure many other things that are extremely important in professional or commercial success.

Overall, the detailed descriptions and the supplementary opinions provided by the three policemen had set a favorable and believable stage on which to set Doctor Lofgren's key testimony. The ball was now back in the other court. It was time for the prosecutor to cross-examine this expert, and it was crucial that the prosecutor neutralize the doctor's testimony.

* * *

When Mike had dealt with the prosecution's psychiatrist, his cross-examination had been brief. He emphasized that this expert had been procured by the prosecutor and that he'd been used repeatedly by the DA's office in the past—to wit, a hired gun. Then he emphasized the limited time spent in examination of the defendant, a numerical fact whose inferior status he could graphically contrast with the many hours spent by the court-appointed psychiatrist. While not necessarily logical, he knew that more time would be emotionally translated by the jury into *better examination.*

We are all programmed to believe that, whether dealing with pills to treat illness or dollars to buy presents, *more is better.* Yet often, a brief examination is quite sufficient to delineate a problem, additional time being unnecessary and sometimes even counterproductive.

Looking at the empty gas gauge of a car that won't start may be quite sufficient to delineate the problem needing attention. And the diagnosis of acute appendicitis made by the surgeon within twenty minutes, may not be productively improved by observing and collecting additional data over the next seven days (and the patient may have died of a ruptured appendix in the meantime). But Mike avoided any direct confrontation with the expert on the issue of how much time was necessary for an adequate examination in this case. He just used the numbers to appeal to the jury's intuitive sense that more is better.

As for the substance of Doctor Koch's direct testimony, Mike ignored it. Why strengthen its appealing simplicity that the defendant knew what he was doing and that he had planned the crime ahead of time? Why ask questions that would allow more opportunity for the expert to underline and reaffirm the common-sense appeal of this line of thought?

* * *

The prosecutor's problem was different. He had to go after the neutral expert, and he had to do so in sufficient detail to make the conclusions derived from this doctor's testimony less than credible. In one way, his task might seem a discouraging one. He would be called upon to do battle in a foreign land, in an area outside his particular competence. How could he be expected to successfully challenge an opponent who knew light years more in the area under contention?

Yet Thornton Miller was not at all discouraged. Muscular in frame and lithe in movement, he had the athlete's natural confidence (a confidence based on being "hosied" first by whoever was picking sides during years of childhood games). But there was an additional reason for his confidence. The subject matter might indeed be a foreign land, but the courtroom was his home turf. He would be asking the questions. He would, therefore, be framing the controversy. His opponent could not gratuitously proffer information or introduce clarifying topics. And the power to choose the data to be amplified in a complex area is the power to shape what goes by the name of truth.

In fact, many an expert witness has ended up feeling after cross-examination like a powerful animal caged in the zoo. Outside his bars, a puny tormentor has confronted him. Were it not for the artificial barrier, he could easily trample right over his opponent. But the opponent keeps spearing him from a distance with a long barb. And when the expert attempts to smash through the bars, his tormentor simply slips around to another side of the cage, continuing to prod and poke until he, the once powerful animal, lies bloodied, exhausted, and defeated on the floor of his cage.

A strange way the courts have of dealing with the expert, or at least the innocent expert who hasn't yet learned to protect himself! But perhaps many years of experience have shown the court that this approach has fewer evils than the alternatives—or perhaps it's just that courts are run by lawyers and by judges who are former lawyers.

CHAPTER 43

"Now, Doctor," Thornton Miller's tone was crisp, "you spent more than fifteen hours interviewing the defendant?"

"Yes."

". . . who is a psychiatrist, like yourself?"

"Yes."

"I'm told it's easier, Doctor, to understand a person of similar background. Is that correct?"

"Other things being equal, it would be a positive factor."

"Was it in this case?"

"You mean, did it help me understand Doctor Kiley better? I suppose so."

"You *suppose* so?" If Thornton had analyzed the reason for his sudden emphasis here (as a boxer might explain in words on viewing the TV replay of a fight why he had spontaneously thrown a certain punch at a given time) the prosecutor might have explained that, as a rule of thumb, emphasizing any show of uncertainty in a witness subtly diminishes his credibility. It helps to build an impression that *"he don't know what he's talkin' about."*

"I don't think it was vital, but it was a factor that additionally helped me understand him." Without at this point fully seeing the direction of the prosecutor's questioning, Doctor Lofgren intuitively sensed it would be better to qualify and downplay his agreement.

"So the similarity of your backgrounds, including the fact that you are both professional men, both psychiatrists, both with successful practices, both additionally of an academic bent, did in fact contribute to your understanding?"

"Yes." (It certainly would have been hard to say "No.")

"Now, Doctor, I'm told that empathy is an important part in the sort of understanding a psychiatrist develops about his patient. Is that so?"

"Yes."

"Would you tell the members of the jury, Doctor, what is meant by that word, *empathy*?"

"Empathy refers to feeling with a person what they're experiencing, the ability to put oneself in their place."

"You mean, *his* place."

"I mean *his* or *her* place."

"But in this case, Doctor Lofgren, were you, during those many hours of interviewing, able at all to empathize with the defendant?"

"Yes."

"In other words, you were able to put yourself in his place?"

"Empathy, as used professionally, has a connotation of being able to feel with the other person while maintaining one's objectivity." Doctor Lofgren now saw clearly the direction of his opponent's thought and was trying to head him off at the gulch.

"Please answer the question, Doctor. Were you at all able to put yourself in his place?"

"I think I understood pretty well where he was coming from."

"Doctor, I sense that you're *avoiding* my question. Is there a reason for that?"

"I want to make sure I'm understood properly."

"That's what we're trying to do right now. Were you at all able to put yourself in the defendant's place?"

"Only in the sense that I could understand what he was going through."

"You could understand what he was going through?"

"To a degree, yes."

"You could empathize?"

"Yes."

"You could, that is, put yourself in his place as a fellow psychiatrist under duress?"

"As a fellow *human being*."

"And a fellow psychiatrist."

"Yes."

"And in empathizing with your fellow psychiatrist, in understanding him, in being able to put yourself in his place, you remained *absolutely* objective and unbiased at all times?"

Doctor Lofgren hesitated. He was aware of his counter-transference. He believed he had made proper allowance for the presence of his own feelings of identification with Kevin, and that he was able therefore to render a reasonably objective report. Should he answer "yes" in an oversimplified way that might make him look absurd (who, after all, is objective and unbiased at all times?), or should he try to explain the nuances of his reaction and risk appearing overly subtle? Finally, he answered, "I remained sufficiently unbiased to render a report that I believe is reasonably objective."

"Doctor, that was a mighty long pause before your answer. I hope *that* didn't reflect your actual degree of certainty in responding to this important point." In transactions among people, everything communicates something. At this moment, the prosecutor was interpreting for the jury the meaning he wished its members to attribute to the pause.

"I wanted to think, in order to give the proper answer," replied Doctor Lofgren.

"Your answer was certainly *very* proper," said the prosecutor, in a tone just this side of snide. "You wouldn't want the jury to think your testimony was at all biased to protect a colleague."

"I object, your Honor." Mike was on his feet indignantly.

"Objection sustained. The jury is instructed to ignore that last remark." Looking directly at the panel members, the judge delivered his words in the third person. Then turning to the prosecutor, he said sternly, "You are asked to conduct yourself professionally in this courtroom, Mr. Miller, and refrain from further gratuitous innuendo."

But how does a person *unhear* what he's just heard? How do the members of a jury go about ignoring an inference that's already been made? How do they go about erasing it from the tape of memory?

Thornton Miller went on as if no reprimand had occurred, turning to a new subject after having pursued his first issue as far as seemed advisable. Often it is better to understate a point, leaving the jury in some doubt, rather than to hammer the point into the ground. Doubt about any aspect of testimony decreases its credibility, and Thornton was out to chip away as much as he could.

"Doctor Lofgren, would you say the defendant was an intelligent man?"

"Yes."

"Highly intelligent?"

"Yes."

"In all the hours while you examined him, did he ever talk ragtime?"

"Ragtime?"

"I'm not sure what *fancy* words psychiatrists use. Did he ever speak incoherently, so you couldn't understand what he was saying?"

"No."

"He was mentally alert?"

"Very."

"And in obtaining a history, were you able to note anything strange, bizarre, or very unusual about his behavior?"

"He had missed some days at work, which was very unusual for him."

"How many?"

"I don't know offhand."

"You don't know *offhand*. Well, this is hardly an offhand matter, Doctor. This is a very serious matter, involving murder."

"That hardly requires me to be a human calculator with total recall of all numerical details, I hope," replied Doctor Lofgren evenly, thus turning the disadvantage of his uncertainty to advantage. The prosecutor now looked more like a harassing nitpicker. "If the exact number of days is important to you," continued Doctor Lofgren, "I'm sure we could obtain the figure from Doctor Kiley's office calendar. At any rate, most of the days were lost in connection with the specific traumatic incidents that have been described in the court already."

"So those missed days at work could hardly be considered bizarre?" Thornton was recovering quickly.

"Under the circumstances, no."

"Well, was there any other behavior—anything at all that struck you as strange?"

"Yes, the whole business of writing a letter with words clipped from magazines, the cloak-and-dagger plans for meeting Mr. Polito and enticing him back to his home—"

Thornton interrupted impatiently. "We'll get to the *murder plans* later, Doctor Lofgren. Aside from the *murder preparations* themselves, was there anything strange or bizarre in the defendant's behavior?"

"Not externally visible."

"That's what behavior means, isn't it? What a person does that we can see."

Doctor Lofgren's inner response at that moment was to debate whether to challenge the prosecutor's definition. For even sophisticated Behaviorists in their efforts to apply the fruit of animal studies to the more complex arena of human beings had started to talk about internal behaviors like his own present thought processes. He decided, however, that it would be an irrelevant ego trip to dispute the definition of behavior with the prosecutor. So he said nothing.

After a pause, Thornton continued his questioning, "Did the defendant have any past history of psychiatric illness?"

"No overt illness, no."

"So we are in agreement that the defendant is a highly intelligent man without any prior history of mental illness; that he is mentally alert, that he is fully coherent, and that he has exhibited no strange or bizarre behavior—other than *the planning and execution* of the murder itself?"

"Yes."

"Well, now, let's get to the murder plans. The cutting out of words from a magazine in order to form a message struck you as bizarre, Doctor Lofgren. Did any other aspect of his murder plans and behavior strike you that way?"

"Every aspect of it. Aggressive, assaultive, murderous behavior was completely foreign to his whole life."

"Then let's focus on the message formed from words out of a magazine. That struck you as bizarre?"

"Under the circumstances, yes."

"Strange and bizarre in the sense that you could see no realistic purpose to be served by it?"

"That depends."

"On what?"

"Well, it's characteristic of these paranoid states that if you accept the patients' delusional premises, the rest of what they think and do often makes sense. In this instance, once the delusional premise is accepted that Mr. Polito is with certainty the culprit, and once it is accepted that society will not afford proper protection, then there's a certain logic in everything that happened after that—including the note, of course."

As Doctor Lofgren was giving his response, Kevin leaned forward toward the table and scribbled something on the pad of paper in front of him.

Thornton Miller continued to pursue his point, "So you'll admit, Doctor, that the defendant's behavior in planning the murder, though strange by ordinary human standards of *moral* conduct, was highly purposeful in effecting the murder—and in effecting the murder so that the defendant would appear blameless?"

"Accepting his premises, the rest of his behavior seems not only understandable, but almost inevitable, yes."

"Yet you choose to look at this cold-blooded, premeditated planning as illness rather than evil?" A tone of heavy incredulousness imbued Thornton Miller's voice.

"Yes—since it was due to his illness."

"Doctor, how precise is your diagnosis?"

"It's based on standard psychiatric procedure, and it's delineated in the current Diagnostic and Statistical Manual of the American Psychiatric Association."

"That's not the question I asked, Doctor. How precise is your diagnosis?"

"Doctor Kiley's condition fits clearly into the criteria established in the current diagnostic manual for Acute Paranoid Disorder."

"Have you ever heard of the current Diagnostic Manual being referred to by other psychiatrists as a *Chinese cookbook*?"

"Yes."

"What does that mean?"

"It's meant, of course, as a criticism."

"By members of the American Psychiatric Association, itself?"

"Yes, that organization's hardly a monolith."

"And what is the nature of that criticism: *Chinese cookbook*?"

"According to the current manual, diagnosis is made phenomenologically. That is, a certain number of observable signs and symptoms have to be present in order to make a diagnosis, and other factors must not be present—must be excluded. This approach to diagnosis avoids the pitfalls of previous classifications that sometimes depended too heavily on unproven and unobservable theoretical factors. It also makes proper recognition that we are not sufficiently advanced yet in our field to have many instances of psychiatric diseases with clearly defined biochemical abnormalities. However, some critics have complained that the present system lumps patients into categories created by more or less artificial groupings of symptoms, selected much as one might pick a variety of dishes from the menu of a Chinese restaurant."

"All of that's a little hard to follow, Doctor. But would it be correct to say then that, among recognized psychiatric experts, your diagnostic system is under dispute?"

Doctor Lofgren hesitated again. Should he even try to engage with this jury of laymen, in a brief educational tour de force, the technical complexities of such matters as validation studies? There would be little chance of attaining clarity by such an attempt.

"We're *waiting* for your answer, Doctor." Thornton was taking advantage of this pause for internal debate to infer that the expert was hesitating before having to make a damaging admission.

Doctor Lofgren decided upon an oversimplified though more or less correct answer. "There is substantial consensus among psychiatrists currently that the present diagnostic system is the best available way of classifying illnesses."

"The best *available* way, Doctor? What does that mean? Garbage might be the best *available* food for a starving man, but there wouldn't be a great deal to be said for it."

"Well, there's a lot to be said for our present method of diagnosis, Mr. Miller! It helps to sort out and put order into what otherwise might remain a chaotic patchwork of disease. It takes advantage of the considerable body of knowledge we have accumulated about psychiatric disorders. Yet at the same time, it realistically recognizes the present limitations of our knowledge. In the future, as we learn more—and the power of sorting things out better provided by the present diagnostic groupings is going to help us know more—a new and more refined diagnostic classification will emerge."

Doctor Lofgren was being too darn eloquent from Thornton's viewpoint. When an expert is dealing with an area so difficult or unfamiliar that the layman can't grasp the subject readily, projection of competence counts heavily. It tends to produce a receptive response: *I can't exactly follow him, but it sounds to me like he knows what he's talkin' about.*

Thornton counterattacked: "Hold on, Doctor! Please. Please. We're not asking you for eloquent speeches to defend the *preliminary* state of knowledge in your profession. What we need is for you to answer the questions, not step around them with a bunch of fancy talk. I asked you if recognized experts in your field do, *in fact*, dispute the current diagnostic system. Now, is that true? Please answer that question."

"Yes."

"Yes, it's true?"

"Yes."

"Yes, it's true that recognized psychiatric experts do dispute the validity of the present diagnostic system?"

"They point out the limitations of the present system."

"Doctor, why is it so hard to get a direct answer from you? Why do you keep avoiding the questions? You're not trying to *downplay* the limitations of current psychiatric diagnosis, are you?"

"I wish to be careful that the limitations of our current psychiatric knowledge are not *overplayed*, so that the jury ends up with an exaggerated idea of our degree of imprecision."

"*Laudable*, Doctor. And I want to help the jury see, on the other hand, that your diagnostic methods are *imprecise*, that your diagnostic categories are *under dispute* within the psychiatric profession itself, and that by your own admission the limitations of the present diagnostic system destine it to be supplanted by a more *valid* one in the future. I think that's pretty important for the jury to understand when the time comes for them to evaluate your testimony—your testimony that *a planning and calculating murderer is not responsible for his crime*!"

"In any case, Mr. Miller, my opinion regarding the lack of criminal responsibility in this case does not rest on the particular label by which his condition happens to be called."

"Please! *Please*, Doctor Lofgren. No *speeches*. You've had ample opportunity in direct testimony to express everything you considered advisable to say. The court listened patiently to all the time you took. Now please limit yourself during cross-examination to answering the questions so we can clarify some important points for the jury."

"I was commenting, Mr. Miller, on the little speech you had just given." Doctor Lofgren spoke with an unflappable ease. Though limited in court experience, he was apparently a natural in this amphitheater.

"All right, Doctor Lofgren. If we take away the fancy label of Acute Paranoid Disorder, what is left of your opinion?"

"What is left of my opinion is the following. It has been known by doctors, for generations, that certain people will develop delusional convictions in which others mean to harm them. Under the sway of such delusions, counter violence will not uncommonly occur. The people subject to this acute state, whatever label one might choose to give it, often have been under severe precipitating stress, and they have tended to be socially isolated. This is the clinical picture presented by Doctor Kiley, and its validity does not rest on any current diagnostic label. The present APA Diagnostic manual simply provides a convenient and widely circulated device to categorize, discuss, and investigate this sort of condition."

Thornton decided it would be best to change tack a little. "Doctor, you keep referring to *delusions* as the core of the defendant's condition. But are there any *objective* tests that help confirm the diagnosis?"

"The diagnosis is based on subjectively stated symptoms and related behaviors. The behavior is externally observable and, in that respect, is objective."

"So it's based primarily on what a patient tells you, and the behavior he shows along with his statements?"

"To a large extent."

"To a *large* extent? What *else* is it based on?"

"The full consistency of the clinical picture, involving everything from vulnerable personality characteristics, social isolation, precipitating stress, and mental status characteristics. An example of the latter would be Doctor Kiley's excellent intelligence, yet his anger at any effort to directly challenge his delusions."

"We'll come back to these factors of *full consistency* later, Doctor. I'd like for the moment to stick with the fact that your diagnosis *to a large extent* depends on what your patient tells you and what he does in conjunction with that. Now, suppose I told you at the present time that I had the absolute conviction I was suffering from a fatal illness? Furthermore, I was convinced that the only thing that could save my life would be the continuing accumulation of money. And suppose, further, that my behavior was consistent with this. Suppose that I went around the room here taking money from the people, by force if necessary, to *save* my life. Would you diagnose me as insane on the basis of my statements and behavior? Or might you wonder if I were *telling stories* to my own advantage?"

"I would always have to weigh that latter possibility. But if, as a man in your position and with your sense of law, you were *actually* to go around this room attempting to beat people up right now—instead of just *talking* about it—I would be seriously concerned about your sanity."

An involuntary titter went through the courtroom and, though inwardly enjoying it a bit, Doctor Lofgren added earnestly, "I meant no disrespect, Mr. Miller. I was responding seriously to your hypothetical question by pointing out the importance of a person's *actual* behavior when taken alongside his *statements* and *previous life pattern*. If you were a habitual criminal instead of the responsible and high-minded public official that you are, I would then much more readily entertain the possibility that you were telling a self-serving story—that you were malingering, so to speak."

This graphic illustration by Doctor Lofgren of the importance of the total setting, plus his apparent magnanimousness toward his sharp-tongued interrogator, seemed to make a significant impression on the jury. It also set the prosecutor back some. It was Thornton Miller's turn now to pause overlong. Trying to recover, he asked with perhaps less than the usual authoritativeness in his voice, "But you do admit then that your diagnosis is not based primarily on objective findings at physical examination or on objective laboratory studies like x-rays?"

"Certainly."

"And that, therefore, it is possible for a patient to mislead at times if it is in his interest to lie?"

"I don't believe that's the case here, for reasons that I've mentioned, but, as a general statement, that would always have to be considered as a possibility."

"Then, if it's a possibility, your diagnosis is not a certainty."

"Not an *absolute* certainty, but a relative certainty, based on a careful consideration of the total clinical picture."

At this point, Kevin again leaned forward from his chair and scribbled a brief note on the pad of paper in front of him. Thornton, meanwhile, was trying to regroup. He referred to his notes, taken during Doctor Lofgren's testimony and organized for the specific purposes of cross-examination. He went on to his next point:

"Doctor Lofgren, assuming for a moment the credibility of the defendant's statements, let's explore the implications of your conclusion.

I guess what troubles me about it is the number of insane people you might diagnose. After all, if someone walks around with his hand in his vest and tells me he's Napoleon, that's pretty far out. That's pretty extreme. I can easily understand that sort of thing as a delusional conviction if the fellow's really serious. Doctor Kiley's so-called delusional conviction was, by contrast, nothing far out in itself. He experienced the persuasive coincidence, after all, of just having given an unfavorable disability report on a patient who then phoned him more than once to complain bitterly about what he considered an injustice done to him. Immediately after that, the crank telephone calls started coming anonymously, and it would have been quite easy for anyone to jump to a wrong conclusion. As far as the *extreme* persistence of his false conclusion is concerned, that type of thing can be seen everyday without having to observe the goings-on at a psychiatric hospital. We call that *pig-headed* or *obstinate*, Doctor. We don't need a fancy psychiatric term like delusion.

"Or if we did, we'd have every father who was convinced his teenage son took the car without permission last Saturday while he was away—but can't really prove it—locked in an insane asylum. We'd have every girl who was absolutely convinced her mother was being unfair to her declared incompetent. We'd—well—when we were through, we'd have no one left on the street. They'd all be *delusional*. Now, Doctor, are you planning to lead us all down this entryway to your hospital?"

"No."

"No?"

"No."

"Please explain, Doctor?"

"Explain what, Mr. Miller? You've just given me your lengthy opinion. Were you asking me to comment on it?"

"Yes."

"Well, then I will. It's obvious that the more bizarre the delusion, the easier it will be for even the inexperienced to grasp its nature. So anyone will get the picture pretty quickly on coming across a person seriously claiming to be Napoleon, or Caesar, or an extra-terrestrial being. But those same untrained people can easily miss other delusional illnesses because the beliefs involved aren't bizarre in themselves.

"Take the person with the hypochondriacal delusion that he has heart disease. Most of his friends won't see this as a delusion. It's a common and understandable fear, after all. So they'll just say: 'Poor Joe, he worries too much about his heart.' Yet Joe may have an unshakeable conviction that he has heart disease, even after complete cardiac investigation proves negative, and he may accompany this belief by behaving in the full fashion of a cardiac cripple.

"As for the two examples you mentioned between father and son and daughter and mother, that sort of thing usually involves passing incidents, though the incidents may be recurrent. If, however, those sorts or convictions were extreme and lasting on the part of one or the other, we might well be dealing with psychiatric illness. Sometimes the line between illness and health, between sanity and madness, can be a fine one. But in my opinion, Doctor Kiley had definitely stepped *over* that line."

"The line, as you judge it, Doctor, seems so fine that it's pretty easy to walk over it!" Thornton felt the snideness in his own voice as he reflexed out this gratuitous retort, more out of frustration than any positive purpose to be served. So far, he was not at all pleased with his own performance in this vital cross-examination.

Still, he was dogged. Hardly pausing for breath, he continued his relentless attack—more like the plodding fighter now who keeps moving forward because he knows no other way, though his counter-punching opponent seems to be punishing him at every turn. "Doctor, what if the defendant suddenly gets *cured*? What if he suddenly sees the error of his delusion—like right after an acquittal on the grounds of insanity?"

"Objection, your Honor!" Mike was on his feet again. "The expert has been called to give testimony regarding his professional opinion of the defendant's mental status *at the time of the crime*. That is the point at issue now, and the point would be prejudicially obscured by a hypothetical excursion into the possible mental status of the defendant at some future date."

"Sustained." The judge peered over his half-glasses at Thornton Miller. "Please confine your questioning of the witness to his findings at the time of examination as they refer to the crime in question."

Thornton was not happy with the ruling, but at least he had said enough to get his point across to the jury. "Doctor Lofgren," he continued, "I'd say that the defendant jumped to a hasty conclusion and then stuck to it in a pig-headed way. You insist on calling that a delusion. Okay, I'm not going to argue with your use of technical terms—though I don't see that all the *fancy* words you psychiatrists throw around have ever done that much good. But how do you go jumping from that to a conclusion that the defendant cannot adhere to the right?"

"Because his psychotic state led to the crime." Doctor Lofgren's tone was as matter of fact as if he were reporting the daily weather.

"That's a gratuitous statement, Doctor. That's your *opinion*. But what proof do you have to support your opinion?"

"Doctor Kiley was suffering from a psychotic illness that distorted both his judgment and his impulse control."

"Doctor Lofgren, did you not say that the reasoning and behavior of paranoid psychotics is quite understandable, quite rational, once you've accepted their delusional premises?"

"Understandable, in the sense that they are thinking coherently and you can follow their reasoning—yes. Rational in that their manner of thinking is balanced and their behavior is temperate—no."

"It's very hard to get a direct answer from you, Doctor."

"I believe my answer was very direct, given the complexities of the issue involved—human behavior."

"Well, let's see if we can sift through some of this *complexity* for the jury, Doctor. Will you admit that the defendant, in his mind, knew right from wrong?"

"Yes."

"Will you admit that he tried to disguise the murder that he had planned out ahead of time to make it look like a legal act of self-defense?"

"Yes, that has to be taken within the context of—"

Thornton interrupted, "Doctor, please—*please*! Just answer the questions. In this complicated matter of human behavior, I am trying to highlight some important points for the jury to remember—some plain points for them to keep in mind after they listen to all the razzle-dazzle *ifs, ands, and buts* of your testimony. I want to make sure they recall that you and I agreed at least on some basics; namely, that the defendant knew right from wrong and, in accordance with that, tried to disguise his murderous action by means of elaborate and premeditated planning."

Now, Doctor Lofgren interrupted vehemently, "Mr. Miller, your simplifications of my testimony for the jury distort—"

"Please, *please*, Doctor! No speeches. *Please!*" Thornton drowned out the expert's next words with a leather-lunged voice that clearly bested his opponent in decibel level.

But timing the brief pause after the last *please* just right, Doctor Lofgren burst through the jamming procedure with a staccato burst: "You're distorting my meaning by omission as if I said 'It may rain next Tuesday' and you changed it to 'It may rain' with the implication of 'It may rain today.'"

Turning to the judge, though really talking to the jury, Thornton said with an almost sigh that gave the impression of trying to maintain his patience with an exasperating witness, "Your Honor, would you remind the witness that he is to limit himself to answering questions now, and that he is not to make gratuitous speeches?"

The judge just nodded his head a couple of times, more with impatience than in affirmation. Continuing to look directly at the prosecutor, he replied simply, "Continue with your cross-examination, Mr. Miller."

Addressing his next remark to no one in particular, though of course targeted toward the jury, Thornton said, "Well, I think that point is clear anyway, and I hope we don't have to hear any more lectures about the weather forecast."

Then turning directly to the expert, he continued, "Now, coming to some of the *complexities* you described," and his voice was heavy with irony as he drew out the word, "you stated that the defendant was very isolated. Did you not?"

"I used that term to describe certain important elements of Doctor Kiley's situation that made him more vulnerable to his illness." Doctor Lofgren had vowed quietly to himself, after the last exchange, never again to be trapped into an unqualified yes or no answer if he could help it.

"Yes, of course, Doctor," Thornton said in mock appreciation. "Now, is it true that the defendant went every workday morning to the hospital?"

"That's my understanding."

"And is it true that he spent his time there talking with his patients, and with the mental health workers, and with the nurses, and with the other doctors, and with the people from medical records, and with other personnel?"

"I assume so, but that's not what I was referring to by the term, *isolated*."

"Please, Doctor, just answer the question. Now is it true that he went to his office from the hospital, and that here he talked with his secretary and a constant flow of people all day long?"

"I assume so, but that's not what I meant by the word, *isolated*."

"And is it true, Doctor, that two or three times each week, he then went over to his club where he played squash and socialized with his friends?"

"That's my understanding; but once again, it's irrelevant to my use of the term, *isolated*."

"And is it not true that he had a . . ." Thornton paused here nicely in midsentence, emphasizing the indelicacy which he was going to have to reluctantly mention "shall we say, close woman friend, a *very close* friend, whom he visited frequently—often staying overnight at her apartment?"

"That's my understanding, though the sort of closeness involved didn't overcome his *isolation*."

"Well, maybe that's the sort of thing you psychiatrists understand more than we ordinary people do, Doctor." Thornton was pleased to hear a faint titter in the room at this point. "But I just want the jury to be aware of all these facts when they think about your statement that the defendant was isolated."

"It's clear that I used the term in a different sense, Mr. Miller. One can be isolated right with people, *lonely in a crowd*—"

Thornton interrupted. "Please, Doctor. You had your opportunity already to explain yourself. Please limit yourself to answering my questions. We're trying to clarify certain aspects of this matter for the jury."

The prosecutor then glanced at his notes and paused for a moment to indicate a change of subject: "Doctor Lofgren, you described an incident of the defendant being bullied as a child. Is that right?"

"Yes."

"From *that* you concluded he had developed a need never to be bullied again—*ever?*"

"I said that the experience had contributed to his overreaction."

"Well, why not reach some other conclusion from that experience? Why not figure that he was a spoiled little kid with a swelled head, and it was probably healthy for him to be taken down a peg or two? I don't think, after all, there's a man among us here who didn't take his lumps as he was growing up. Why do you want the defendant to get special consideration because he got his too?"

"I don't want the defendant to get special consideration. And I'm certainly not defending excessive narcissism as a virtue. I was simply explaining to the jury some of Doctor Kiley's life experiences and underlying personality structure as these factors actually existed—and how they made him more vulnerable to being unhinged by the recent stresses in his life."

"Doctor, do you consider factors like divorce, unsatisfactory relationships with children, or disillusion with the Vietnam War, to be rare or unusual?"

"No, not at all."

"Yet you seemed to be weaving theories from things such as these. You seemed to be saying, 'Poor boy, see all the unfortunate things that happened to him in life. He shouldn't have to be held accountable for his actions.' Doctor, would you excuse everyone on the grounds of being unhinged by unhappy life events? Would you, in short, open all the doors and empty all the prisons?"

"I was helping the jury to understand one particular human being in terms of how his past experiences in life helped to shape him into the person he was at the time when the recent events began. It would be a gross distortion, Mr. Miller, to say that I would *excuse* anyone on account of unhappy life experiences . . ."

"Please, Doctor Lofgren. I must ask you again. No speeches."

"If you will do me the courtesy, Mr. Miller, of allowing me the opportunity *to fully answer* your questions, please! I had described a paranoid psychosis suffered by the defendant that had disturbed his judgment and impulse control. I said this illness could be *precipitated by* severe stress in a *vulnerable* personality. The factors you have recounted now were simply background incidents that I had brought to the jury's attention to illustrate one element in the chain, namely, a vulnerable personality."

* * *

The conflict between Thornton Miller and Doctor Lofgren wore on undeterminedly, and it seemed at times, interminably. The prosecutor attacked additional details of testimony, and the expert tried to parry the blows. When they were finally through, Doctor Lofgren stepped down from the witness stand, wearied from the intense effort of his sustained concentration. At the defense table, Mike Grady leaned over reassuringly to Kevin.

"The doc did all right," he whispered quietly but with obvious satisfaction. "Miller really had to discredit him, and I don't think he did it. Of course, you never know what a jury's going to do, but I'd say we're ahead on points."

Kevin did not return Mike's effort at eye contact. He simply remained grim-faced. Then, he said, "Mike, I want to testify."

"No way!"

"Why not?"

"We're in pretty good shape right now. Really, Doc."

"Maybe *you* are."

"Well, if I am, you are too. We're on the same team."

"In some ways, yes. In some ways, no."

"What do you mean?"

"Mike, I have to testify. I insist on it. It's my right."

A sinking feeling hit the bread basket of the usually unflappable defender. For what seemed a long while, he said nothing.

CHAPTER 44

Mike's request for time to confer with his client fell near the end of the court's day. When appraised of the reason, the judge approved and gaveled the afternoon session to an end.

From her seat on the first spectator bench behind the defense table, Linda had sensed something wrong. She had noted the mask of strained tension on Kevin's face during Doctor Lofgren's testimony. And she had seen his lack of response to Mike's enthusiastic overtures after the completion of cross-examination.

When she found out later that Kevin insisted on testifying, over the stringent objections of his defense attorney, Linda was distressed. She felt in her heart that this was the time she had been preparing for. Yet as the hour grew closer, she found herself less and less confident. It was one thing to know, in theory, how to proceed. It was quite another thing to execute one's plan when the person nearest and dearest in life actually collapsed with rosy cheeks onto the hardwood floor amidst the sweetish aroma of almonds. Finally, she decided she would bring in reinforcements for the big day tomorrow.

* * *

The conference with Kevin had been a difficult one for Mike. His client seemed bent on snatching defeat from the jaws of victory. Kevin started his explanation this way: "I've been sitting there every day during this trial, and I've come to some conclusions."

"Like?"

"Like when . . . I killed Joe Polito, I did what I *had* to do. I'm not ashamed of it. I'd do it again. Because no matter what you folks think, I know *he* was the one who almost killed me. And I know, given more time, he would've completed the job.

"I should probably be indifferent to what that jury thinks of me. I know they're just twelve little people trying to get by in life. But you know what? I find that I *do* care. I'd like to be completely indifferent to the opinions of others, but I have to face the fact that I'm not. Not that they *agree* with me. I'd like that, of course, but it's not the crucial point. If they say, 'You shouldn't have done it, no way! You've got to be locked up,' okay, I can handle that. But somehow, I can't stomach the notion that they should take one of my most carefully deliberated human acts, perhaps the most carefully thought out decision I've ever made, and judge it to be the nonhuman act of an insane creature."

Mike shook his head. "Doc, let's not get off the track onto some technical question of sanity. You don't think you're really guilty of a crime here—just something you had to do. I don't think you're guilty either. You were all prepared to use one of society's loopholes, the defense of self-defense. So we're just using another loophole instead. What's the difference, as long as you're found not guilty of something you're not guilty of?"

"Mike, do you think I'm insane?" Kevin looked straight at his attorney.

His defense counsel returned his gaze firmly—and paused.

Waiting a brief moment, Kevin continued, "You have to think about that one, huh? Well, that's what's important to me, Mike. More important than a *not-guilty* verdict. I may not be able to convince you, and I may not be able to convince Bill Lofgren, but I want the chance to convince a jury of my peers."

All Kevin was managing to do at this point, however, was to convince Michael Grady that his client was crazier than ever. "So suppose, Doc, that you're able to convince the jury, with the aid of good ole Thornton Miller, that you should be found guilty? Will that prove anything? Will it prove your sanity? Remember, that jury more than anything else is a swaying reverberating pool of human emotion. There's a sadistic element in that protoplasmic mass, ready to throw the book at any defendant in order to *restore law and order* in their lives. There's a primitive element there that harkens back to the crowds at the old Coliseum in Rome, waiting bloodthirsty on the edges of their seats to cast thumbs down on the life of the luckless gladiator before them.

"Tell them you did what you had to. Look them straight in the eye as you defend your action. Explain to them your reasonableness, and I don't doubt they'll turn their thumbs down on you as a cold-blooded instrument of infamy. The whole *insanity* business will insanely drop out of sight. You won't have proved a goddamned thing, except that people are temperamentally programmed computers, and that you just pushed all the *thumbs-down* buttons."

"Sometimes, Mike, I realize that you're even more cynical than I." Kevin laughed with a lightness of heart totally out of keeping with the situation. "Let's just say," he concluded, "that you and I will interpret the data of their verdict differently."

CHAPTER 45

The following morning, as Kevin filed into court, he nodded *hello* to Linda who was sitting in her usual seat. Then he noticed Bob Upton sitting beside her. Smiling a little, Kevin waved, but he was too preoccupied with his planned testimony to give the matter further thought. Bob, an anesthesiologist, who administered Pentothal and muscle-relaxant medication intravenously as part of the modern procedure for shock treatments, had been friendly with him for several years, so it was not totally odd to appear in court as a sign of support.

In fact, that relationship had given Linda the sense that she could call on Bob for help in this extreme situation. As an anesthesiologist-expert in the use of life-support systems with the unconscious patient, he was the ideal companion for this morning's venture. He had even brought with him, inconspicuously placed at his feet, a small carrying case containing an Ambu bag. This apparatus consists of a rubber face-mask attached to a spongy air bag. Forming a close seal with the mask around nose and mouth by firm pressure with the left hand, the right hand can rhythmically squeeze air in and out of the lungs by means of the air-bag bellows. The efficiency, not to mention the aesthetics, far surpasses mouth-to-mouth resuscitation.

Bob was motivated by his regard for Kevin, as well as by his friendship with Linda, to take the time from his busy schedule to be present for this possible crisis. He was also motivated by the potential excitement of publicly saving a life in a tense courtroom drama—though he did not admit this last element to consciousness. Strong motivating factors are not always acceptable to a person's sense of dignity, which is much more enhanced by allusion to altruistic factors.

As Kevin sat at the table with his legal defender, he thought of their conversation after the previous court session: "Mike, what are you going to ask me on the stand?"

"Not much," was all his lawyer had answered. "You're the prosecution's witness. I'm sure Thornton will ask you questions to your heart's content during his cross-examination."

Kevin was not completely unaware of his lawyer's dilemma. How often, as a psychiatrist, had he been confronted with a patient who was resistant to following an optimal treatment program? How much should he compromise then before resigning from a case, especially when dealing with a patient whose illness was of such a nature as to becloud awareness of its very presence? And Michael Grady had, in fact, considered the ultimatum: "Either follow my advice and don't testify, or get yourself a new lawyer!" He knew though that this would be tantamount to resigning from the case, and he still felt a commitment. This was just another obstacle, like a bad trump split that had come up in the play of the hand.

So he tried to figure out the best way to compensate. He would make his own direct examination brief, trying to help the jury understand that a normal person does not go out of his way to testify against himself. Then he would hope for the best in regard to cross-examination. Mike did not have the highest regard for Thornton Miller's abilities, and he allowed himself to hope that the prosecutor might plod on counter-productively in his questioning.

Mike had also contacted Doctor Lofgren, who expressed no surprise at this turn of events. He agreed to provide additional testimony that a delusionally psychotic patient, by the very nature of his illness, cannot have full insight into the fact of his condition. Or as the doctor expressed the point: "If he knew his delusion was a delusion, it wouldn't be a delusion."

After the usual formalities of opening the day's court session, Kevin took the stand.

"Doctor Kiley, why did you want to testify today?" Mike asked.

"To talk to the jury."

"And what did you want to say to the jury?"

"I wanted to assure them that I was in my right mind." Kevin smiled at his own words, inappropriately perhaps under the circumstances, but aware of the absurdity of his position.

"And do you recall my advice to you?" Mike was matter of fact.

"Yes."

"What was that?"

"You advised me not to testify, because it would be against my own best interests to do so."

"Thank you. Your Honor, that will be all."

Mike took his seat, and Thornton approached the witness stand almost greedily, aware that he'd been given an opportunity equivalent to a turnover on his opponent's five-yard line with a minute left to the game and only three points behind.

"Doctor Kiley, you're aware that the court-appointed psychiatrist came to the conclusion that you were insane?"

"Yes."

"And you disagree with that?"

"Yes."

"Why?"

"May I take the time to explain?"

"By all means."

"My diagnosis of Acute Paranoid Disorder depends basically on Doctor Lofgren's judgment that I am delusional. Specifically, that my conviction about Joe Polito as my alleged tormentor was incorrect and *rationally uncorrectable*. Yet I am certain"—and at this point, Kevin turned to eye the jurors directly—"if matters had turned out differently—if I were a free man today—I would also be free from my previous terror, because my actual assailant would no longer be around to perpetrate his outrages—"

Thornton interrupted, "Doctor Kiley, I don't think it's necessary to drag the name and reputation of a dead man in here like this—"

Kevin interrupted back sharply, "You told me I could explain. Now *let me do it!* I wouldn't have had to take this stand in the first place if you had demonstrated any competence in your cross-examination of Doctor Lofgren. It's just my luck to run across a young star in court when I needed a dunce, and a dunce like you, when I needed competence!"

Thornton stood incredulous for the moment. He could scarcely believe that he was being badgered by a witness. Then a patently suspicious glint dawned slowly in his eyes. His neck drew back, and his face-line lengthened in indignation. "Doctor Kiley, I must ask you to show respect for the court if you cannot do so for the person. What are you trying to accomplish?"

Kevin laughed derisively at him. "I can see what's going through your pea-brain right now: 'Maybe this guy's out to look crazy as a clincher for the jury.' Well, let me assure you, that's hardly the case. In fact, the only thing you and I have in common is the wish to prove my sanity. It's just that I've been frustrated, sitting here impotently during these proceedings. And I have little reason to be tactful about your performance. I just felt like calling a spade a spade, so I did."

"Doctor Kiley, let's stick to the issue then." Thornton was absolutely raging underneath, especially since the defendant's criticism had hit a nerve.

Kevin went on, "Mr. Miller, you took exception to my—shall we say—highly derogatory remarks toward the deceased Joe Polito. In other circumstances, I might admire your chivalry in admonishing me, in effect, to speak well of the dead. *Dice Bonum Mortuorum*," Kevin added, "But in the present case, we can't afford to cushion the realities about Mr. Polito too much without making my behavior seem incomprehensible and, therefore, lacking sanity."

"I see the logic of your point." Thornton had decided to stand aside for the moment and give the defendant enough rope to hang himself.

"Mr. Miller, you yourself referred to the timing of the predations I experienced as a *persuasive* coincidence. So let's start with that. I had been in practice for over twenty years and I had never—*not one time*—ever been directly threatened by a patient. Then I was threatened by one specific patient, Mr. Polito, about a specific issue. The subsequent harassments then continued in an unbroken and progressive chain from that time on—harassments which I had never been subject to before in my life. That certainly fills the bill of your *persuasive coincidence*, by which is really implied: *no coincidence at all!*

"Returning to the complaints and threats: the phone calls started and were repeated in a continuous series. In his first phone calls, Mr. Polito identified himself directly. Then there was a transitional call in which he misidentified himself in the original message, but identified himself directly during the course of our conversation. Following that transitional call, he never identified himself again directly by name. But I could identify that voice and its perturbations *anywhere* by then—much better than the face that I had seen only once, and which I admit I was tricked into misidentifying by a clever lawyer.

"Each of you on the jury might think"—and Kevin looked at them now with increased intensity—"that you can't identify a voice on the phone that flawlessly. But believe me, concentration is the key. When someone makes his calls *that* important to you, you pay attention.

You pay *close* attention. You can recall *every* fluctuation and intonation of that voice, because it grips you without distraction.

"There were external factors too that were corroborative. Mr. Polito had, in fact, been emotionally unstable. He had a strong tendency to be paranoid. And, in fact, the incident that led to his job loss involved his assaulting a fellow employee while under the influence of his paranoid thinking.

"As the phone calls continued, so did the magnitude of the threats. And as they crescendoed, the off-phone harassments started. When that person fired at me from the rim of darkness in my parking lot, I recognized his voice as well as you might recognize the voice of the one closest to you in life speaking from several feet away.

"And, finally, when I offered blackmail or *protection* money to him, he understood perfectly why I should be anxious to do so. He had every reason to believe, from his inside knowledge of what had transpired, that he had me thoroughly frightened and intimidated.

"Now, what about his wife's alibi? Let me ask you, how would each of you react when called upon, in effect, to protect both your spouse and your family's good name? If you would have even some hesitation before telling the truth, then put another person's alibi in that same context. Measure the degree of credibility you can attribute to it.

"Mrs. Polito said her husband was *always* home. But in the random sample of his behavior for the few days I incurred the large expense of monitoring his activity, I discovered that he went out for a goodly part of *every* night. The police must have known that. My defense lawyer knew that. But perhaps in deference to her widow's grieving—which I can understand—no one challenged her in court on the issue.

"Perhaps as you're listening now, you're saying to yourselves, 'He's got a point there. He doesn't sound way out. He had good reason to believe that this Polito fellow was the culprit. But that's not the same as being *really certain*.' Well, if you're thinking that, let me ask you what we ever mean by that term?

"Mr. Miller asked the good Doctor Lofgren if he was certain about my diagnosis, and he replied, quote, 'not an *absolute* certainty but a *relative* certainty.' That, ladies and gentlemen of the jury, is a word game. *Certain* means sure, *definite*, established beyond doubt or question. Why then admit to degrees of relative or absolute certainty?

Either a thing is certain, or it's not. I only wish Mr. Miller here had brought that to the attention of the expert witness.

"The fact is, *relative certainty* does not mean certainty at all. It's euphemistic for a very high degree of probability—sufficient to justify practical action. And that is what we're forced to operate on in life for the most part. Doctor Lofgren was telling you in effect that he considered his diagnosis probable enough that he would act on it with appropriate behavior—namely, that he would come to court and testify in that regard.

"In a much more momentous matter, I did likewise. So I lacked a mythical *absolute certainty* that Joe Polito was the culprit. Let's say for the sake of argument that the *degree of probability* of my conviction was equivalent only to the probability that no one in the major leagues next year is going to bat 600 for the whole season. Well, tell me, how would you like those chances for living out the year—pretending for the moment that your life depended on someone reaching that batting average? Your chances would be better with a malignant melanoma spread throughout your body! Yet you can't say with *absolute certainty* that no one will hit 600 next year. It is theoretically possible.

"Well, that's what I was faced with—the *overwhelming* probability, a *relative certainty*, certainly exceeding that of my confidence in Doctor Lofgren's diagnosis, that Joe Polito was the culprit—that he might well have killed me already when he sideswiped my car, and that he *would* kill me after a little bit more time for torture.

"Now I'd like to address another aspect of my so-called delusional premise, naively put forth in testimony by Doctor Lofgren and bizarrely ignored by Mr. Miller. The good doctor stated, and I quote verbatim from the notes I took: *'Once it is accepted that society will not afford proper protection, then there's a certain logic in everything that happened.'* That, ladies and gentlemen, was put forth, I remind you, as part of my delusion. Well, just picture the following scenario. Suppose that a desperado like myself were let free to wander the streets. And suppose that all the fury of my alleged madness were to be directed at the good doctor, insulted as I was by his report. And suppose, further, that my madness were to be galvanized by the discipline of a single purpose, to wreak revenge craftily and skillfully on my unfortunate adversary. Evidently, Doctor Lofgren has the *unshakable conviction* that he would be adequately protected by the State."

Kevin paused at this point, then stared intensely at the jury, his eyes scanning each member successively in both rows. Then he continued, his voice dropping momentarily to a lower pitch, almost of intimacy, "Do you think so? Do you think he would be?" Then rearing back, he exclaimed loudly, "Well, think again! In our society, he'd be a *sitting duck*. Sure, he could get a restraining order against me so I could be arrested if the police found me on his premises. But unless all you good folks wanted to quadruple your tax expenditures for police protection—which'll never happen—the police will *never* have the manpower to keep every crackpot like that under protective surveillance. Why, the police departments can't even muster enough men to keep a visible presence on our city streets. The *Thin Blue Line* ought to be renamed something like the Ethereal Blue Vapor!

"If the good doctor were a multimillionaire, he could hire his own bodyguards. But even doctors, whom we all know are rich bastards, don't have that kind of bucks. No, ladies and gentlemen, if I were careful, patient, and crafty, I could harass and hassle him as much as I wanted—slowly turning the screws tighter over a salaciously sadistic interval of my own choosing." Kevin illustrated the last point by a slow and exaggerated twisting motion of his right thumb and crooked forefinger against the opened palm of his left hand.

After a brief pause to let his point sink home, Kevin continued, more briskly now, "Mr. Miller knows the workings and limitations of the police departments better than I. Why didn't he correct Doctor Lofgren's naive mis-supposition? Why didn't he point out these facts of life to the good doctor, perhaps correcting his pre-delusional conviction of degree of safety providable by the state? This would have enabled the expert to rethink part of his conviction that *my* conviction was delusional.

"You may think the answer to that question lies in Mr. Miller's mental torpor." And, here, Kevin almost laughed. "Well, after listening to him for all this length of time, I can't say you'd be wrong. But I think there's an additional explanation. In public, even in the courtroom, Mr. Miller is a member of the *Law Keeping Club* of our Society. There are some fictions which, as a member of good standing in the Club, he is honor-bound to keep. One is that *Society can protect all its individual members*. He would have had to violate his sacred trust as a law-enforcement official to challenge Doctor Lofgren's naiveté.

"And after all, think of the unfortunate awkwardness that would flow from the explosion of such a myth. People might start to say things like: 'Gee, what choice did this fellow, Kevin Kiley, have? It's true, he really was exposed like a soldier on open ground out there in no-man's land. We, the State, couldn't really protect him. If anyone was going to do it, he had to be the one. He had to depend on himself!'

"Well, you can see how pernicious—not to mention seditious—that line of thought might be. So it has to be squelched, ladies and gentlemen. It has to be *ignored*. All members of Society in good standing must avert their gaze. We must all huddle together and accept a comforting falsehood—a group delusion, one of the insanities of Society itself: 'He was *safe!* He was *protected!* Only his own willfulness caused him to take the law into his own hands!' Now put him away quickly before we all have to see the truth!"

Kevin, who had worked himself into a crescendo, now let it fall away like a composer not yet ready to finish his piece. He paused reflectively while Thornton Miller looked on, indecisive as to whether to let his witness ramble unchecked. The issue uppermost in Thornton's mind lay sharply circumscribed. Was the defendant's unfettered testimony convincing the jury of his sanity? Or were his ravings coming across to them as manifestations of a deeply troubled mind?

While the prosecutor was still debating inwardly, Kevin resumed his harangue, "I'd like to return, for a moment, to the issue of *certainty*. I've said to you that, almost always in life, this comes down to a *high degree of probability*. We use the word *certainty* then to comfort ourselves because, in truth, we are always called upon to choose our upcoming actions on the basis of our *best estimates*—on the basis, that is, of *probabilities*. We are forever being called upon *to certainly act without certainty*.

"In a little while, you will be called upon to render a verdict about me. You will be told to be certain *beyond the shadow of a reasonable doubt*. Fine sounding words! An exquisite turn of phrase! No wonder it's been incorporated into our legal rituals. How could you ever turn down such a handsomely stated concept? But what does it mean? Stripped of the rhetoric, it means: 'If it's very, very probable, vote it!' But how probable is *very, very probable*? That depends—on a lot of things.

"If the testimony allowed is controlled tightly to protect a defendant's civil rights, if the jury is of a temperament to bend over backward to make sure that no innocent man is ever sent to prison, then there will be few false convictions—but a whole bunch of criminals walking the streets. If looser standards are applied to prevent that latter evil, fewer criminals will be freed, but more innocent men will be convicted. It will always come down, however, to a choice based on *probabilities*.

"Now let me paint the following scenario for you. Suppose a jury has to make its decision—conviction or acquittal—in the case of a certain alleged assassin. The jury members are conscientious folk who want to give the defendant every benefit of the doubt. The evidence mounts, however, to a sufficiently high degree of probability that the jury members finally reach a point where they're near ready to convict. Yes, the fellow certainly gives every evidence of guilt. However, there might still be the tiniest shred of lingering doubt. How is the jury going to vote, my friends?"

Kevin paused, and then added, "Oh, yes, let me throw in one additional factor here. There's a special peculiarity that applies to the jury I'm telling you about. You see, if they acquit this alleged assassin, and if he is *actually* an assassin, he is going to murder each and every one of them.

"Of course," and Kevin changed to a lighthearted tone at this point, "if he's not guilty, they don't have to worry because he won't murder them. Now, friends, do you think, in my little scenario, that these good and conscientious jurors are going to be influenced at all by this fact? Are they likely to peg a guilty verdict at a slightly lower level of *relative certainty* than if they were *above it all?*"

Kevin waited for the jury to reflect on this for a moment—he had their attention—then he added whimsically, "You know, folks, I was on such a jury once." Then he turned back to the prosecutor and said with quiet firmness, "That's my answer to your question, Mr. Miller—why I disagree with Doctor Lofgren's opinion about my sanity."

Thornton hesitated. He thought he should question the defendant further, but he couldn't think of what he should ask. Finally, he turned to the judge, and said, "No further questions, your Honor."

Bob Upton had been spellbound by the whole performance. He turned enthusiastically to Linda and whispered loudly: "*All right!* Old Kev is right on there. They ought to let him go."

Linda smiled at Bob's enthusiastic support. It pleased her, though she was too much of a realist to delude herself. She knew in her heart now how the verdict would go. Guilty! But at least, she thought, Kevin looked brighter. The chance to tell his side of the story seemed to have released a poison, like pus drained from a finally opened abscess. She knew that at least for this moment she did not have to fear his suicide. After the verdict though . . .

CHAPTER 46

After Kevin's testimony, the court session was adjourned until the following day, in order to allow further testimony by the court appointed psychiatrist. Doctor Lofgren duly documented for the jury the paradoxical nature of a delusional illness that prevents a patient from having insight into the fact of his illness while in its throes. He summed it all up neatly again: "If a person with a delusion *knows* it's a delusion, it isn't a delusion." He noted that highly intelligent patients will reflect this quality of mind in the subtlety of their reasoning and the cleverness of their rationalizations: "So they may *seem* to make sense even when they're quite ill." He also expressed the opinion, which he granted to be of a more speculative nature, that Doctor Kiley's inner sense of guilt about the murder had driven him to, in effect, seek punishment by proclaiming his responsibility for the crime as forcefully as he could.

Then the time came for the prosecution and defense to render their final summations to the jury. The prosecutor's turn came first. Beginning in low-key fashion, Thornton suggested the evil in this man. He pointed out how the defendant's intemperate hostility had come out even in the courtroom, once the defense had taken him out of wraps; that even being the prosecutor and an officer of the court had not provided protection against the defendant's abuse; that a dead man had been maligned as if himself on trial and without even the opportunity to defend himself; that the dead's man widow and grieving family had been assaulted with a malicious charge tantamount to the accusation of perjury. And all this, suffered at the hands of the *admitted* murderer!

Thornton expressed recognition of the defendant's intelligence and clever eloquence. He emphasized though the one basic fact at issue, "Doctor Kiley is the admitted murderer of Joseph Polito. That fact is *certain*," and he intoned the last word with almost a snide snarl, in obvious juxtaposition to Kevin's discussion of the term. "The only question for the jury is one of *responsibility*. Is this highly intelligent man who coldly and calculatedly planned such a heinous crime to be held responsible for his actions?" Thornton's suggestion to the jury was a resounding, "Yes."

On his side, Michael Grady was pretty much saddled with his original game plan despite the unexpected appearance of the *prosecution's* star witness at the trial's end. Mike emphasized his defendant's lifetime record as a responsible citizen and highly regarded physician. He recounted the terrible stress that his client had been subject to, stress that had ultimately caused his breakdown. He underlined the fact that the court's own impartial expert had diagnosed an acute psychotic illness, and it was this illness alone that could make in any way comprehensible the performance of such a violent act by a man of peace, by a physician who had proudly devoted his lifetime to the sustenance and nurturing of life.

Mike granted to the jury that his client's madness bore the eerie appearance of rationality. But he pointed to the expert's testimony indicating the subtle nature of psychosis in such a person. He also pointed out, more by innuendo, that an intelligent person in his right mind does not go out of his way to send himself to prison for life.

So the jury retired to debate its decision, and Linda waited to spring into action when the time came. She was convinced now that the crisis would occur in the courtroom, right after the verdict. Kevin was, as she tried to experience it from his point of view, in a *no-win* situation. He obviously could not tolerate the notion of being not-guilty by virtue of insanity. Nor would he accept a life of incarceration at Walpole until—so she hoped—he had more time to adjust to the idea and to the anticipation of eventual parole. She had to see to it that his immediate response of rashness would not be fatal. She had to play for time.

* * *

She waited, and waited, and waited. Kevin waited. Michael Grady waited. Thornton Miller waited. The whole court waited. Everyone had expected an early verdict, which never came. At day's end, the judge discovered that eleven members of the jury had reached a consensus expeditiously. However, one juror dissented and seemed absolutely adamant in his opinion. Finally, the judge ordered the jury sequestered for the evening, to continue its deliberations on the following day.

CHAPTER 47

By the third day, it had become abundantly clear that the jury was hopelessly hung. It turned out that a unanimity had easily been reached that the defendant was not insane. Doctor Lofgren's testimony had seemed overly subtle, and Doctor Kiley had appeared much too *with it*. For most of the jurors, the alternative was so obvious that it hardly needed debate. If he wasn't crazy, then he was guilty. Maybe there were extenuating circumstances. Maybe the judge would take this into consideration in terms of the sentence imposed. But the basic facts remained. He had committed the crime. He bore responsibility for it. He was guilty.

The fly in the ointment came in the form of one Juan Gonzales, a 28-year-old, free-spirited, sometime-carpenter. Born and raised in the Jamaica Plain section of Boston, he was quick-witted although he had never settled down in school, finally receiving his high school equivalency diploma while on active duty with the Army. Divorced at the age of 22 after a short and tempestuous marriage, he had an extensive circle of friends from a similar ethnic background, though he lived alone. He was a hard but intermittent worker. He also played hard and was somewhat of a lady's man. His friends would not have been surprised to hear about his stubbornness. As one of his acquaintances said to a reporter later, laughing as he spoke, "When he gets his head set, man, look out!"

Juan said to his fellow jury members, "Look, I don't care what our instructions are. I buy that guy's story all the way! I don't think he's crazy, but there's no way I'm going to find him guilty. I'd have done the same thing to some bastard who got on my case like that." There was simply no reasoning with him. Or rather, there were three unsuccessful days of trying to reason with him. Long before the judge finally called the mistrial, his fellow jurors realized that Juan was hopelessly intransigent.

But another strange thing happened. Though a judge is often seen by professional prosecutors and defense lawyers as malignantly biased in favor of the other side, the average citizen often thinks of him as an impartial referee, trying to render justice fairly and above all personal bias. Yet many of his rulings reveal well his own personal judgments—

his own verdict, so to speak. Kevin had been detained in hospital and jail settings until the trial's end. Now the judge set a $50,000 cash bail, a figure readily accessible to Kevin through an emergency loan from his retirement fund. The effect was to give Kevin his immediate freedom for the next several months, the probable interval until his new trial would be initiated.

Kevin was well aware of the message behind the ruling. The judge obviously did not consider him a maniac too dangerous to be let loose in the community. But most of all, Kevin felt deliriously euphoric about the jury outcome. He had hoped only for a *guilty* verdict as the lesser of two evils. He was completely unexpecting and totally overwhelmed by the final result. In his mind, he tried to fight the spontaneous surge of euphoria by pointing out to himself the reality that the hung jury meant but a temporary respite, and that he would eventually in all probability be found guilty. That's a relative certainty, he joked to himself.

But no thoughts could abate his euphoria, as Linda and he publicly embraced before leaving the courtroom. In the corridor outside, a local TV news-coverage team was waiting with bated breath. Young and handsome Clinton Ellis brushed back his blonde hair and threw his left arm around Kevin in an act of aggravating intimacy, holding the microphone with its umbilical cord to the world in his right hand. Close floodlights in the corridor washed out their faces. "Are you satisfied? Are you satisfied, Doctor, with the outcome?" Clinton was asking with the delight of a local newscaster who has found something different from the three-decker fire or placard-pacing-protestors to report on.

"Amazed," said Kevin.

"Do you think it was fair—to all concerned?"

"I think I did what I had to do."

"What do you think about the dissenting juror? What do you think about Juan Gonzales?"

"It was important to me that I explain to a jury of my peers that I did what I had to do, as a rational act, under terrible duress. I can't tell you how it feels to be understood by another person—*really understood*—by a person who had come into a position of importance in my life. I wanted a chance to talk to a jury of my peers, but Juan Gonzales was more than my peer. No matter what happens in the future, I will be eternally grateful to him. I have never felt less estranged; I have never felt more understood; I have never felt more a member of human society than I do today."

"Do you have any message you'd like to give?" And handsome Clinton worked the microphone back in front of Kevin who looked at the broadly smiling young man beside him, amazed at himself that he could still be amazed after all these years at a fellow human being's vacuousness.

"Sure, Clinton," he said in his irrepressible euphoria of the moment, "how about something really fresh like: you can fool all of the people some of the time, and some of the people all of the time, but you can't fool all of the people all of the time."

"Yes, Doctor Kiley. Now tell me, what will you plan to do until your next trial?"

"Minister to my patients." Kevin smiled broadly. "Though I don't think I'll be overwhelmed with new referrals right now. And I think I'll leave the disability evaluations to someone else, so I'll have time to tend to my homestead and"—looking over at Linda, he continued—"redefine some of my personal relationships."

"Thank you, Doctor Kiley. This is Clinton Ellis, reporting from . . ." and his voice trailed off, as Kevin moved away from the plastic smile toward the courthouse steps and the outside air. Linda was beside him again, arm in arm, as they walked. Mike caught up, jostling Kevin's shoulder spiritedly. "See what happens when you don't take your lawyer's advice!" he called out with a laugh as he headed toward the officials' parking lot around the corner.

Kevin and Linda headed down the street toward her car, and neither one seemed to touch foot to ground—it is truly one of the perversities of human nature that people can find moments of absolute bliss while their whole worlds actually lie in cataclysmic disarray around them. As they drove off, Linda said, "Kevin, I thought that was just beautiful . . .what you said to the newscaster about Juan Gonzales and how he made you feel."

"Well, it's true," Kevin said happily. "I do feel more as if I belong. Anyway, I can see that the Insanity of a Society is probably no worse than the sum of little insanities among all its members. And lots of times, I guess it's a whole lot better. The lesser of two evils, maybe. An individual's own dissociated craziness or the Organized Craziness of Society, they're the only alternatives we have."

Then Linda glanced over from the driver's wheel and asked, "If the verdict had been different, would you really have killed yourself?"

"Who are you asking?" Kevin replied expansively, "The me you're talking to right now or the me who would have been there. They're different enough, you know, that they should qualify as two distinct illusions."

Linda laughed jovially. "You always make things so complicated. I guess you always will."

"An enduring meta illusion among my illusions, huh?" Kevin replied playfully. Then more seriously, he added, "But it is comforting to think that, whenever the time really comes for it, I do have Seneca's option—and yes, I can envision circumstances under which I think I would have exercised it right there in court."

"Really?"

"Certainly."

Less than even a *relative certainty*, Linda thought. But she said nothing of the contingency plans she'd made to obstruct the exercise of that option. She just beamed exuberantly. And as they shared a moment of silent togetherness, The Elusive Dreams song echoed in the background of Kevin's mind, guitar chords strumming the last chorus of "Blue Cowboy":

Ride, Cowboy, ride, though you can't find your place
Ride, Cowboy, ride, till you've played your last ace
Lookin for somethin' that won't have to end
Meanwhile—I'll tell you—Life is your friend.

Milton Keynes UK
Ingram Content Group UK Ltd.
UKHW030018180324
439604UK00001B/295